Annalise

Venus Rising

ELLORA'S CAVE
ROMANTICA PUBLISHING

An Ellora's Cave Romantica Publication

www.ellorascave.com

Venus Rising

ISBN #1419954261
ALL RIGHTS RESERVED.
Venus Rising Copyright© 2004 Annalise
Edited by Briana St. James
Cover art by Syneca

Electronic book Publication January 2004
Trade paperback Publication March 2006

Warning:

The following material contains graphic sexual content meant for mature readers. *Venus Rising* has been rated *X-treme* by a minimum of three independent reviewers.

Ellora's Cave Publishing offers three levels of Romantica™ reading entertainment: S (S-ensuous), E (E-rotic), and X (X-treme).

S-*ensuous* love scenes are explicit and leave nothing to the imagination.

E-*rotic* love scenes are explicit, leave nothing to the imagination, and are high in volume per the overall word count. In addition, some E-rated titles might contain fantasy material that some readers find objectionable, such as bondage, submission, same sex encounters, forced seductions, etc. E-rated titles are the most graphic titles we carry; it is common, for instance, for an author to use words such as "fucking", "cock", "pussy", etc., within their work of literature.

X-*treme* titles differ from E-rated titles only in plot premise and storyline execution. Unlike E-rated titles, stories designated with the letter X tend to contain controversial subject matter not for the faint of heart.

About the Author

෨

Annalise is the pseudonym of two multi-published, award-winning authors one of whom is Liddy Midnight. Their success requires that they spend their days dripping with diamond jewelry, nibbling expensive bon-bons, wearing gorgeous designer gowns, and dictating their stories to hunky male assistants who type up the steamy prose and ship it out to panting publishers. Alas, the truth is far more boring, but who wants to read about that? They certainly don't.

Also by Annalise

෨

Equinox II *(Anthology)*

Venus Rising

ဆ

Annalise

Chapter 1
ဆ

Link examined the small shop wedged between two monolithic office structures. The hand-painted sign read, *The Fantasy Shoppe*. Not part of a chain, he was sure of that. This aged storefront had never appeared in a glossy vid or holo-ad. He'd bet his last credit the grime coating the windows was the result of genuine age and neglect, not a resin or synth mockup.

"Have you ever seen this place before?" he asked Brad, his lieutenant.

Brad glanced up and shook his head. "Nope. Looks like a junk shop. Something you'd see in one of the older city centers."

They stood in the capital of New Virginia. Built atop the reclaimed land from the previous century's chemical wars, most of the buildings followed the new style of architecture, their soaring entrances catering to both land and air craft.

"I'm curious. Want to come along?" Link asked.

"Not me. All this walking has made me thirsty." Brad jerked his head in the direction of the mammoth hotel adjoining SpaceFleet HQ. "I'm gonna see who I can scare up in the Drowning Pool."

"How can you drink in a bar that has the word 'drowning' in its name?"

Brad shrugged. "To each their own. And you watch your UV. Don't go nuts out here."

Link tapped the badge on his sleeve and then his sunglasses. They darkened another degree.

Brad nodded and raised a hand for a cruising roller. When his friend was gone, Link took a moment to gaze up at the megalithic structures that typified the new cities. Called cities within cities and connected by tunnels or shielded walkways, the structures allowed residents to move about without exposure to the harmful rays of the sun. Link had spent too much time breathing the metallic tang of recycled air.

He took a deep breath. He smelled dirt. Maybe a woman's perfume, though that must be imagination–or just the side effect of too little sex too long ago. There wasn't a woman in sight.

He lifted his hand. His spread palm was slick with sweat.

Although the sky overhead and the street were crowded with vehicles, he was the only pedestrian in sight. Like their fellow shuttle passengers, who'd been set free after three years at the Mars Station, he and Brad had craved new faces, new places. Brad had gone straight to the hotel, while Link had picked up his personal flier, or PF as he'd discovered they were now called, from the officers' hangar.

Once unpacked, even though the headquarters hotel was more than spacious by interplanetary standards, he and Brad found they had the same itch to explore.

They wanted to stretch their legs. Or Brad had, until his gregarious nature made him bored of walking around on synth pavement radiating temperatures over one hundred degrees.

For Link, the thick New Virginia air, as steamy and heavy as a tropical jungle, was welcome after the controlled atmosphere of the Mars dome.

He moved closer to the dusty shop and peered in the window. It was filled with an odd assortment of objects, from dishes to toys. He let his gaze drift from item to item, until he caught sight of a familiar shape and grinned. There, looking poised to leave dock, was a model boat. The long, sleek lines mirrored a few he remembered watching speed over the ocean as a child. Not that he'd ever piloted one of those; by the time he was old enough, the safety bureaucrats had banned open cockpits as being too exposed for day use and the power models too dangerous for night use.

For a moment, Link was transported to his family's summer home in Maine. He could almost feel the cool breeze on his cheek as he maneuvered his skiff from the dock. What he wouldn't give for a few days on the bay.

The scent of water at low tide filled his head. He glanced around, but saw only the stark edges of city buildings, the flat expanses of reflective glass surfaces.

"You've been off-planet too long," he said to himself, turning his attention back to the shop. "Or out in the sun too much." A glance at his badge revealed a current level of UV exposure that gave him a few more hours to explore before he had to seek shelter.

The shop window before him had a wonderful museum quality to it.

Link harbored a secret love of museums. He liked their smell and the muted lights that protected ancient paper and fabrics. There was something soothing and peaceful in the knowledge that so much endured from past generations. It counteracted the grim nightly news and gave him hope that Earth—and the humans who teemed over its surface—might still be around to see the third millennium.

Link pulled the shop door open and jumped when a bell rang over his head. "What the hell," he muttered.

The scent of dust and mold permeated the shop. Grime on the windows filtered the midday sunlight and cast the shop shelves in shadow. Link eyed a jumble of objects, sorted by some system he couldn't divine. The chaos of the window display extended throughout the shop. Toys rubbed shoulders with jewelry and dishes. A T-shaped stand held a dazzling array of necklaces, strands of gold and silver sparkling amid colored beads. Some of the longer chains spilled into what looked like an iron cooking pot, decorated with a woodland scene around the outside. Pine trees and bears. He liked the handle shaped like a pinecone atop the lid. Who had a use for cooking pots these days? Perhaps a restaurateur like his grandmother might be interested in this, but only to serve a specialty dish. Automated cookers did most of the work.

He picked up an old-fashioned screwdriver, its wooden handle worn smooth and bare of paint. When was the last time that someone had actually used such an antiquated tool? He laid it next to something that looked like a candle, but when he picked it up, it was too hard and had no wick. From browsing in museums, he knew what it was, although his peers wouldn't have. Sealing wax, of all things. Sure enough, not far away lay the little metal seal used to imprint the hot wax.

Racks of clothing along one wall seduced him from the jumbled objects. He couldn't resist skimming his finger over a garment similar to his dress uniform tunic—only this looked as if it was made of leather. To contain animal products, the coat must be old indeed. Gently, Link shifted the lapel open and peered at the label. It was dark with age but legible. *Genuine Leather*.

He ran his fingers along the sleeve. It was still soft and supple, despite its antiquity. How much must such an exotic jacket cost?

"That's real leather, son," said a voice behind him.

Link turned. A small man, or small compared to Link who topped two meters, smiled up at him. The fellow looked further diminished by his large, corrective lenses. Another anachronism, but one fitting the nature of the shop. Link couldn't think of anyone he knew who wore spectacles; only a few eccentrics refused the quick and painless procedures to correct vision abnormalities.

Then Link had a cynical thought. Probably just costuming to go with the shop. The funny little guy had an infectious smile, though, and Link found himself grinning back. "Some shop you have here."

"Thank you." The old man beamed a smile. "Would you like to try it on?" he asked, taking the coat from its hanger.

"Ahh," Link began to protest, but found himself slipping his arms into the sleeves. The coat fit well but lay heavily on his shoulders. He shrugged to redistribute the weight and found it didn't help. "I thought animal products were illegal."

"Not antiques. Of course, many these days would disdain wearing it. But you won't find a warmer coat."

Link shrugged out of it. "No, thanks. I work off-planet. I'd have no use for it." And neither would anyone else in New Virginia. Winters weren't as cold as they used to be.

The man took the coat without comment. With a deft motion, he replaced it on the hanger and slid it back into the rack of clothing.

"I'll just look around." Link moved away. He'd always hated hovering servants and didn't do much shopping for himself. He valued his personal shopper; he supplied just about anything Link needed before he realized he needed it.

The proprietor beamed another sunny smile and whipped out a stick with fluffy stuff on one end. Could that be a bunch of feathers? The man ran the fluffy end around and over a stack of assorted dishes that no self-respecting cook would ever use, and Link decided it must be some kind of cleaning tool.

He examined the overloaded shelves on a freestanding rack across from the clothing, handling one thing after another, turning them over in his hands. Many of the objects he recognized only because he liked wandering through museums. Old tools fascinated him and many of the items he picked up belonged behind glass, in controlled conditions. Then a stray sunbeam glinted off an object he knew well.

He picked up an iridescent plastic card. The surface was featureless, except for two words across the top, in fancy black script. *The Palace.* These cards, which had fallen out of use for a few years, were back now that hard currency had finally gone the way of the solar engine.

Link tilted it, frowning. Usually they held the maker's name or mark somewhere. With the exception of the elaborately drawn letters, the card was blank. When he gripped it more tightly, it gave only a bit. Not new, then. The ones in use now were far thinner and more flexible. Some space stations even used cards for certain security areas, but he'd never seen one quite like this.

"What's this for?" he asked.

The shopkeeper peered over his glasses. "It's a credit card."

"Of course, I know that, but it's unusual. This one feels old, but it looks new." He ran a finger lightly across both sides. The surfaces were completely smooth.

The man took it and flipped it over. A small blush colored his round cheeks a pale pink. "Oh, dear. A bit of both, I'm afraid. Old-style card. Ah, hem. To go with old-style service, you see. I'm sure I have no idea how this found its way into our shop. If my wife saw this she'd be making a coat out of someone's hide."

"So, what's it for then?" Link asked, plucking the card from the man's gnarled fingertips.

The old man cleared his throat, his skin flushing an even deeper shade of scarlet. He hid his face a moment behind the fluffy end of his cleaner thing.

Link thought of all the unusual credit cards he'd seen or even heard of, and couldn't account for the old guy's reaction. "Come on. I've used lots of cards but I've never seen one like this. What is it?"

The shopkeeper leaned close, his eyes darting toward the back of the shop. Link found himself glancing that way, too, half-expecting the man's wife to pop into view.

"A brothel card," the little man whispered.

Link laughed out loud. "A brothel? You mean a pleasure center?"

The shopkeeper glanced again toward the back of the shop and paused before he answered. "Oh, no. I mean a true brothel, in the old sense. The pleasure centers of today offer little to compare with a true brothel—not that I know from personal experience," he rushed to add.

"And this is what? A membership card?"

"It looks to be. Unlikely to have any credit on it anymore. Perhaps one of my dealers bought it for its unique design."

Link angled it to the light again, but could make out nothing more. "Looks pretty dull to me." He offered it to the old man, losing interest.

"Oh, it's not dull. They never are." The old man pushed it back toward him. "Rub it briskly, *then* tip it to the light."

Link rubbed the card between his thumb and fingers before tilting it toward the sunny window. He laughed. With each tilt, the colors on the card shifted and changed. A penis appeared, rising to rigidity.

Oh, yeah, he could imagine the old guy's wife wouldn't like this. He moved closer to the front window and shifted the card about again, rubbing it harder. This time, the penis not only rose, it spouted a gush of semen. "Clever."

He turned to the shelf where he'd found the card, but when he set it between a dusty book — *Black Beauty* — and a small purse stitched with a beaded floral design, he found he couldn't bring himself to let the card go.

The plastic remained warm under his fingertips. He stood there a moment, the card flat on the shelf, his fingers held as if glued to the glossy surface. An urge swept through him to know the difference between a pleasure center and a "true" brothel. It was less physical than mental, but he had an uncanny feeling that if he let go of the card, the urge would die.

Impulsively, he slid the card off the shelf again and flipped it over. The back was plain white. There was no modern gold square indicating a chip was embedded in the plastic.

"How much?" he asked before he could stop himself.

"Oh. I imagine it's worthless but for the holo."

"Yeah, but what a holo. I'd like to show it to some of my men," he lied. "How much?" Link could not say why he felt a compulsion to keep the card. It still retained the warmth of his fingers.

"Oh, seven credits should do it."

Link lifted an eyebrow. "Seven? That's a bit pricey for a card that's practically worthless."

The man sighed and shot another glance toward the back of the shop. "Six? Five?"

"Five." Link tapped his personal commerce code into the shop's communication console, the only thing in the place that was neither dusty nor anachronistic, and debited his liquid account five credits.

Moments later, he was on the street and heading back to his hotel. The card remained in his hand, safely tucked deep in his pocket. He stroked the smooth edges while questions ran through his mind.

Could he coax any information out of the card? Just how old was it? Was it encrypted, and if it was, could he break the code? If he did, could he find the brothel?

If he did manage to read any of the data, likely the brothel that issued the card had gone out of business or had relocated off-world somewhere. It wasn't on Mars or Luna. There were sizable stations at each LaGrangian Point, but they all belonged to private corporations. When those stationary points between the earth and the moon first opened up for development, one of the megacorps had seen a bonanza of credits in creating a secure and restricted environment for "special" business interests. The Palace sounded like it could be a "special" business. No way could he talk himself into one of those.

Link's hotel, attached to HQ, offered all the conveniences of a civilian lodging but was run with military efficiency. The decor emphasized comfort over pizzazz. It was decorated in muted beige and gray, which unfortunately reminded him of the camouflage gear worn by lunar pilot wannabes.

As befit his rank as a colonel in the Planetary Air Force, SpaceFleet Command, he had a suite to himself at government expense. It featured the best of technology, so he could work even when off duty, and the latest in ergonomic beds and chairs, designed for the comfort of those accustomed to artificial environments.

At least his room was not beige. Its cool blues and whites reminded him of sails skimming across the cool Maine ocean.

He slid his fingers over the panel of controls by the bed and saw he had ten minutes of shower water available and four minutes until that water was heated to his specs.

After he'd taken his shower he wandered around the chamber, toweling off. The urge to try to access the data on the card was almost overwhelming. The need just to pick up the card was strong, and inexplicable. Uncomfortably so. That troubled him. He was not a man to give in to pressure.

To resist the impulse, Link forced his attention to other tasks. He tucked the towel more firmly around his hips and sat at the communication console. He requested the cleaning of his dress uniform and completed a report on a young woman in his unit who was up for promotion. He'd put off the file work long enough; she'd make a fine second lieutenant.

His attention didn't wander until he began recording his expenses. His gaze returned again and again to the card. Without realizing he'd done it, he found himself staring out the window, rubbing the card between his fingertips. He looked down at it and frowned.

No cleverly embedded image of a penis appeared. Nothing happened. He enclosed the card between his palms, chafed it quickly, and looked at it in the light. Still nothing.

"Damn. I've been cheated," he muttered and went to the communication console. It held not only the necessary equipment for work, but also anything a person could want for entertainment. Or almost anything—brothel services excepted. He held the card as he would his security pass.

Nothing happened. He tilted it back and forth, but nothing appeared on the screen.

"Fuck that." Five credits down the drain. Not a fortune, but a useless card was not what he'd planned to blow it on. He tossed the card to the floor. He stretched out on the bed and said, "News."

The large screen blinked to life on an infocast, just starting a fluff piece on the increasing lifespan of the average human. A proposal had been introduced to the Americas Council to raise the age of majority to 25. He snorted at the discussion of what those twenty-somethings who were not yet of age should be called. An improved-to-perfection brunette interviewed two experts, a common culturist and a linguist. Neither of them brought up the military term he'd always used, AOA, an acronym for Almost Of Age. Leave it to the corps to invent a TLA that worked in any legislative environment. Remarkably efficient.

He half-dozed through an hour of the same-old, same-old news. Protestors had broken up a meeting of the North American Weather Guild in Ponca City. Lunar mineral rights issues had stalled mining operations again. Three children had been recognized for their contribution to fire safety in one of the worst sections of Old London.

When he woke, he sat up and groaned. He'd forgotten to adjust the bed to suit his off-world back. As he stretched his tight muscles, he caught sight of the card on the floor.

The same urge he'd felt in the shop swept over him. Impulsively, he plucked the card from the carpet.

"I must be stupid," he said aloud, realizing that although he was expecting old technology, whatever access system was used on the card might not be. He went to the comm unit. "Read card."

The screen shimmered and glowed in a swirl of gold and white. Two magnificent doors appeared. *The Palace, Where You are Royalty*, read a superimposed text. The glowing letters faded as the doors swung open to reveal the lobby of what looked like an opulent hotel. The decorator who chose the brilliant palette of fabrics and furnishings was clearly not a fan of camouflage.

A woman appeared, standing behind a gleaming reception desk made of pink marble. The receptionist was lovely, with large dark eyes and glowing skin that hinted of tropical isle genetics. She smiled.

"Welcome to The Palace Hotel. It's been a long time since you last visited us." She shook her finger at him. "You have very few credits left. You'll find you have only limited selections today, I'm afraid."

The beauty's face faded and a menu appeared. He almost swallowed his tongue. The menu read:

Massage pleasures

Oral pleasures

The choices were displayed on lozenges of shifting patterns. After a moment, he realized they were slices of bigger scenes, scenes that depicted his choices.

Fascinated, he looked more closely. He could make out hands, mouths, and both male and female organs.

Oh, yeah, this was nothing like the pleasure center on Mars. What had that one corporal called it? *The Plug and Play.* No mechanicals or holos at The Palace, from the looks of it, just warm hands and hot mouths.

Real hands. Real mouths. His cock stirred.

"Massage," he managed to choke out, thinking of his back, but he was pretty sure it wasn't his back he'd get massaged at a brothel. At least he knew it wouldn't be at a pleasure center, not that he'd ever been in *The Plug and Play*.

Not many women chose the Mars rotation, but Brad and he made sure none of them ever regretted it. Even avoiding the women under his command, he'd never gone long without feminine companionship on the station.

And there was Erica on the few leaves he spent earthside. Or there had been Erica. She'd had the audacity to tell him it was a formal life partnership this time or nothing. That's how he'd found himself living at the base hotel.

The screen remained as it was before. Two options.

"Massage," he repeated, but nothing happened.

He groaned and walked to the screen. He touched the words *Massage Pleasures*.

Sure enough, as he suspected, another menu appeared. A damned touch screen! *What a nuisance*, he thought as he looked over the selections. Somehow, touching the words gave them an impact that speaking them did not.

The next few menus were pretty simple. *Massage, Therapeutic or Erotic.* "Massage, erotic" was penis and testicles by the hour or the orgasm. He opened the therapeutic menu and laughed when he saw he really could have his back worked on under the supervision of the orthopedic staff.

He noticed that his credit on account only allowed him either an hour of therapeutic back massage or a penis/testicle massage resulting in one orgasm.

His balls throbbed at the thought. It had been a while. Erica had met him at the door with her demand. One minute he was kissing her, tongue halfway down her throat, hard where she ground her hips against him—and the next he was climbing back into his PF with his duffel, heading for the hotel.

When he reached for the screen, his heart began to beat a little more quickly. He opted for the penis/testicle massage. Another screen appeared and a sultry voice said, "Select your server, please."

The screen filled with rows of thumbnail images of women and men—what he thought was called a *headshot*. Although they appeared to be of different races and ethnic origins, both the men and the women wore their hair the same way, long and brushed straight back from their faces. The similar hairstyle made them monotonously alike.

He skimmed his fingertips over one face and it enlarged. With an idle interest, he browsed through the headshots, examining the servers available, marveling that there were so many, at least fifty, who were willing to crank his carrot for him.

Then he paused. He tapped an image and the thumbnail expanded.

"Not possible," he said softly.

The image filling the screen was that of a woman with dark, long hair and finely arched brows. Beneath those aristocratic brows, her large, almost almond-shaped eyes were framed by thick, dark lashes. Her lips were full and well-shaped. Subtle makeup enhanced her beauty.

It was a face he'd examined up close many times but hadn't seen in years.

Cadet Sara Evans. PeaceKeepers Academy, Class of '43.

His class.

His Evans.

"Not possible," he repeated. Then he noticed words beneath her image. "Unimproved?"

He worked his way back to the beginning of the images and found the help screen. There he read a note he'd missed the first time through. Those labeled unimproved were servers who had undergone no body-enhancing procedures, which was a rarity these days. That meant the woman or man might have flaws and, as the disclaimer informed him, satisfaction was not guaranteed.

Link tapped the screens until he had Cadet Evans—a woman who should be a full colonel by now—back on the screen. What the hell was a first class officer doing in a home-planet, old-fashioned brothel?

Unimproved.

He remembered the soft weight of her breasts in his hands, and the feel of her gasp in his mouth as she climaxed. There had been nothing wrong with her unimproved body then, and he imagined not much was wrong with her now. Without thought, he reserved Cadet Evans, listed as Server G752H, for one penile/testicular massage to orgasm.

His heart began to pound again. The screen went blank. For a moment, he thought that was it. The card had failed in some way. Then gold and white swirled across the screen and the original receptionist coalesced from the misty effects. As she thanked him for his patronage and reminded him to bring his card along to his appointment, the room printer spat out a flimsy instead of updating his personal data unit. Another odd combination of old and new.

He picked the appointment reminder off the desk and examined it. G752H. An address, a date, a time.

An asterisk.

*No refunds for unimproved attendants.

Link folded the reminder and tapped it on his palm. "Well, hell. I'm a bit unimproved myself."

Chapter 2
❧

Link tried to watch the news again. He tried to work on the various reports that were due at the end of the week. He tried and he failed. He ordered a meal, but when it arrived, he found himself staring at a plate of pseudo-steak, not sure if it was what he'd actually ordered.

Finally, he admitted defeat. He used the room controls to pay the high premium on an extra shower, full jets, no time limit, stripped, and stepped into the tiled shower stall. Jets of water gushed from all sides. He hit a pump and filled his palm with the hotel's liquid soap.

He lathered his chest and belly, his mind on Cadet Evans. Not the swept-back hair and expertly made up server G752H, but the Evans he remembered from training. He closed his eyes and wrapped his hand around his erect penis.

With the ease of years of practice, he stroked his cock, his mind on very clear, very precise memories: Evans pulling down her uniform trousers, back to him, her heart-shaped ass tight with well-honed muscles.

And then the slow turn.

He'd forgotten nothing. Not the unvarying, soft ivory of her skin. Not the glimpse of the tiny mole high on her inner thigh. Not the profile of her small breasts.

Natural breasts. Not improved.

Tight, sweet nipples. Not improved.

Link leaned one hand on the wall and moaned. She'd been tight and wet each and every time he'd fucked her. She'd bitten his shoulder the first time she'd climaxed around him.

For a moment, he was back there with her. He could smell the wonderful womanly scent of her. He could feel the scrape of her teeth on his skin, the slick tightness of her body around his cock.

He came in a near-painful rush. When he opened his eyes, he was in the hotel shower, water pouring over his skin, his come swirling away down the drain.

* * * * *

Evans waited in the long corridor for the latch to click on the door in front of her. Other than featureless rows of beige doors, spaced far apart in ivory slick walls, there was nothing to look at. No visible cameras. No exits.

One end of the corridor was a blank wall. The other ended in a heavy metal door. That door opened to another long corridor lined with more doors. Those each led to a cell.

Evans wished she knew what lay behind the other doors lining this hall.

Her door bore a hand in red with a number fifteen stenciled over it. Hands meant massage chambers. Stars meant special client chambers. What was special about them, Evans didn't know. She hadn't been "ordered" for anything special yet. Some doors had cryptic signs, arrows, birds, symbols that must mean something to those in the know.

Unfortunately, she hadn't progressed to such privileged information.

A way out was what she wanted. Privileged information was what she needed.

Her heart began a rapid tap in her chest. She took a few long, deep breaths to steady herself.

"Wait a moment," said a voice behind her.

Evans turned and saw a tall woman striding toward her. She had the dull, gray hair of an elderly woman, though she could not be over forty. She wore the starched white garb of the medical staff.

Medical Aide Jennel. The tyrant of cleanliness. Now, where had she come from?

"I need to fill you in on your next guest." Jennel tapped a stylus against a datapad. The readout displayed what looked like a client contract. Evans knew every guest was required to sign a special contract for an unimproved attendant.

"I read the appointment codes," Evans said. "No conversation. Total silence."

"That's not all. He's not taking any sperm suppressors."

Evans felt her stomach dance. What else could go wrong with her day?

"You'll get a special kit for clean up after he ejaculates. Be sure to seal the cloth in the pouch provided and report for disinfection afterward."

Evans heard a click as the door to her chamber unlocked. She nodded and left Jennel in the hallway. The tap of her stylus didn't falter before the door shut the sound out.

The small massage chamber was devoid of objects except the chair in which she sat. It was of some exotic wood and showed that for the client, all things must be of the finest quality.

Opposite her was the door for the guest's entry.

She shifted on the hard chair. This was her second task of the day.

Task.

Laughter bubbled in her throat, but she clamped down on it and schooled her features. *Think of them as tasks, nothing more,* she told herself.

It was the only way she could get through them. She shivered, although the chamber was warm, as was her loose robe. The warmth "encouraged" the guests. The chamber was also dimly lighted with a soft yellow glow from the floor. Each attendant's light color depended upon which best reflected their skin tones or the robe they'd been given to wear.

She waited for her guest.

Guest. If it weren't frightening, she would laugh. They were just men or women who wanted sex and were willing to pay well for it.

She'd been in this place three weeks and learned very little more than that—and how many doors lined each corridor.

She still knew nothing of what had happened to Angel Martinez, the missing twenty-year-old daughter of the Secretary of the Department of Homeland Security. If Angel wasn't found in the next six weeks, she would be beyond her twenty-first birthday. At that point, as she would be an adult, The Palace could claim she was there voluntarily. Under the influence of the drugs Evans knew were in the food, Angel would hardly be in any condition to argue.

The two agents who'd gone in as guests had learned zilch, far less than she'd learned during her first few days. They'd known nothing of the drugs, or how isolated attendants were kept.

Evans's heart beat rose from tap to thud. She shifted and licked her lips. At least this was the simplest of tasks. Jerk the guy off and be done with it.

And clean up. Her mind shied from what preceded the clean-up part. There had been only one guy in her life who had not used sperm suppressors.

Don't go there, she chastised herself. Think of Angel.

She kept her expression neutral and her gaze dutifully on the floor in case anyone was observing her.

They watched everyone, everywhere, at all times, and it was not considered good service to look at the guest's face. If and when he wanted eye contact, he'd say so. So far, no client had wanted to meet her gaze.

The guest door opened. A man's shadow stretched across the floor. He wore the long, belted robe into which each guest changed after check-in. A twin of her own, though more luxurious. She heard the familiar sound of his card sliding into the service slot. The credits would begin to tick off right away.

To the public, this building looked like any luxury hotel from the outside. From the interior, which could be gained only with a membership card, it still looked like an expensive hotel. All services were obtained privately, through the use of an old-fashioned card. And old-fashioned service was what could be had behind the many closed doors. She didn't know the full extent of the available services, but she suspected that enough credits could buy almost anything at The Palace.

The man waited, standing before her, his hands at his sides. She could hear him breathe. Slightly fast. He was nervous. Perhaps it was his first visit.

She lifted her gaze to the belt of his robe. Slowly, to both relax and entice him, she pretended to have difficulty working the knot, skimming her fingers against his penis and testicles as she slowly drew the belt open.

The robe parted. His skin was pale, what back in the Academy they'd called spacer-white, but his body was rock hard, honed and toned, every muscle defined. It was a pleasure to look at — and touch — someone so healthy.

He had a large cock, thankfully already erect. The relief she felt was almost overwhelming. Her last guest had been unexcited and harder still to arouse. He'd cuffed her twice when she'd failed to stimulate him to satisfaction. Her nipple still ached from the pinch he'd given her.

She slid her hands over the guest's penis. The skin was smooth beneath her fingers, the head dusky in its engorgement. His testicles were heavy and warm as she gently palmed and kneaded them. He arched a bit under her ministrations and his breathing quickened.

The smell of expensive soap emanated from him along with his body heat. She had discovered that even wealthy guests could be repulsive in their personal habits. This man's skin was clean. A blessing for one in her position.

She let herself relax and her mind wander. This was a healthy male specimen, which most of The Palace's guests she had served were not. She hadn't seen his face, but with his physique, surely women would be falling all over him.

Why was he seeking pleasure for hire?

Perhaps he was one of those men who enjoyed sex more if they paid for it. Perhaps he couldn't reach an orgasm unless he paid for it.

By all appearances, he was enjoying her touch. She stroked down the hard length of his penis, letting her fingers tangle in his damp curls, exerting pressure right *there*, as she'd been taught. He hissed in a breath as he jerked in her hands.

His knees trembled and he placed a hand on her shoulder. She jerked her hands back and the room's yellow glow flared into stark white.

A man's stern voice said, "No touching of the attendants is permitted. A second violation will result in a five hundred credit fine." The light dimmed again to soft yellow and she reached for him.

"Sorry," he said, barely above a whisper.

She wrapped her hand around his penis and stroked him gently. If they saw *him* touch her, then they were watching right now and would take note of her technique, mark any inconsistencies with the manual. She lavished gentle sweeps of her hand up and down the fine long length of him. He shifted and spread his legs a bit. He jammed his fists into the pockets of the robe.

She cupped his testicles and squeezed them with rhythmic gentleness and slipped her fingertips behind his sac to tease the smooth skin there.

His thighs were dusted with dark hair. So many men indulged in hair removal these days that to see a man with body hair was unusual. It told her he was not up on Earth fashion. He shifted his legs further apart. The flex of his thigh muscles was a pleasure to watch. Since her hand was inside the concealment of his robe, she let her fingers drift up and down his inner thigh. She grasped some of the soft hair there and tugged.

A guttural sound escaped his throat.

The disembodied male voice said, "If you're enjoying your experience, we have an upgrade special today with a discount on fellatio for only another eight hundred credits. Simply step away from the attendant, touch the two on the keypad by the door and the amount will be automatically deducted from your account. This offer is good only for the next five minutes."

He did not move. And she did not break the rhythm of her strokes. His penis was so stiff, she knew it would be but moments before he came.

The voice said, "For maximum pleasure, be sure to tell your attendant how you wish to ejaculate. Choose from within the attendant's hands, across the attendant's breasts, or on her face. Enjoy the pleasure of seeing how far your semen can go."

Oh my, Evans thought.

"Simply state your desire and your attendant will see you receive the best of care."

"Breasts," the man said in a half-whisper. His voice was deep, and touched a chord of familiarity she couldn't stop to examine. She feared she might not get her robe open before he finished. As she caressed the turgid length of him, she tugged at the fabric.

The robe was designed to fall apart with a light touch. The man's body shuddered and she had barely time to direct his cock before he climaxed.

His come arched across the small space between them. It spewed hot across her breasts. He groaned, rocking on his feet.

Her overseer said, "We hope you enjoyed your massage. Please allow the attendant to adjust your robe and then exit by the door through which you entered."

Evans did as she'd been taught. She stroked the man's penis, massaging until every vestige of his erection was gone. Making sure to caress him with every touch of her hands, she pulled his robe closed. She followed procedure, massaging his testicles and cock through the soft fabric as if she could not bear to part with his equipment. Lastly, she looped his belt.

His semen was growing sticky on her skin. She was not permitted to close her robe until he left. She risked a glance up as he turned away.

And gasped.

He turned back. The surprise she choked back was not mirrored on his face. His expression remained as blank as the walls of her cell.

Heat rushed across her skin. Involuntarily, her hand went to her breast—and his semen. His gaze dropped to her hand. Slight color touched his high cheekbones.

Then he was gone. The door whispered closed before it locked with a click.

The yellow glow in the room rose to the stark white it had become when he'd been reprimanded for touching her. A soft whisper of sound accompanied a panel sliding open in the wall. A shelf glided forward. Evans examined the supplies. A damp cloth to wipe the semen from her breasts and a pouch in which to seal the cloth. A sweet, medicinal smell filled the small space as she wiped the thick semen from her skin.

Just as she ran her fingertips along the bag's seal, there was a click from behind her and she knew the door to the cells had opened. That was her signal to leave.

A guard led her to a washroom where she dropped her robe and, under the woman's impassive scrutiny, washed away the medicinal odor and the memory of Link Taylor's semen from her breasts. She set aside the sense of shame that he'd seen her here.

Back in her cell, she carefully hung her robe on a hook. It was all the clothing she possessed in this place. Each day the robe was exchanged for a new one. She climbed under the covers, lay on her back, and tried to sleep.

Even when the lights blinked out, she could not close her eyes. She stared up into complete darkness, seeing another time and another place in her mind.

More than ten years ago.

She'd scorned her enlisted quarters as Spartan when she first joined the PeaceKeepers, but after several weeks in the attendants' accommodations here, she remembered that tiny shared cabin as luxurious.

Busy and bustling, her life then had been one new experience after another, each greeted with eagerness. She was one of many recruits, young and fresh and ready to serve.

Then a new enthusiasm entered her life.

Link Taylor.

He'd been as young as she, and just as ready to save the world. They'd freely shared their dreams and their bodies. Or had until they graduated.

Their graduation had coincided with the beginning of Luna Corporation's catastrophic bid to be recognized as independent of any planetary control. After that, other corporations, some much wealthier than the nations that spawned them, bid for independence as well.

Link's dreams took him into the Planetary Defense Force, to fight and preserve Earth's colonies. She'd been recruited into the United American Department of Homeland Security, where she worked undercover to keep dissident corporate forces from tearing apart other planetary alliances.

She'd liked to have married — or to be completely politically correct, to have formed a formal life partnership — and started a family, but no man had ever measured up to Link.

At least she could say she was good at what she did. And she assumed he was, as well. Occasionally she saw him mentioned in a report, always to his credit. He'd even made the infocasts a few years back for orchestrating an end to the smuggler standoff at Luna Station and preventing further bloodshed.

She'd never expected to see him again, least of all here.

How many times had she tasted his skin, buried her face in the soft hair at his neck? How many orgasms had they shared during their years together at the Academy?

She'd never bothered to count but she could bring every one to mind, from the first time they had coupled, slow and sweet, to his departure for space, when they'd fucked furiously, knowing it was their last chance.

She slid her legs apart and touched herself. She was slick with desire, desire for a man she'd not seen in ten years. Finally, she closed her eyes. Her hand stroked in rhythmic circles while her mind shifted from the feel of his penis in her hand today to how it had felt filling her so long ago.

How she had hated the thought of some man's come on her when Jennel had said the guest did not use sperm suppressors. And how she had denied the ripple of arousal as she'd realized the semen on her skin was Link's.

Her climax came quickly. With the ease of practice, she concealed it by coughing and turning abruptly to her side.

She could never count on being unobserved.

Chapter 3

ഇ

Link sat on his hotel bed, eyes closed. *Evans.* It was definitely Evans. Her breasts were unchanged. Small, dusky nipples, uptilted. Definitely unimproved, the left breast slightly larger than the right. The only change had been a dusting of freckles across her chest that she'd acquired since their Academy days.

Freckles slick with his come this afternoon.

He shifted uncomfortably on his bed. He resisted an urge to head for the shower and masturbate to the memories. Not memories of the quick hand job today, but of the times they'd made love. Freely, enthusiastically — if not with much technique.

Today, she'd had technique. Mechanical technique. And when she'd finally looked up, her eyes and gasp had betrayed her recognition of him.

And the presence of drugs.

An hour later, he activated the card. The same greeting and admonition that he had very few credits left showed him he could only have a therapeutic back massage. The available attendants included the unimproved Evans.

Moments later, the communications console silently printed the date and time of his appointment. Two days away. With an aching cock and a mind full of memories, he crawled into bed and tried to sleep.

* * * * *

Evans slid her tray along the mess hall railing and frowned at the choices. Everything on the menu was synthetic, nothing natural. No fruit, no fresh veggies. The sign on the wall extolled the nutritional benefits of the entrees, listing the vitamins and minerals provided by each item. Evans figured the only things not listed were whatever drugs they added.

She knew she was being drugged, she just didn't know with what. She tried to eat as little as possible, but the counselors had admonished her twice for loss of weight. That was something an unimproved attendant could not afford. Attendants had a duty to keep their allure, which meant firm, plump flesh.

She sat with Cloud9, a small attendant who was enthusiastic about her work. Or else she did a good job of pretending to be. She talked about technique. A guest's pleasure. The rewards that came with being in the top ten requested attendants. Evans smiled and tried to look interested.

"Do you know an attendant named Angel?" Evans asked. "I think she specialized in bondage. And was kinda young."

She hazarded a guess at the bondage. None of Evans's guests had showed any interest in bondage, but sexual acts involving an AOA indicated that dominance might be in the mix. And if the girl was unwilling, bondage might be necessary.

Of course, she didn't know if Angel was unwilling. She was sure "they" could concoct a drug cocktail that would ensure cooperation with anything.

"Angel? Don't know the name," Cloud9 said. "Why?"

"She's the one who turned me onto this place," Evans lied as she forced herself to load her spoon with vegetable puree. At least, it looked like vegetable puree. It didn't taste like much of anything. "I kinda thought I'd thank her, but I haven't seen her anywhere. I don't know what they call her here."

She had been christened Bliss6 by The Palace. The names were stupid. Guests ordered the attendants by code numbers and letters, but Evans supposed it gave everyone some convenience when they chatted to one another, such as now. It also allowed someone to hide.

Where was Angel hiding?

"Oh. You could ask a counselor."

Cloud9's eyes were particularly beautiful, the turquoise of the Caribbean emphasized by drug-contracted pupils. She bent her head and swayed closer, so close that her shoulder-length hair, blonde tinted with a soft red, brushed against Evans's breast.

"I think I'm ahead of Ecstasy11 this month," Cloud9 whispered.

Evans forced herself not to move away. She leaned her head closer. "Really. Wow. I'm so new, no one has asked for me as a repeat yet."

"They will. Now, with your looks, if you were improved, you'd already have a following. You should at least shave off your pubes. Then you could decorate with some cool body art. I'm having golden snakes done tomorrow." Cloud9 paused and licked her spoon. "Or are you working the fetish menus?"

Evans shook her head.

"Yeah. Didn't think so. You don't have the improvements for that—slick skin is the best."

Cloud9 leaned back to get a better view and eyed her up and down. Evans squirmed inwardly as the girl licked her spoon again, this time with a lascivious manner not targeted at the pureed peas.

"You ought to consider a facial, having that mole on your thigh removed, getting your breasts balanced, oh, and you gotta get nipple enhancement. Since mine, I'm ready to climax with the flick of a client's tongue. Now, that's the sort of thing that gets you noticed. I almost have enough credits in my bonus account for a clit enlargement. That'll get me moved up in price and demand. You can clamp lots of goodies to a good-sized clit."

Cloud9 dropped her spoon beside her empty plate. "Your ass and thighs could be a lot tighter, too. Let's face it, not many men like older women, and without the enhancements, you're showing your years. Young guys won't want you. As you are, you'll probably be stuck with all the old farts."

"Great." Evans rolled her eyes. "Maybe I need to rethink the surgery thing."

"Of course, some like the old ones. They usually have credits out their asses. Some of my best tippers have been old, y'know, in their fifties even."

"Hi, Cloud9, Bliss6." Another young blonde, improved to perfection, came up and nodded. Evans thought she was called Grace8. Of a top-heavy, athletic build, she had an annoying way of looking down her nose at everyone. She sat down on the other side of Cloud9, claiming her attention. They looked like sisters, both blonde, polished and perfect, Cloud9 with her aquamarine eyes, the other with the deepest green eyes Evans had ever seen.

The product of enhancement, or genetics? She couldn't be sure, but she suspected the former. The two sat like lovers, arms and fingers linked, heads tilted close together while they whispered.

Evans took the opportunity to slip away to the gym. She wasn't going to get any information about Angel from either of these sources.

Cloud9 had a pretty good idea of exactly what Evans needed to have improved, though. More than could be expected from their occasional, casual interaction. Did that imply that some attendants were able to make use of the hidden surveillance equipment? And what about clients?

Certainly the agents who had posed as guests had not been offered that opportunity. Not for the first time, Evans wondered if there were levels of membership, with exclusive services offered to a select few, an elite group that no government agent could infiltrate.

As she turned in her robe for some workout gear, a thong brief and tight fitting bra, she remembered the training vids. Had they been captured live encounters or ones planned for filming? Thoughts of Link ejaculating on her breasts and being watched by a training class of eager or drugged out attendants made her head straight for the free weights.

As she curled the heavy weights, she wondered if it had been a glint of desire in Cloud9's eyes just before she'd brushed her breast. Had the little blonde moved closer to her on purpose? Could Cloud9's interest prove useful?

All through a rigorous workout, designed to tighten her thighs and lift her breasts, Evans worked on other ways she might locate Angel. Every minute of the day was regimented, with exercise, meals, and training worked around the guests' demands. Her limited contact with others came during meals, the one hour of weekly free time she was permitted in the rec hall, and here, in exercise sessions. She wished she could soften up one of the silent guards who escorted her to and from her appointments. Was that how Cloud9 knew such intimate information? She was *intimate* with a guard — or perhaps a counselor?

None of the attendants busy in the workout room resembled her quarry. Mostly in their thirties, her fellow attendants were an odd mix. Some sported elaborate, changeable body art, some strategic piercings, others were enhanced to fantasy proportions. Some fit into all of the above categories.

A tall brunette, who chose to work out nude, sauntered past Evans, carrying a shiny rod with bulbous ends. Surely she hadn't been born with those massive breasts? No, that wasn't right. No one was born with breasts. Evans giggled aloud at the thought of the woman as a baby trying to fit through the birth canal, hampered by huge boobs, and earned a stern look from one of the exercise counselors.

The woman's body art wasn't evident until she turned away. It was all Evans could do not to gape at the phoenix draped across the woman's back. The wings spread from shoulder to shoulder, framing the bird's colorful body. The coiled tail undulated as the brunette walked, drawing the eye down to where it disappeared between the woman's cheeks. The art undoubtedly continued on out of sight. This was no ordinary skin decal. This was hand-painted art. How many hours had it taken?

Although she tried to look away, Evans found her gaze locked on the woman as she mechanically did her own routine. The woman could press a sizeable weight while splayed on a weight bench, and at the same time, pump the shiny rod in and out with vaginal contractions. The common exercise area was supposed to be used for strength and endurance training, not sexual response training.

That occurred under the tutelage of specific instructors, in private. Or had, as far as Evans knew, until today. The brunette evidently had decided to make her exercise session do double-duty. With boobs like those and her vaginal talents, she probably had a full schedule of guests.

From her unshaved pubis, given Cloud9's comment, Evans guessed the woman catered to guests on the expensive fetish menus. The woman's abdominal muscles rippled as the smooth metal rod disappeared into her dark curls, reappearing a moment later, slick and wet. How did she manage to grip the thing?

Boy, am I a slacker, Evans thought as the woman double-pumped both the weight and the vaginal bar in time to the lively music that floated from hidden speakers.

Then the woman moved to one of the machines.

Evans had to admire her strength and control, as well as her concentration. Two gold piercings on her labia winked through her pubic hair as she went through her drills.

Her massive breasts hardly moved. More than gravity was holding those babies up. Evans wondered how they hid the struts and cables, and tried not to giggle again.

Shit. These strange thoughts kept distracting her. What drugs had they been giving her in her food? She had a hard time concentrating on her mission.

The woman ended her routine, reached down and drew out the rod. Evans gulped as she saw the thing was longer than she'd thought.

Link cock-sized, in fact. Thoughts of Link grounded her from her fugue. The brunette looked square at Evans and winked. Holding eye contact, the woman raised the ball to her lips and ran her tongue languidly across its curved surface.

Evans flushed and switched her attention to her own exercises. First in her peripheral vision and then in the mirrored wall, she was aware of the brunette sashaying out the door, still carrying the rod.

What if Link ordered that woman next time?

Next time?

Her insides quivered at the thought of the brunette's internal muscles sucking the sperm out of Link like a geo-tube sucked up rock samples.

She forced her mind from Link and concentrated on the counselors. She'd been trying to counteract the drugs and keep her mind sharp by recognizing the staff and attendants inside The Palace. She might need to know how many there were, what positions they held, and be able to recognize them later. She had also tried to talk to them — to no avail.

The two counselors in the exercise room were busy with administrative tasks at the moment, one working with his wrist panel and the other punching in codes on a communication unit. The display looked like a table of attendants, exercises, and reps.

She'd give a lot to get into The Palace's database. So far, she'd had as much luck breaking into the brothel's systems as she had chatting with counselors. There had to be cameras in her cell but she hadn't been able to locate them yet. Until she could, and disengaged them, she didn't have a prayer of working on a comm panel.

When she finished her routine, the counselor who'd frowned at her giggles came over. "You are to report to the medical center."

"Why? I just had a disease check three days ago." Evans mopped the sweat off the back of her neck.

"It is not my place to worry about that. I only know you have been summoned."

She turned in her towel and workout garments for a robe at the checkout window, pulled it on and followed the counselor to the door, who told the guard, "Take her to the med center."

It was like an out-of-body experience. Between the exercises and whatever drugs they'd given her, Evans had a hard time negotiating the hallway. They'd round a corner and the floor would pitch at an angle. The guard had to support her several times or she would have fallen. For some reason, giggles kept burbling out of her.

"Come on, sister. I'm not paid to haul you around," the guard grumbled. "Give me a troublesome client over a slap happy whore any day."

Evans did her best to straighten up, but the occasional giggle still slipped out. Inside, she was horrified. She'd never, even as a teenager, been a giggler.

They entered a corridor she'd not been in before. Following her mental map as she always did, and despite the drugs, she knew the moment they walked into unfamiliar territory.

They'd moved far outside what she had thought the boundaries were for that floor. They paused at a door to allow a counselor to pass. On Evans's mental map, they stood deep in what had been a blank area. She adjusted and expanded the floor plan as they went. The door clicked open to a short hallway with five doors on one side and none on the other. The fifth door opened into a gleaming white exam room exactly like the one in which she'd had her last check-up.

The guard pushed her through and remained in the hall. The opposite door opened, and Evans sighed. It was Jennel again. Med-Aide Jennel. Evans took one look at her hard face and lost the persistent urge to giggle. Instead, she felt heat flushing her skin. Sweat broke on her forehead.

"Come along with you, up on the table." Jennel's smile didn't reach her cold eyes.

"What am I here for?" Evans stood her ground, just inside the door. She tried not to sway.

"Blood work. You did service a client with live sperm, you know." With efficient movements, the med-aide slid a tray out of the wall and put together a syringe.

"Oh." Evens worked to pull herself together while she watched the preparations. No way could she think of Link as a client. Was it possible she'd conjured him up from some drug-induced dream and mentally superimposed his face on another man's?

"Have you been eating well? Have you lost weight?" Jennel cupped Evans's chin in her hand and twisted, tilting Evans's face toward an overhead light. The woman examined her skin and had her open her mouth before releasing her.

"Why?"

"Just answer the question."

"I'm fine."

The sideways slide of the woman's eyes told Evans she thought she was lying.

"Sit. Or not. If you don't want to make yourself comfortable, that's up to you."

Evans sat, and the woman slid a tournicuff up her arm. She was more gentle with the syringe than Evans expected, which brought back the giggles. The med-aide gave her a sharp look as she sprayed sealant on the needle mark.

Back in her cell, Evans giggled again when the door clicked shut behind her, locking her in. What drug had they given her, and how? Had it been in her meal? Why hadn't her exercises helped her metabolize it more quickly?

She didn't believe they were checking to see if Link's sperm was tainted with disease-causing microbes.

Was the blood work to check up on how her body reacted to the drugs? *Shit.* What if The Palace was conducting rogue clinical trials? What if The Palace was involved in developing illegal drugs?

If that was the case, she had to get Angel out before the place blew wide open. If some local force busted the place, Angel's name and relationship to the top dog in Homeland Security would be the lead item on every infocast. Drug officers were notorious news hounds.

Angel's father wanted this kept quiet. Homeland Security couldn't afford blackmail, at any level.

Evans marshaled her thoughts, trying to pierce the mental fog and focus on the floor plan she'd been building in her head. She expanded it as often as she could, every time she peeked through a new doorway or was taken down a new hallway to serve a guest.

It was essentially a prison, this brothel. No one mentioned the locked doors, the punishments for any sign of disobedience, or that many of the attendants were criminals. They'd opted for doing their time in this "assignment" rather than a real prison. But not all of them were convicts. Some wanted the credits one could earn from selling sex. Others were reputedly street kids and runaways who'd been coerced into the life and hadn't a hope of escaping once the doors locked behind them.

What had become of Angel Martinez? The thought sobered Evans, driving away any remaining impulse to giggle. According to Angel's father, she'd been a troubled child and grown more troubled as she went through her teens. According to her friends, she'd been hanging out with a man known for "recruiting" young talent for The Palace. However, none of them knew his name, or else they were too frightened to admit it. The only other evidence they had indicating Angel was inside was a fleeting glimpse of her on a street cam located in front of The Palace's outer doors.

The view screen on Evans's wall blinked on, informing her she had a guest in one hour. Suddenly, the giggles were gone and the accelerated heart rate was back.

It's only one task, she told herself. Only one.

And if it was a short one, she could get to the rec hall early enough to question a few more of the attendants about Angel. Her gaze shifted back to the screen. The assignment was a number seventeen on the menu of pleasures available to members. Number seventeen was a back massage.

Her heartbeat settled down to normal. Back massages were innocuous.

Chapter 4

❧

Evans eased the door closed on the massage room. Her guest was already stretched out nude on the bed, a length of heat cloth drawn up so it didn't quite cover the cleft of his buttocks. The intention was that she could better tease him a bit below the waist. When the overseer offered an upgrade to a full body massage, the guest would be that much better motivated. Upgrades were supposedly, along with undefined treats, a way for attendants to earn more time in the rec hall.

Cloud9 had spoken of tips from clients, but Evans had never seen any evidence of monetary rewards. She suspected all of the rewards were empty promises, but she didn't know for sure. She'd yet to have a guest even agree to an upgrade.

The room was warm and suffused with her usual yellow glow. Music played and the scent of a pine forest filled the chamber. A small table filled with bottles of fragrant oils and lotions and a few sex toys stood near the head of the table. When she neared the bed, a jolt of awareness passed through her.

Link.

His head was propped on his folded arms, his face turned away. What the hell was he doing here? Why had he chosen her again?

An unaccountable fury swept over her and the unmistakable burn of tears filled her eyes. Anger because he complicated her mission and tears that he must think she was what she looked to be—a whore.

The chamber overseer informed Link that the attendant was required to test his skin for sensitivity to the various oils and creams used during the massage. His patience was requested during the process.

She picked up the allergy cloth and ran it over his skin. When the cloth turned orange, the overseer informed Link the lubrications she used would be tailored to his sensitivities. He was also informed that if he ejaculated during the massage, he must tell his attendant so she could offer him the appropriate cleansing cloths before he left.

At the word ejaculation, Link clenched his buttocks and shifted his hips. Evans strove for a mind block, but the drugs in her system made concentration almost impossible. She found she couldn't turn her attention inward the way she'd like to; she had no choice but to pay attention to what she was doing.

Link's body was superb. He had two scars along his ribcage from heat weapons. She remembered his eagerness to get into the corporate wars. She wondered how and where he'd been wounded.

He showed no evidence of allergies. Gently, she oiled her fingertips and worked her way along his shoulders, keeping her attention on her hands.

Warmth filled her as she explored the strong, honed shape of his upper body. She trailed her fingertips down the deep indentation of his spine, edged with hard muscle. In truth, there was nothing therapeutic about the massage. Its purpose was arousal, pure and simple, and its goal orgasm. The guest was the one who was supposed to respond, but she found herself becoming aroused.

She poured a line of warm oil into the valley of his spine and spread it to left and right in gentle sweeps of her flattened palms. His muscles bunched. Evans shook as heat flared in her belly. Her eyes were drawn to the rise of his buttocks. She remembered anchoring her hands on them to ride out the incredible orgasms he'd drawn from her. The memory made her hunger for his touch. She struggled to keep her hands moving smoothly and shifted her hips. Her fingertips skimmed lower.

He turned his head from left to right, burying his face in the crook of his elbow. No face-down hole to stare through here. No real pretense that this wasn't a bed either, when the usual male voice spoke.

"If you wish to upgrade your pleasure, there are various options available today." Evans kept her hands moving in the prescribed languid sweeps. "We are offering a special full-body massage for an additional five hundred ninety credits. Or take advantage of your position and select from an array of insertion devices for the same price. Your attendant is fully versed in their use."

Link said nothing, but his back muscles tightened under her hands.

She kept up the exploration of his body at his waist, coming closer each time to the edge of the sheet. Her unimproved breasts brushed against the inside of her robe with each movement she made. The material, soft as it was, rasped across her sensitive nipples. How much longer could she go on without revealing her own desire? She struggled to control her breathing, to keep it even and steady.

"Please remember that it is not permitted for back-only massage guests to turn over without increasing their credit total. There's a keypad on the massage table so you will not need to change position should you wish to make an upgrade. All attendants are well versed in the art of fellatio. Just eight hundred more credits today."

Link's whole body tensed. She imagined his cock was rock hard against the table. Sweet Sol, she wanted him to turn over, pull her up and fill her the way he had when they were escaping the drudgery of their first year at the Academy.

She threw herself into her work, putting all the hunger she felt into each touch, willing him to feel the longing that racked her. His ribcage reacted as she slid her hands along his sides, skimming far enough under to tease his nipples with her fingertips. He made a guttural sound in his throat.

But he didn't upgrade.

He fisted his hands and remained almost frozen on the table, his eyes closed. She increased the pressure and tempo of the massage, and fought a growing desire to lean down and kiss his scars. He shifted under her hands. His skin, reacting to the oils, was hot and running with sweat. Her fingers left visible paths across his skin as she stroked and teased him.

Evans knew Link's time was almost over. Her insides were liquid hot, her nipples so swollen they were chafed from shifting against her robe. How could she face the aftermath of this massage? She dragged her fingers down the center of his spine, to the cleft of his buttocks. He shuddered and moaned.

Her upgrade buddy spoke up right on cue. "Your time is up. Thank you for choosing a therapeutic back massage. We hope you've enjoyed your attendant's services. The table sensors indicate you need a cleansing, which is offered at no additional charge."

Link shifted to his side and sat up, drawing the heat sheet across his loins as he did so. She kept her gaze on his feet. Feet she recognized all too well. Big feet she'd played toe games with in the aftermath of sex, usually when they lay tangled together and talked of their future and dreams.

Where had Link gotten the credits for his visits to The Palace? Was he on the take? She rejected the idea as absurd as soon as it occurred to her. Not Link. Anyone but him. But then, he was the last man she'd expected to see walk into The Palace as a guest.

She didn't need another mystery to solve. Her mission centered around a missing AOA, one whose life might be in danger.

A panel slid open in the wall, revealing several of the cleansing cloths she'd used on him the last time. They lay on top of a large disposal pouch.

With hands that were not quite steady, she approached Link's lap.

This was not a task. This was torture, she decided as she worked to wipe away the evidence of his climax. She desperately wished to look up and see how he was handling this.

Would she see the same blank look on his face as the other day? Or would she see disgust?

"Look at me," he said softly, as if he read her mind.

The magic words that allowed her a punishment-free look at him had been said. She lifted her gaze.

His eyes were still the shade of an old pewter tankard from one of the museums he used to love to haunt. His brows were dark straight slashes over his eyes. He looked hard.

Link Taylor *was* a hard man.

He examined her face, but without the flush she knew must be so evident on hers. He watched her with a cool, detached expression. He might have been any client, one who had chosen her at random, for no particular reason.

His hand fell to the bed, and she returned her gaze to his lap. His cock stirred as she swept the soft cloth over him and the longer she took, the harder he grew. She longed to stroke him with a real caress, but he'd not upgraded, so she kept to the required cleansing.

She held up the heat cloth when the job was done. He wrapped it around his hips as he slid from the bed and headed for the door. She took her time wiping down the massage table for the next client, willing the tumult within her to subside and ignoring the cold-sounding click as he left without a word.

Questions about what had happened to him in the intervening years of their separation swirled in her head. Why had he come to The Palace? How could he possibly afford it?

Once she had finished with the table, she packed all of the cloths into the pouch then put it, the oils, and the unused toys into the little cupboard. When she slid it closed, another click, for her door, signaled to her that her task here was done.

She followed the guard back along the corridor. A soft chime startled her. What concerned Evans more was the guard's reaction. The beefy woman jerked open a door and thrust her through it into an empty guest chamber. In the instant before the door closed, Evans saw two guards rush past. They pushed a gurney carrying a draped form. A limp arm hung out from under the sheet. In the brief glimpse she had, she couldn't tell if it was a man or a woman.

Evans stood in the dark, wondering what had happened. She plotted the gurney's course in her head. It had come from an area she'd never entered. Were they headed for the infirmary? Had a fetish scenario gone horribly wrong? Or had some out of shape client gone too far for his health and stamina? Was it a guest or an attendant who lay under the sheet?

When the guard opened the door again, and beckoned her out, the hallway was clear.

Back in her cell, Evans pondered the gravity of her situation. She still had no idea where Angel might be. Because of the ticking clock on Angel's age and the lengthy application process for volunteers, Evans had come in as a convict, but she now knew that severely limited her movements. There were far fewer opportunities to make contacts than Intel had told her to expect, and she had no backup, no support. She was entirely on her own.

And now Link Taylor had discovered her.

She could deal with the mission stalling. She wasn't sure she could deal with Link Taylor.

She glanced at the view screen, blank at this time of night, and not for the first time wondered if it was also a view cam. Just in case, she rolled herself up in her blankets and buried her head under the sheets.

And cried.

Chapter 5
୫

Link woke up remembering the touch of Evans's hands on his back. And on his cock as she wiped away his semen. Despite that ejaculation, he'd left her with a hard-on and lacked the credits to do anything about it. He'd tamed his erection in the dressing rooms adjacent to the massage chamber.

Shit. He had to talk to her.

What the hell had happened to the most promising cadet at the academy that she now gave blowjobs for a living? He punched the mattress. He wanted to know what had pushed her out of the service and set her on that course. Her family was dirt poor, but those circumstances had not been the impetus for her to join the PeaceKeepers. Zeal, honor, duty had.

And Link knew it. The same ideals had brought him in, and they'd talked about old-fashioned principles for hours—and rued the cynicism that tainted the patriotism that had recruited them.

What the fuck had happened to his idealistic cadet?

How long had she been in that place, catering to the desires of the needy wealthy?

Who was he kidding? He was neither needy nor wealthy and he wanted her services.

Badly.

He tried the card after his cold shower and was directed to add to his balance. He didn't have enough credits left on it to allow him even one drink at The Palace's lounge.

Reviewing his personal assets gave him a stomachache. He had little in the way of liquidity. That was no surprise—who on the Mars Station needed pocket credits? Right after the war, he'd invested in long-term vehicles, set up to mature at his retirement. His investment in a shipping partnership supplying the off-planet stations wouldn't come up for confirmation for another five years.

On paper, he was fairly wealthy.

In actuality, he was almost broke.

The card purchase was typical of his investment luck. For a mere five credits, he'd gained entré into an exclusive sex club, complete with one masturbation experience and the most erotic back rub he could imagine. Not bad for a measly five credits.

So spend another five credits!

He smacked his forehead. He'd go back and see if The Fantasy Shoppe had another card — or maybe two — for sale.

Why hadn't he thought of that before?

He finished dressing in record time. Wolfing down his breakfast, he barely tasted the real scrambled eggs and ham before he scalded his throat with coffee. Muttering curses under his breath, he raced out the door, onto a waiting lift, through the hotel checkpoint, and out the doors.

Dodging traffic, he crossed the street in the shadows of the soaring mega-structures. At ground level he passed the blank walls of the great foundations, heading for the gap formed by two support columns, and the old shop nestled between them.

There he stopped and stared in disbelief. Between the towering supports, where The Fantasy Shoppe had stood, he faced an empty alley. His head spun. He shook it to clear his vision. A few scraps of paper blew along the slick pavement, now deep in shadow, where the shop had been.

He walked back to the corner and checked the signs. Yeah, this was the street. Directly across from a PeaceKeepers recruitment center, now that he looked around.

He walked the length of the block, down to the gleaming door of a Personal Improvement Center in the lower level of the city in a city overhead. All he passed were the street-access doors to the lower levels of a few other store fronts, the

PeaceKeeper recruitment center, a travel planner, a restaurant filthy enough to make him keep moving under any circumstances, and back to the other support structures of the overhead complex.

There was no one on street level to ask for directions. The PeaceKeeper recruiters raised wary eyebrows as he walked back and forth, and he was sure it was only his uniform that kept them from reporting him for heat stroke.

Overhead, PFs zipped around, jostling for space and docking on upper floors. If he recalled correctly, and he could swear he was right, the little shop had not extended up to a second story. Only a pedestrian would have noticed it, and they were in short supply.

He walked back and forth one more time, but didn't see anything resembling the quaint shop where he'd bought the card. He swore it had been right where the alley was.

Brad. Of course. His lieutenant had seen it.

That thought was immediately tempered by the memory that Brad's interest had been in drinking, not shopping. He hadn't actually entered the place. Would Brad look at him the same way the recruiters were eyeing him now, if he asked about a disappearing shop?

Frustrated, Link kicked the curb. So much for his investment luck.

He slowly made his way back to the headquarters hotel. There, he asked the officer on duty and one of the guards if they knew of any local shops where he could buy something unusual. The guard recommended the hotel gift shop. The duty officer directed him to her favorite shop, the nearest Glimmer Gifts outlet.

There was only one more place he could look. He hopped a slide-way into the bowels of HQ.

There, he checked in and was assigned a communications console, one of the desks available to whatever officers happened to be on base. A slew of messages popped up on the screen when he identified himself. Link ignored them and called up his banking records.

His liquid account showed no record of a five-credit debit to The Fantasy Shoppe.

Transactions were instant. *Shit.* He was out of options.

Almost.

With reluctance, he went in search of Brad. He found him tipped back in his chair, eyes closed, dictating a report to his comm panel

Link tapped him on the shoulder. "Brad. Did you know that huge synth-stone building on the corner of Oxford was a brothel?"

Brad dropped his feet to the floor and tapped a pad on the console to pause his report. "I've heard it rumored. Not a place you or I could ever afford, is my understanding. It's for diplomats, four-star generals, CEOs, INCs, you know, all those letter and number types."

"Well, I found a membership card to the place...in the street." Link crossed his arms over his chest in an effort to look casual. "I'm thinking of trying it out."

Brad made a rude noise. "You can get it free anytime, any port. So what are you thinking?"

"Of something different, if you get what I mean." Link wagged his eyebrows to keep the moment light. "I just need some way to put credits on the card."

"You'd have to have credits up the ass to afford that place. Why spend a month's pay for a blow job you can get from Pfc. Harkins in Supply anytime for free?"

"I don't think Harkins is up for what I'm looking for. And Harkins is doing Lieberman in personnel. She can't see past his Shuttle Relay Team silver medal belt buckle."

Brad laughed. "Can you say that three times fast?" He rose and slapped Link on the shoulder. "You know, I'm bored.

Maybe I'll check your brothel out. If we can get credits on your card, maybe we could make a twosome."

Link watched Brad leave the security area. He returned to his own space.

Make a twosome. The idea of Evans massaging Brad's equipment made his mouth go dry. Link forced his mind from the images he'd conjured up.

An hour later, as he was giving a last look over the roster of officers available for his next crew on the Mars Station, Brad burst in, breathing expensive Mars-tini fumes down his neck.

"You won't believe what I learned from the bartender at The Drowning Pool."

"Try me." Link kept his gaze on the roster and hoped his tension didn't show.

"The brothel is a private club, like I said. Some mighty exotic stuff in there, if half the rumors are true. But you won't get past the door without that card. Now, here's the good news. If you give him the card, the bartender knows a guy who knows a guy who knows a guy who can put double your credits on it— no questions asked. All you have to do is find some credits, this guy does some magic... and bingo, we're being sucked and fucked."

No, Link thought, *only I'm using the card.* He studied a heat scar across the back of his hand. "Great. I'll get the credits. You introduce me to the bartender."

* * * * *

Link activated the card. The gold and white swirl seemed to take longer than usual to disappear. A cat-eyed woman, this time with lavender hair, welcomed him with gushing enthusiasm. He suspected the enthusiasm of her greeting had ratcheted up in direct proportion to the number of new credits on his card.

The menu was much more extensive, though not exotic.

So what was exotic? Flowers up his ass?

He sorted through the menus again and again, almost caressing the view screen with his fingertips as he contemplated the options for an hour with Evans. And he'd thought the touch screen was out of date. For this application, it was appropriate.

Fellatio.

Anal sex.

Partner Pulsations

Gusto Grannies

Dozens of terms he'd never thought about in connection with sex.

Shower Fun.

The listing caught his eye. He tapped the words and reared back as a very realistic gush of water shot at him. He laughed at his overreaction. It betrayed the state of his nerves.

The water "dripped" down the screen and then the screen fogged as if it were the glass wall of a shower. A woman's finger drew the list of options with agonizing slowness. Each word revealed a little more of her sultry nudity behind the shower door. As the list of options and prices appeared, so did more of her. By the time she traced the last word on the menu, he could see every luscious inch of her—and the huge dildo she plied in her free hand.

Without hesitation Link touched one of the options.

Shower with attendant, sexual activity (barring violence).

Another screen appeared. A simple accounting of cost. He opted for two orgasms and gulped at the number of extra credits he had to fork over for the privilege of getting off twice in one visit.

Lastly, the screen shifted and fogged over, then a hand wiped it clear to reveal the usual bevy of attendants ready and willing to suck and fuck him under the sensuous spray of a ten-jet shower chamber.

Evans was there.

His cock twitched at the thought of more time spent with her. He flattened his hand on her image.

Another image came to mind. Pulling back the cheap plastic curtain of the barracks shower stall. Watching her soap her breasts, watching her turn and smile at him.

And hold out her hand.

* * * * *

Evans examined the shower chamber, an authentic marble-tiled room with a retraction toilet and sink. A long counter held a basket of supplies chosen by the guest to enhance the bathing experience. She grinned. The basket was empty except for a bottle of liquid soap and a cloth. So, her guest was a no-nonsense man... or woman.

Shit. The room shifted. She gasped and grabbed the counter.

"Are you ill, Bliss6?" asked the ever-present chaperone's voice.

"I-I think... that is." She sat abruptly on the toilet as it slid from the wall.

"Take deep breaths. And drink some water."

Her hand shook as she reached for the cup that had appeared behind a sliding panel in the wall. It held cool water — and something else. Something minty. She drank it down and leaned forward, putting her head between her knees.

With each breath she felt better. Not clearer in the head, but less nauseated.

"Are you ready for your guest?" the voice asked.

"Sure," she said, standing up and testing her balance. She blinked and suddenly the soft peach and gray colors of the marble shower chamber came into focus, sharp and clear. She heard the whoosh of water as the shower jets began to spout, out of sight behind the wall she faced.

She discarded her robe and took up the little basket with its lonely bottle of bath soap and cloth. Walking into the shower was like walking into a spiral shell. The circular center had jets coming from all heights. Several curved ledges protruded from the slick walls, sculpted to nestle a bottom or support a leg. She set her basket down. Here and there, bars offered a guest someplace to hang onto if necessary. Around the top of the enclosure hung hand straps. The floor beneath her feet was made of a resilient, warm material, and the inner chamber was wide enough that even a man as tall as Link Taylor could lie down and get screwed in complete comfort.

Evans felt her heartbeat escalate and shut her mind on the image of Link stretched out on the floor and her lowering herself on his erection. She stepped into the jets and allowed the blood-warm water to wash away her anxiety. Or was she feeling the minty drug begin its intended work?

She slicked back her hair. It hung down to the middle of her back, the only improvement the establishment had forced on her. She was surprised Link recognized her.

After twelve days of injections, her hair had gone from military crop to bumper crop. She giggled at her mental turn of phrase, then sobered. A shift in the air pressure told her the guest had arrived.

She would think of Link as she pleasured this guest. She would close her eyes and conjure the hard masculine lines of his body. It might be the only way she could get through the task — especially if her guest was like the last, a sinewy woman in her eighties.

A hand fell on Evans's shoulder. She forced herself not to cringe or recoil. Eyes closed, head down, she turned. Opened her eyes. And saw his feet.

Link's feet.

A soft moan escaped her. He gathered her hair and smoothed it from her brow, back over her shoulders. The touch of his hands liquefied her insides. As he stroked her shoulders, she knew she wanted nothing more than to feel him buried inside her.

"Look at me," he said.

And because he made the request, she was permitted to do so.

His expression was no longer blank. His pupils were dilated, his eyes almost black in the soft light of the peach and gray chamber. His nostrils flared.

He cupped the back of her neck and drew her close.

For a moment, her heart went wild. When his mouth settled on her brow, she shivered and grabbed his forearms to hold herself upright.

The last time he'd kissed her temple, feathering his breath across the skin, he'd also driven his cock so deep inside her she'd screamed.

He made an inarticulate sound. Did he remember that time as well? The last time they'd seen each other before he'd shipped out? How he'd held her against the wall of the departure room? How he'd banged her so hard against the wall that the parting couple in the next room had roared with laughter and shouted their encouragement?

She quivered when he skimmed the backs of his fingertips down her cheek.

"You are lovely," he said.

"Thank you," was all she was permitted in response. His preference profile said not to speak unless spoken to.

He scrutinized her face, touching the small marks he found in her unimproved complexion.

"Lovely," he whispered, leaning down and pressing his lips to her wet shoulder.

She drew him into the arching sprays of body temperature water. She had a job to do.

And someone to watch over her.

"What's first?" he asked, rubbing his palms up and down her arms.

"You've chosen free expression in a shower scenario. As long as you don't hurt me, you're free to do as you please. I'm here for your pleasure." She found her throat thick and her tongue clumsy on the prescribed words. "You paid for t-two or-orgasms. You have whatever time you need."

"As long as I don't hurt you." He ran his hands from her shoulders to her breasts. Slowly, he stroked the water drops around her nipples. "Who decides what's hurtful?"

She met his gaze. At the same time she covered his hands with hers and pressed them to her nipples. They were hyper-sensitive and she wondered if it was the drugs or the tension of being in Link's company, of being touched by him again after all these years.

After all her fantasies.

"If I say that something hurts, you must stop or the scenario will end."

And two burly guards will remove you if you don't cease hurting me immediately, she thought. Of course, he knew that. The instructions were given to him when he checked in.

"I understand." He ran his fingertips down the center of her body to her navel. And further on down, between her legs. She anchored herself by gripping his biceps and took a deep breath.

He found her clit and rubbed her gently. Much as he might have years ago. He slid first one finger, then a second, inside her. "You're wet as a whore."

She opened her eyes and stared at him. His face was in shadow, too dark for her to read any intent in his expression. She clamped her jaw tight on a retort, but could not stop her body from stiffening.

"Do you always get wet for the customer or do you use a lubricant?"

"I'm unimproved," she said, her voice hoarse. Her fingers bit into his rock hard arms as he rhythmically stroked two fingers in and out of her.

"Is that so?" He pushed with his hand and with his fingers so deep inside her, she had to stumble back against the wall. A jet was in the center of her back, gushing warm water the way her insides gushed the fluids to ease his way.

Abruptly, he let her go. "What's this?" He moved to the basket and looked inside.

"Those are the items you selected," she said. The urge to put her hand to her crotch and press on the ache left there by his touch was almost overwhelming.

He grunted and tossed her the soap bottle. She fumbled the cap open and poured a generous amount in her palms.

He held his arms out wide and said, "Wash me."

Standing there, he looked magnificent and dangerous. Sparkling beads of water misted his dark hair. Water ran in narrow rivulets along the defined muscles of his upper torso, into a stream that parted about his engorged penis.

Sweet Sol, was he engorged. Ten years might have taken a little of the lift out of his penis, but the way it swelled and moved told her he was unimproved as well.

Just as he was not on sperm suppressors, so he'd obviously not taken any of the many pleasure drugs available, legal or illegal. Some of the drugs were as expensive as the scenario itself. The ones offered by The Palace were engineered to last the specific time needed to move clients through their programs. A natural erection had its own time and rhythm. The term of some drugs was as short as thirty minutes, but they were said to yield an orgasm forceful enough to make a grown man scream himself hoarse or pass out.

The drugs also had side effects that were not so enjoyable. Some men experienced impotence for days or weeks afterwards. Others found themselves at the opposite end of the spectrum, suffering continual tumescence for an extended period of time without achieving relief. But even healthy men could become addicted to the incredible increase in stamina.

Evans remembered Link's stamina. Ten years hadn't changed him much, from what she could see. A new gush of hot liquid flooded her insides.

She slicked the soap across his chest, teasing his nipples, pinching them. He grunted and turned around.

She did as she had in the massage room. She rubbed his back, the soap generating a slick and slippery surface for her hands to slide across.

But unlike in the massage chamber, here she could do as she pleased with him.

Her fingers skimmed down the valley of his spine and into the cleft of his buttocks. She used the side of her hand and ran it up and down. He clenched his muscles and propped his hands on the shower room wall.

She soaped her palms again and knelt behind him. She lavished the suds on the inside of his legs, up and down from ankle to groin.

Then she stood up and soaped her body. Next, she leaned against him, matching her legs to the backs of his, holding his hips. He was a head taller than her, so she stood on tiptoe to get as much of her skin against him as she could.

Holding his hips she slid up and down, teasing his body with hers, shifting her pubic hair across the back of his thighs, rubbing her nipples, tight as stylus points, across his back.

"Enough," he gasped.

She stepped away.

He turned around, one hand wrapped around his cock. He was squeezing beneath the head and she knew he'd almost lost it. She almost smiled. No, he hadn't changed that much.

"Come here," he said and held out his other hand.

She stared at the outstretched hand. And wanted to take it and hold it again to her breast. Instead, she leaned forward and pressed her lips to the center of his palm. He cupped his hand and she captured it and held it to her mouth. She tongued him, from his palm to the inside of his wrist.

From the corner of her eye she saw him let go of his cock. She wrapped her hand around it and stroked him.

"I'm not ready," he said, covering her hand and stopping her caress. "I don't think I feel adequately... clean."

Then he grinned at her. It was the old Link Taylor smile. Lots of white, fine teeth, improved in his youth, she was sure. A flood of memories swept over her. Other smiles. Other showers.

She forced herself into her meek attendant demeanor and picked up the soap bottle. This time, she soaped the cloth and very meticulously washed his body. Down his beautiful, rippled abdomen, then to his penis. It was hard and unyielding through the cloth. It wouldn't take much to set him off, but she wasn't ready for the ending, either. Even though he had paid for two climaxes, the faster he reached the first one, the sooner he'd go.

And she couldn't bear to part with him.

She went down on her knees. The water sluiced his penis clear as quickly as she soaped him.

He cupped her head as she slid her mouth over the head of his penis, shielding her from the direct spray of the water jets.

Every lick up and down the shaft of his penis drew from him a guttural sound that she remembered well.

"Are you pleased?" she asked as she was required.

There was a minute pause before he said, "Yes." The word came out with a gust of long held breath. She smiled.

He rhythmically smoothed her hair from her brow and when she tipped up his cock to lick the underside, she stole a look up. He was watching her.

Her insides quivered. She shuddered as a small spasm, the beginning of a climax, rippled through her. Oh, she hadn't changed that much herself, had she?

He leaned against the wall and propped one foot up on a conveniently placed ledge. It allowed her to lick and nuzzle deeper between his thighs, gave her the ability to suckle his testicles. She pulled the warm weight of one after the other into her mouth.

Water ran down and over her mouth and cheeks.

"I'm going to come," he said, holding her head and gasping.

His come spurted hot and thick into her mouth. She let it flow down his shaft and over her fingers.

The water sluiced it away, down his thighs.

Then he jerked her to her feet.

His mouth closed over hers, his tongue sweeping in and rolling across the remnants of the semen in her mouth. She felt devoured.

Possessed.

He turned her and backed her to one of the little ledges. Then it was him on his knees and her bottom cradled on the curved ledge. He spread her legs. Clever, carved ridges and the contours in the seat kept her comfortably in position.

The tip of his tongue found her clit.

Despite the contours of her perch, she was unable to lean back enough to give him the access he needed. With a growl of frustration, he lifted her and placed her gently on the shower floor. Water gushed over his back and across his shoulders when he buried his face between her thighs.

His tongue was talented, his technique unchanged by their years apart. He licked and stroked her with catlike efficiency. She struggled to keep still as he probed her deeply. Trying to relax made the sensations harder to resist, the orgasm more difficult to stave off.

Sweet Sol, she'd missed him. Memories of other times, other places combined with the present, propelling her to familiar heights.

She swallowed a scream and bucked her hips against his mouth, the ripples of the climax shooting from her groin to the soles of her feet. Somehow Link followed the heaving movements of her hips, sucking her labia into his mouth as she trembled in the throes of the aftershocks. When she went limp as the discarded washcloth on the shower floor, he caged her by straddling her on his hands and knees.

They stared at one another. She licked her lips. He licked his.

"One down. One more to go," he said softly.

And grinned.

Chapter 6
❧

He thought he might be able to feast on her all day, but she'd ended that idea by coming in but a few moments. He'd scarcely started and she'd fallen apart. Did the drugs she took include something to heighten her sensitivity, increase her response to stimulation?

And artificially give the impression he was quite a guy between the thighs?

He'd refused the erection enhancers he could afford, telling the counselor he was allergic to them. That was true, but he would have risked the reaction if it had increased his time with her. The drugs doubled the cost of the scenario, but the aspect most important to him was the short lifespan, no more than thirty minutes, of the ones he could access. It simply wasn't enough time with her.

He knew this session wasn't going to be enough time with her, either, no matter what he did. He had to draw out his next climax. As the thought entered his head, she reached up between his legs and squeezed his balls. He took her hand and slid it to his thigh. "Not yet, sweetheart. I'd like a little clean-up first."

She obliged him. To gain control of his erection, he had to close his eyes and calculate the amount of fuel needed to make it to Mars and back in the new Z-282 fighter. Then he calculated the cost of that fuel, both at current prices and with a 13.6 percent increase.

He couldn't keep his hands off her. He loved the feel of her small breasts. Loved the way her nipples peaked under his touch. He wanted to lick them raw.

He soaped his hands and mirrored her motions, rubbing her wherever she rubbed him. If she slipped her hands between his thighs, he slipped his between hers.

If she stroked his buttocks, he stroked hers.

He cupped her chin, held it still, and licked each drop of water that beaded there. She opened her lips and put out her tongue. He slipped and slid his over and around hers, just barely touching the tip.

There was no stopping his cock from filling with blood or his balls from aching.

"Bend over," he finally managed to say, and she did, planting her hands on her knees.

"I'm just going to admire the view for a moment," he said, stepping away to catch his breath and subdue his arousal.

Water hit her back and ran into the cleft of her buttocks. She was shaved down to not much pubic hair, but the soft tuft left behind was dripping and he watched the water for a moment. He thought of soaping his fingertips and probing her anally, but didn't.

He'd paid for whatever he wanted, but he knew her, he knew what she liked. Or rather, he knew what she'd liked once. Now she was a cock jockey. She was paid to take whatever the client wanted.

Memories still held him back. He did soap his hands and did massage the sweet globes of her ass.

She turned and reached for him, and he said, "Don't touch. I'm still playing back here."

Her buttocks clenched. He continued his massage, wanting to suck proprietary passion marks on her firm ass, so her next guest would know she'd just made love to someone else.

But he'd lost sight of something: they weren't making love. They were fucking. And he was paying a fortune for the privilege of watching her suck his cock and in a moment, maybe take a ride on his joystick.

"I want to fuck you. Face to face," he said without further thought.

And it really was what he wanted. She turned around and came into his arms as if no time had passed for them.

Her kiss was sweet as he lifted her high.

"Keep your eyes open," he ordered when she wrapped her legs about his hips.

He guided his cock into her. She moaned and her eyes flickered shut as he slid deep. "Keep them open, I said."

"As you wish," she whispered.

Then he had to close his. She was feather light in his arms. Her thighs quivered and she began to pant as he raised and lowered her on his erection.

"Come for me," he said, kissing her mouth, her chin, her throat. "Come for me."

She rode him frantically, bucking against him. And then he felt her climax ripple through her slick body. Nothing fake about it. He remembered every nuance of her reactions. The hitch in her breathing gave her away. If he opened his eyes, he was certain he'd see the familiar telltale flush across the pale skin of her throat, spreading down to cover her breasts.

He felt her orgasm ripple and grip his cock, and the answering clench deep within his body. Way down in his balls. It made his own climax erupt from deep down, too. He buried his face against her neck and groaned. He shuddered, shook with the force of the blast off.

Her whole body trembled in his arms.

He bent her back and licked her nipples, licked up the drops of water running between the small sweet mounds.

"Thank you for choosing the shower scenario," a cheery but familiar voice said.

For a mad moment, he almost shouted at the guy to go fuck himself. Then he remembered he was simply a client.

Evans slid gracefully out of his embrace.

"The attendant will be happy to assist you in the cleansing process."

"Don't," he snapped when she reached for the washcloth. "Leave it."

He watched her go, her hips swinging in that sensual rhythm he remembered so well. Anger pumped through him almost as hard as his come had pumped into her.

Why was he angry?

He knew why. She might be taking a shower with someone else in the next hour. Having orgasms, sucking someone else's cock.

He hastily washed and left the curled cleverness of the shower unit. In the outer chamber a urinal and toilet slid from the wall along with a wash basin. The chamber was empty.

She was gone. Nothing of her remained behind, not even the scent he remembered on her skin as though it was yesterday. It struck him that he had never been aware of her smell, during any of his visits to The Palace. They'd once made a game of finding each other in the dark, without touch. He had known her bunk by the lingering scent of her skin, her hair, her essence.

How had they erased her scent?

The hell with that, how had they broken her spirit? The Sara Evans he'd known ten years before would never have tolerated this *don't look him in the face, give the guest whatever he desires,* bullshit.

* * * * *

Evans spread her thighs for the elderly doctor. He had a full mane of luxurious white hair, but his face was as lined as the Mars surface. Over one hundred, maybe even one-twenty. Med-Aide Jennel glowered at the man's side.

"What's this for?" Evans asked for the second time.

"Shut up," Jennel snapped at the same time the doctor said, "Routine."

"Don't question Dr. Owen," the med-aide instructed.

Evans swore under her breath as the doctor swabbed her insides out and Jennel sealed the samples in pouches. Once the swabbing was done, the doctor barked, "Irrigation." Jennel retrieved a pouch of fluid with an attached tube and a basin. While the doctor flushed her vagina with a soothing wash, the med-aide caught the outflow in the basin.

Good-bye, Link spermies, Evans thought and giggled.

The doctor stood up and dipped his hands in a fluid that dissolved his sprayed on protective shield. She hiccuped.

Dr. Owen lifted his eyes to hers. His faded blue eyes held a touch of amusement, and a touch of yellow in the whites.

"I think you're receiving too much B12, young lady," he said. "Jennel, make a note to decrease her dose. We want her healthy, not giddy."

B12, my ass. Evans headed for her cell. And why all the health checks? Surely one test of Link's come would show he was squeaky clean. Or had something popped up? That thought killed the giggles.

Who knew who Link had been probing these last ten years?

As she drifted to sleep, she felt her mood slide toward depression. *It's just the drugs,* she thought. *It's just the drugs.*

* * * * *

Each morning when she read her list of tasks for the day, she wondered if Link might be on it. Two days had passed since the shower scenario. Two sleepless nights spent aroused almost to the point of screaming, remembering the fullness of him inside her, the force of the climax that had been sparked by his demand that she come for him.

She donned her robe and went to her first appointment. Her mind was half on Link and half on Angel Martinez and the hopelessness of finding out what had happened to the young woman. She'd at least found one attendant in the mess hall, a man who remembered Angel from his induction and early training but hadn't seen her since. He was wildly handsome and strutted like a peacock, puffed up that he was now the third most frequently requested male by women fifty and over. And tenth with men under thirty.

Evans shivered. What had become of Angel? Who was requesting her services?

Her first client of the day, a well-built man who, from his sun damaged skin obviously risked excessive UV exposure to pursue outdoor activities, did not wait for her to open his robe. He pulled it open as he crossed the chamber.

* * * * *

If it weren't for thoughts of Angel Martinez and her agonized father, Evans knew she might have been tempted to tell her last client, the arrogant asshole, that she knew fifteen very efficient — and painful — ways to kill a man. She'd settled for pinching him beneath the concealment of his robe.

When she was back in the bathing room, washing her hair for the next client, the door behind her opened. A tall woman in a robe like hers entered. She was also an attendant, but one who had achieved the privilege of directing others. Her name was Heaven4.

"You were not very polite to your guest."

Evans stood under a gently blowing current of air and jerked a brush through her hair. "He was hurting me. I thought someone was supposed to intervene."

"They decide when to intervene. Not you. This is not your first lapse of manners, is it?"

Evans didn't answer. It was, in fact, her third "lapse" of manners.

"You will pretend to enjoy all facets of every encounter or the guest will not be properly served. Do you understand?"

She swallowed her ready retort and lowered her head. "I do," she said with pretended meekness.

Heaven4 came up behind her. "Get on the bench and open your legs."

Evans did as directed, lying back on a soft, padded bench and suffered the indignity of the woman spreading her nether lips and inspecting her.

"You're a bit chafed." On cue, a panel slid open in the wall. Heaven4 took out an iridescent bottle with a short nozzle. She sprayed a cold blast of liquid across Evans's clit.

She went numb.

Heaven4 ushered Evans back to her cell. As she turned to go, she said, "That will wear off in about forty minutes. If you have a guest, fake it."

Chapter 7

ഇ

Link obtained a loan at a financial center. He put every credit on his brothel card through Brad's bartender connection, thankful that once sober, Brad never mentioned accompanying Link on any adventures.

"I'm addicted," he muttered as he activated the card in his chamber. He'd be eating the proverbial beans from now on.

He'd learned how to cut through the magic bullshit of graphics and enticing women to the matter-of-fact lists of services and prices—and attendants.

Like a man hooked on the latest ecstasy drugs, he chose Evans and, with a hard swallow but no regrets for the upcoming loan payments, selected a full night in a bed, with a level two privacy option.

He didn't care that the disembodied voice might invite him to upgrade or might warn him from touching or speaking at the wrong moment. He cared only that it was the most time he could get with Evans for his credits.

The room he entered looked much like a luxury hotel room—a room that glowed with golden light. A *very* expensive hotel room. The opulent furniture, crafted of actual wood and upholstered in soft, gold-hued fabrics, was nothing like that found in his government-budget room.

Across one wall stretched an array of tech devices for vids and music. He opted for a miscellany of piano pieces and set them on uninterrupted repeat. He crossed to the wall of glass, ignoring Evans, who, garbed in a long white robe, sat on one of the golden chairs.

They were eight stories up in a thirty-story brothel. The building surrounded an inner courtyard. From the street, The Palace looked like a cube. Now, he saw it was more like a square doughnut.

The gardens below were drenched in flowering bushes and plants. No one strolled on the meandering paths or occupied the benches in the center swath of grass. No one would dare, on such a blindingly sunny day. Too much exposure to UV rays. The maintenance crew must work at night. No sheltered areas were visible, so Link assumed the garden was solely ornamental — a pleasure for the eyes only.

He turned from the view to Evans and stroked his fingertips down the shiny length of her hair. She turned her head and nuzzled his hand, her eyes closed.

His male irritant announced the company's joy that he'd selected the rich experience of free expression for a night. Link half-listened to admonishments against violence of any kind and a reminder that since his server was unimproved, he could end the session at any time if he chose, but, regretfully, no refund would be given.

He couldn't wait. He bent down and scooped her into his arms. They fell across the bed, her robe hiked up to her thighs. She fumbled beneath his tunic, tugged down his uniform trousers and wrapped her hands around his penis.

To his complete and utter joy and embarrassment, he came.

Evans stifled a giggle. When Link smiled and dropped his head on her shoulder with a sigh, she let the giggle warm to a soft laugh. She kissed his ear and stroked the hair from his brow.

His weight was comfortingly heavy across her.

His breath was warm on her brow as he whispered, "That was a surprise. I guess the anticipation got to me."

They lay nose to nose. His pewter eyes were beautiful. She traced the shape of his brows, his nose, his lips.

He captured her fingertips in his mouth and sucked.

She couldn't speak until he asked her to. Words crowded inside her mouth. *Touch me. Lick me. Kiss me.* Heat shot across her skin. Not being able to voice her thoughts made her hotter. *Fuck me. Love me.*

Love?

She'd loved him desperately once, but they'd agreed they had careers, dreams to satisfy themselves before they could satisfy anyone else. He'd gone off-world; she'd succumbed to the seduction of working as an agent for Homeland Security. And she'd never seen him again.

A thickness gathered in her throat. She looked away from the probe of his gaze. There were hidden cameras here somewhere. There always were.

She was an agent on a mission, she reminded herself. She was supposed to be investigating the sexual exploitation of AOAs at The Palace.

She was a miserable failure, a foolish woman who masturbated at night while she wallowed in memories of this man, a woman who held her breath each morning while she searched her list of tasks for an indication he might be among her clients.

"Talk to me," he said softly, gripping her chin, rising on one elbow, and forcing her to make eye contact.

"Thank you for selecting me." It was the required opening line, but she heard the need in her voice. Surely he could, as well.

Link bent his head and kissed her lips. Softly at first, then not so softly. He kissed her neck, her chest, nuzzled aside her robe and pulled it open. Cool air washed across her skin, swiftly followed by the heat of his mouth.

He kissed her navel, probing it with the tip of his tongue.

"Do you like that?" he asked, lifting his head.

"Yes. Very much," she said the prescribed words, but she let her emotions fill her voice. This time, she was not lying to a client. She was speaking to a man she had loved. She ran her fingers through his dark hair. Thick hair, rough as raw silk.

"What would you like?" he asked.

Her watcher spoke, "The attendant may not express preferences. Feel free to indulge your every fantasy. Enjoy the pleasure of sexual gratification without heed to your partner's needs or cares. Explore your partner's body with the knowledge she is here to serve you."

"Fuck you," Link said to the voice. "What would you like?" he repeated to her.

She answered as she knew she must, but she took his hand as she said, "Whatever most pleases *you*." She pressed his hand between her thighs.

"You're very wet," Link said, delving into her inner spaces with his talented fingers. He slid down her, licking a path to where his hand played.

He paused to trace a circle around the mole on her thigh. He'd always paid special attention to that particular spot, one of her many flaws. The Palace had wanted her to consent to its removal, but she'd refused. Now she was glad she had.

Link murmured something into her thigh and she knew what he'd said might reveal their previous acquaintance to the watcher had it been audible. The possibility added a fillip of danger to their situation, fueling her excitement.

He turned his head and, Sweet Sol, she was coming apart under his mouth as he sucked at her clit. How could he know exactly what to do to her?

Her orgasm would be a tearing joy. She knew it. She felt it building, giving rise to an intense, grinding need to scream. She stuffed the belt of her robe into her mouth and bit down in anticipation.

Link left off his ministrations and stood up. Teetering on the edge of completion, feeling robbed, bereft, she stared at him as he pulled off the rest of his clothes.

He took an inordinate amount of time to remove each garment and hang it up. Each fold was fussed over and adjusted until he was satisfied. His grin told her it was a deliberate move.

A memory of him doing the same thing years ago made her smile back.

"Take off that damned robe," he ordered. When she stood up, he embraced her and tore it off for her. The seams parted with a ripping sound. In one swift motion, he wadded the pieces up and tossed them over his shoulder. He held her tightly against his body and sealed his mouth on hers.

She moaned as she relaxed against the hard length of him. How she'd missed the feel of him, the flex and flow of his sculpted muscles under her hands. The other encounters he'd purchased had not permitted her to touch him like this.

Locked in each other's arms, they ended up on the floor, but he wouldn't enter her when she grasped his cock and tried to guide him into her.

"Not yet. I want to watch you come. And I want to hear you. Loud and clear." Link leaned away from her and grasped her nipples between his fingertips. "Don't touch me again until you come."

Her upgrade buddy interrupted. "For only a few extra credits you may avail yourself of a variety of restraints for your attendant. Maximize your pleasure by saying upgrade."

"Not right now," Link growled.

She tossed her head back and slid her hands under her buttocks. If she didn't look away and didn't restrain her hands, she would never be able to obey his order.

He licked her from chin to clit. The heat of her excitement was tempered by the damp trail his tongue left. Ripples of sensation spread out over her skin. Excitement sizzled as she struggled not to reach out to him. She wanted to lock her hands in his hair and guide him where she willed. She wanted to watch him as he feasted on her. Not being able to participate drove her crazy.

He teased her. He nuzzled and licked her. Each time she lifted her hips and prepared for the onslaught of her climax, he withdrew, turning his attention to her hip or her knee or her inner arm.

If he didn't let her climax soon, she'd pull muscles or ligaments or something equally painful.

Wound tighter than she believed possible, she suffered his teasing in increasingly difficult silence. Unable to take the strain, she lifted her head and begged him with her eyes. His answering grin sent her into a frenzy.

Finally, silently, she arched her back off the carpet. Ecstasy swept through her, painful in its clenching power and intensity. She screamed.

Blindly, she groped for him, drew him into her arms, and cried out again as he thrust his cock deep into her sensitive body. He cradled her head in his arms, kissed her mouth, and thrust. Over and over. Quickly. Then slowly. Deeply, then just with the tip of his cock.

She grabbed his ass and hung on.

His body went slick with sweat. His testicles slapped her with each thrust. He sliced into her, carving a bloody trail, she was sure.

Then he came. He was silent as he shuddered under the onslaught of his climax, his body plunging into her in arrhythmic strokes.

The instant he was done, he fell asleep across her.

She stifled a curse and composed her features to neutral. Whoever watched must see only a bland indifference.

Link snored in her ear for an hour before abruptly waking and jerking out of her embrace. He rose on his knees and grimaced.

"Shit," he said. "How long was I asleep?"

"About an hour," she said, rising. "May I use the bathing chamber?"

"Sure. I'll come with you."

He leaned on the wash basin that slid from the wall and looked into the mirror, watching her as she sat on the toilet.

"I can't believe I went to sleep at these prices."

Link watched her face turn a blotchy red. He heard the hum of the toilet washing and drying her.

"I suppose you'd have let me sleep all night," he said.

"I am not permitted to interrupt your rest," she answered.

There was a sweet red imprint of the toilet seat on her ass and thighs when she turned away and headed for the bedroom. He didn't need a target to know where to aim, but if he had, there it was. Just thinking about it gave him another hard-on.

"Go lie on the bed," he ordered. She didn't even hesitate an instant. When he finished with the facilities, taking a long shower and getting a grip on his desire for her, he found her curled on her side, cheek in her palm. It was her turn to sleep.

He lifted the bed covers and got in. He woke her by sliding his hard cock into her. Her breathy little gasp took him back to another time, deep in the woods. They'd been camping, of all the fucking things — one of the few ways to get away from prying Academy eyes and ears. He'd awakened her the same way, thrusting into her wet core. She'd been wet all the time then, and naturally. Come to think of it, she was wet all the time now.

"Are you lubricated?"

"I am unimproved," she said, her fingers curling over the edge of the mattress as he fucked her.

And he fucked her as hard as he could. He lifted her uppermost leg and buried his face in her hair. "Rub my balls," he ordered and groaned when she reached between their thighs and did as he wanted.

But he couldn't sustain the harsh tone or the quick thrust when she moaned. He heard not a moan of pleasure but a sound that told him he was the only one getting any satisfaction from their activity.

He jerked out of her and rolled to his back. A series of recessed lights dotted the ceiling. He wondered which ones also held optical equipment.

She turned and straddled him, sitting lightly on his cock. She licked his lips, kissed his cheek, and then took his earlobe between her teeth. Her words were but a whisper against his ear. "They will punish me if you are displeased."

He thrust his fingers into her hair and tugged back her head. Her eyes were huge, glistening. Pleading.

"Sorry I pulled away," he said, "My back hurt in that position. This is much better."

Question filled her gaze, but then he couldn't read anything in her eyes for she closed them, shifting delicately on his swollen penis.

His hands looked huge covering her small, sweet breasts. No signs of childbirth marred her skin. They'd wanted children, they'd agreed, but not until they'd been as far as man could travel in space, seen it all, done it all.

Fuck. He wanted to tell her that his first thought on leaving Earth had been of her. And he'd put her firmly from his mind soon after, seduced not by another woman but by the sensations of floating untethered in space, the earth but one planet in a sea of stars.

She leaned over and kissed his mouth.

"I'm hungry," he said. "What's available?"

"Whatever you wish. Simply speak your desire." She kissed him again.

"That's a double-entendre if I ever heard one," he said, slapping her thigh, "but I meant I'm hungry hungry. As in needing a meal." He dumped her onto her back, pulling free, and crawled out of bed. With an eye on the communications console, he said, "What's to eat?"

A screen flared to life. "We have a wonderful array of choices today," said a perky blonde with the same hairstyle as Evans. This woman was also wearing a uniform that said, *Chef.*

"I'll have a bloody steak — and none of the ersatz stuff — and a good red wine. Slap something green on the side. Don't ruin it with dressing or sauce, okay?"

"I think you'll be as pleased with the gastronomic offerings as with the sensual ones." The chef disappeared.

He and Evans ignored each other while waiting. She remained curled in bed while he stood by the window and admired the garden below, trying to identify the flowers. They were really too high to permit him more than wild guesses. A bird flew into the window.

"Damn." He watched it plummet and disappear into the foliage, he assumed, though the angle was wrong for him to know for sure.

"Oh no," Evans said, appearing at his side. She spread her palms on the glass and peered down. The sight of her, lean body tipped so earnestly toward the glass, arms spread, head bowed, hair a dark curtain concealing her face, stiffened his cock.

He stepped behind her and grasped her hips. Her head bumped lightly against the glass as he fucked her. He leaned forward and cupped her breasts, deepening his thrusts, staring out the window at the setting sun.

The buzzer alerted him that his meal was ready. He quickened his pace, then fell still. He'd wear himself out before his time was up at this rate. He wasn't eighteen anymore. He hadn't taken any drugs and had no credits to buy them if he discovered he couldn't get it up hours from now.

The harsh sound of his gasps filled the room while he stood, hands on hips, and tried to control his lust. She slowly turned, leaning against the glass, her mouth open, her chest rising and falling as rapidly as his.

"That would have been a good one. For me at least," he said. "But dinner calls."

A hatch near the door held his meal. With chagrin he realized he'd not ordered anything for her.

As if he intended it all along, he plopped the tray, with its huge steak and mammoth bowl of salad greens in the center of the bed.

"Come here," he said when she showed no signs of joining him.

She crawled across the mattress and knelt opposite him. And licked her lips. He poured the excellent red wine into the only wine glass and held it out to her.

"Attendants are not permitted to drink alcoholic beverages," said his ubiquitous monitor. "There is an array of beverages for her selection beside the bed."

Damn. He'd forgotten the drugs. Either they didn't mix well with alcohol, or else her drinks were laced with more of whatever they'd already given her.

To his relief, Evans made no move toward the refrigerated hatch. He sliced a piece of steak and offered it. She leaned over and slowly closed her mouth around the tip of the fork as carefully as if it were the head of his penis.

His erection, not quite tamed, reared its head when she slowly settled into a cross-legged position. The pose revealed all of her to him. Her curls were damp. There may not be any sauce on his steak or salad, but she was dressed with an intoxicating mix of his come and her juices.

A shaft of primal pleasure sliced through him. He cut more steak, bit it off the fork with a growl and offered the next to her. But he held the fork just out of her reach and she had to lean on her hands to reach it across the wide tray. He held the steak out with one hand and slid his fingertips into her curls with the other.

She licked her lips and wriggled on his touch.

"Wonderful," he muttered.

The salad was a peppery mix of greens he didn't recognize. He plucked one feathery leaf from the mix and reached out and teased her nipples, first one, then the other, until they were tight points.

As she nibbled her next piece of meat, he combed and separated her tiny curls so he could see her better, see the swollen, elongated shape of her clit.

Back and forth they shared morsels of steak. His cock stood hard at attention throughout. Between the meat courses, he used pieces of greens to tease and tickle her clitoris, nipples, lips, and belly.

Slowly, she relaxed and began to smile. Her lips glistened with the juices of the meat. Her clit and nipples were taut and when the plate was empty, he shoved the tray aside, pulled her by her knees to the edge of the bed and spread her legs.

He knelt before her and pressed his face between her open thighs. Her scent filled every breath he took.

The heady Sara Evans scent he remembered so well. Whatever they'd done hadn't erased it completely.

Her desire slicked his tongue, fingertips, and face.

"Please," he said, coming up for air. "Climb over me."

He put the tray on the floor and stretched out on the bed. She gifted him with her body, straddling his, giving him total access while taking his penis into her mouth.

He alternated watching the swing of her small breasts with laving and teasing her clit. No matter which he paid attention to, he felt the tremors of her desire. Small sounds issued from her throat and she suddenly froze over him, her body stiff, and quivering. It was a tremor he knew she held in check.

He wanted the wild abandon he remembered from the past.

Capturing her hips in his embrace, he pulled her hard against his mouth and did not let up his teasing. She began to wail, buck and thrust against his mouth. He was awash in her juices.

He came in a quick pump of his seed into her mouth. He shouted at the ball-aching, gut-twisting, pure thrill of it.

Chapter 8
༄

Evans watched Link sleep. He had a bruised look about his eyes. Simple fatigue. He'd made love to her four times. The agony of not being permitted to awaken him made her resort to subterfuge. She shifted sharply on the mattress and coughed.

As she'd hoped, he finally turned bleary eyes toward her and for a moment looked disoriented.

She licked his ear. "Wake up. You have only thirty minutes remaining."

"Let's eat." He groaned when he sat up.

"Shall I order for you?"

"Us." He said it simply. "What would you like?"

"An orange." The words were out of her mouth before she could stop herself.

"Okay." He shrugged as if he did not remember the time he had sectioned an orange and fed the wedges to her one at a time, dripping the juice down her bare chest, then lapping the nectar off with his tongue. It had been the prelude to one of their sweetest lovemaking sessions.

Or had it only been sweet to her? He didn't appear to remember.

The breakfast tray held her orange, already sectioned, arranged like flower petals around a strawberry center. His food, burned toast and black coffee, looked as stark and uninviting as a lunar landscape.

"Takes care of the wine," he said, munching on the toast. He'd donned his robe. Distancing himself, she supposed.

As she ate the strawberry, she realized she would starve if she didn't see him again. Starve from the want of him. The intervening years had dulled only her need for him—not her desire. This latest session had brought the need back to her, through vivid memories undimmed by time.

Link reached across and stopped her hand when she reached for the first orange section. When he held it poised over her nipple and squeezed the juice so it dripped on her breast, she knew he remembered.

* * * * *

The Assistant to the Assistant Undersecretary of the District Attorney of New Virginia's office sat across from Link and shrugged. "I'm sorry, Colonel. The Palace operates quite legally. The men and women employed there choose the life willingly."

"I don't think so. And I can only prove it if I speak to her out of their control." Link tapped an official graphic of Evans from her cadet days, found in a search of the corps databanks. God bless his high security clearances.

"I'm afraid we can't help you." The AAUDA rose. "Perhaps you might seek counseling."

"Counseling? What's that supposed to mean?" Link shot to his feet.

"I suspect you've overindulged in The Palace's pleasures and have become a touch obsessed. Particularly in light of your current financial situation."

Link got a grip on his anger. "Thank you for your time." *And fuck you.*

Outside in the vestibule connecting the civil law offices with the PeaceKeepers', Brad leaned over a desk, flirting with a young corporal. She was definitely improved, her large breasts straining her uniform tunic in sharp contradiction of the regs.

"Let's get out of here," Link growled. He barely paused for the required visual inspection before stepping into the street.

Brad almost ran to keep up with him. "Whoa. Slow down. You won't believe what I found out."

Link jerked to a stop. "Let me guess. The serial numbers on her breast implants?"

Brad frowned. "Nothing like that. Something really good. You can buy the attendants from that brothel you're hooked on." The men wove their way through a labyrinth of government buildings, under the canopies that limited pedestrians' exposure to harmful UV rays.

"I am not hooked on anything," Link growled, resentful of two men making such an assumption within moments of each other. "What the fuck are you talking about?"

"I'm saying that most of the attendants are working off prison time. Not many people know that. You can buy their time and keep them as... well... glorified slaves, I guess. Pleasure servants would be the politically correct term."

"You're nuts." Link powered up his personal data device and checked his appointments. How long before he could book another session with Evans?

"Link." Brad grabbed his arm. "Listen to me. You're obsessed with a cock jockey. A penis pro. Buy her." Brad dropped onto a nearby bench. "I'd check up on her crime first, of course, in case she's in for something like castrating lovers or poisoning her commanding officer."

Link gave his friend the finger and walked away, still poring through the information on his device. He waited until Brad's laughter faded behind him before accessing a few criminal databanks.

No Sara Evans showed up on any of the lists he could access. That meant she wasn't a criminal, didn't it?

Even if she was, what possible crime could ethical, dutiful, loving Evans have committed?

Cock jockey. He and Brad used the phrase for the loose station women who were happy to ride whatever penis was handy. Evans was *not* a cock jockey, no matter how many men she fucked or sucked in encounters arranged by The Palace.

He started another search, this one into what options he had to borrow against his pension. Just in case he had to buy her.

"*Shit.*" Link stumbled. What if someone else bought her?

* * * * *

Evans was asleep when a chime sounded. She opened her eyes to find the lights already up to full and one of the counselors standing in the open door. It was a woman she'd never seen before, but she wore the gold robe of a senior counselor. She brushed back a strand of her long red hair over one shoulder and gave a quick smile.

"I apologize for disturbing you. Come with me." Without waiting, the counselor turned and headed down the hallway.

Evans pulled on her robe, stuffed her feet into the waiting slippers and followed. "What's going on?"

"An attendant has fallen ill and you have the privilege of taking her place. I'm very excited for you." The redhead checked her wrist pad. "It's a very generous guest. You won't regret losing a little sleep." She touched a few keys and frowned. "Hmmmm... I didn't realize you're unimproved, but this gentleman did select you, so that's his choice. You haven't had any fetish training, either. Well, you scored high on the intelligence test, so you should be able to improvise."

She paused at the end of the corridor. "When did you eat last?"

Evans had to think for a moment, her mind still foggy with sleep. "First shift."

The counselor pushed through the door and held it for Evans. "Good. You'll need to drink. He always requests a full bladder in all the attendants."

Evans felt her insides churn and not from lack of food.

The counselor stopped and touched the wall. A hidden panel opened, revealing a keypad and a food hatch. Her fingers moved over the pad quickly. Buzzing, clinking and a swishing sound came from behind the hatch before it slid up to reveal a glass.

Evans accepted the drink and they set off again. The glass held cool water. She couldn't taste anything else. She hoped there weren't any exotic drugs needed for this task.

The counselor went back to consulting her wrist pad. "Through here." She opened a door to another corridor.

As she stepped through, into new territory, Evans updated her mental map. Something good would come of this midnight encounter. A door opened at the end of the hall and she glimpsed a plebian staircase. A very ordinary man dressed in coveralls peeked out and set an ornamental but functional trash receptacle on the floor in the hallway. When he made eye contact with Evans, his cheeks flushed and he hastily shut the door.

The attendant clicked her tongue and shook her head, but Evans was pleased to see that some doors led not to chambers of pleasure, but to maintenance shafts. And where there was maintenance, there were exits. Even in light of the modern methods of nearly instantaneous fire-suppression, regulations stated that every building needed an emergency exit. This stairwell wasn't marked as one, but it might fit the bill.

Evans thought that the world might have come a long way, but trash was still trash and still required collection. And removal. To where?

"Drink up, young lady," the attendant said. "You know, you're going to be the envy of your friends. There were quite a few attendants who were available, and this guest chose you."

With this trip, Evans was beginning to fill in some of the blank areas on her mental map, especially around the med center. Here, the doors were much farther apart than they were where she worked. Larger chambers? They turned another corner before the counselor stopped before a door stenciled with a tree. Now what could a tree mean?

"Since you haven't had the fetish training, I'll give you a few tips. Keep your chin down. Do what you're told. I know that's the first lesson you learn in training, but in here, it is vital. This guest is paying ten times what you normally command. Ten times."

Evans sucked in a breath. That was a hell of a lot of credits. Her stomach knotted tightly and she had to force the water down.

"This client has contracted for two hours. During that time, he gets total command over *you*. Most of the restrictions are lifted for him. Anything goes, including pain. Injury isn't allowed, but anything else is permitted. So behave yourself. He's as well known for his insistence on compliance as he is for his generosity. Relax, do what he wants, and you'll wake up tomorrow with a hefty deposit in your tip account."

Every word chilled Evans, though her skin felt suddenly hot and sweaty. Any remaining vestige of sleep had fled, leaving her a bit dazed and panicked.

The counselor opened the door and indicated she should enter.

For the first time, Evans wondered if she'd recognize the guest. With that kind of available wealth, his face might be on the nightly news. Of course, that meant nothing in the halls of The Palace.

Keeping her eyes focused on the floor, Evans stepped into the room. At the last minute, the counselor gave her a push from behind that sent her to her knees. Keeping in mind the woman's use of the word "command," she stayed there.

She got the impression of a much larger area than she'd thought. The room was starkly lighted with a glaring white. All she could see from her subservient pose were feet.

"Ah, our last participant in tonight's games. Bring her in, Dominique5." The man's warm voice rolled over Evans. She suppressed a quiver of unease. The timbre was deep and sexy, but it held an edge of danger. A sense of familiarity tugged at her. She'd heard that voice before.

A pair of bare feet came into her field of vision. To her surprise, the nails were painted baby blue, startling against coffee-colored skin. No stereotypical black boots here. Of course, this wasn't the man in charge.

The blue-toed woman pulled her to her feet.

As she rose, Evans saw the body art. It began below the knees, swirls of color like scarves wrapped around the woman's dusky limbs. Color framed her shaved mons and assorted piercings, and parted again to reveal four silver barbells quartering her navel. Her upthrust breasts were likewise bare of art. Her enormous dark nipples sported more silver barbells, in front of large metal shields in gold molded to the shape of her breasts. It all reminded Evans of the Roman armor worn on ancient statues — ones she'd seen in museums.

Oh, Link. Where are you?

Evans didn't dare raise her eyes to look at the attendant's face.

"Come, don't delay, Dominique5. Bring her to me." Although Evans was prepared for the power in the guest's voice this time, she couldn't suppress another shiver. She desperately wanted to look up and see the owner of that voice.

Dominique5 took Evans by the hand and led her into the center of the room. Her fingernails were long and wide, painted the same blue as her toenails.

"Remove her robe," the guest said.

Dominique5 pulled back on one of her fingernails to reveal a small blade. She slit the shoulders of the robe, letting it part and fall to the floor.

Cool air washed over Evans. Her nipples puckered from the cold... or was it the sight of the blade? A shifting and shuffling alerted her that more people were in the room than she could see.

The man with the incredible voice and others were scrutinizing her. She wanted to cover herself but didn't dare.

"Look at me."

As she raised her gaze, it was not the man who caught her attention. It was a small girl on her knees in a pose of supplication, hands and feet bound behind her with lavender ribbons.

Angel Martinez.

Chapter 9

ഔ

Evans forced her attention away from Angel.

Sweet Sol. A breakthrough. Damned if they didn't happen in the most unlikely places, at the most unlikely times. And here she was, in no position to take advantage of it.

"Look at me," the man repeated.

The man who stood before Evans was one of the most ordinary men she'd ever seen. He bore no marks or scars. His hair was a common brown, his features "improved" so much they were almost rendered undistinguished. The man looked like a doll, bland and generic.

She knew him instantly.

Alexander Kennedy had occupied a seat on the American Council for all of his working life. His constituents kept sending him back to the Chamber, as they had his father, and his father before him. No one knew just how many generations of the Kennedys had been elected public servants; the early records were lost along with so many others from before the First Hacker War.

She blinked when she realized he was fully clothed in the nondescript garb of one who worked in the commercial world. Plain gray tunic. Gray trousers.

"Dominique5, I think she's perfect." The councilor traced Evans's cheek with the tips of his fingers before moving down to her breast. "No piercings. No improvements. I love a blank canvas." He drew circles around her nipple. "Her profile says she's a novice, unawakened to our delights. Old-fashioned, but perhaps we need some new distractions. Do you agree?"

"Yes, my lord." Dominique5's voice was as exotic as her appearance. Evans couldn't quite place the soft accent.

"Then I'll keep her," he declared. "Get her introduction set up, and we'll continue with our little friend over here."

Dominique5 picked up something from a case on the floor. The man turned away, blocking Evans's view.

"You may look at anyone, but do not speak unless asked a question," Dominique5 whispered.

Evans took the opportunity to examine the room. It was larger than she'd expected, and filled with people. Most of them were attendants. Grace8 was there, along with two attendants she'd seen before but didn't know, waiting off to one side.

The ceiling was hung with straps and hooks and pulleys. Evans shivered a little when she realized some of the possibilities those fixtures presented. In one corner hung a rope chair, with padded parts and clips for adjusting height and position. There were assorted blocks and a couple of chairs lined up along one wall. Several cases and duffels sat in a cluster near where the man stood with his back to her.

"Relax and spread your legs. We were a little late arriving, but he's in a good mood this evening. So is Mistress." The woman fitted Evans with a thong that held a small piece of plastic. She fussed for a moment, until she had the device positioned just at the top of Evans's mons.

Evans watched her, wondering what she'd gotten involved in. Her contract with The Palace had no restrictions on what she would do barring injury to herself, but so far an unimproved, over-thirty, average woman wasn't in demand for much but the basics.

As Dominique5 snugged the thing into place, Evans felt a little tingle run from her clit up into her womb. She couldn't suppress a jerk.

Dominique5's head snapped up. "Are you truly new to this?"

Evans gave a little nod, hating the blush that heated her face. She looked down at the device. "What is it?"

"There's a powerful vibrating bee inside, keyed to a control Master wears. It concentrates your attention on him when he approaches. He uses it on new attendants, to train them to respond to him." She glanced down at the buzzing plastic and sighed. "They're incredible at getting you going. I miss mine."

When Dominique5 moved away, Evans glanced across the chamber at Angel who still knelt and hadn't moved. Her ribbon bonds bit deeply into the flesh of her ankles and wrists.

Evans forced herself to look away from Angel. Would she have an opportunity to talk to the girl?

Dominique5 went to kneel at the feet of a woman called Mistress. Evans gulped.

"Mistress" was the brunette with the phoenix tattoo.

Everyone's attention was focused on another spread-eagled attendant. The blonde stood up on blocks, holding onto the straps hanging from the ceiling. The position left her elevated and fully open to view. And reach.

A jolt of sensation through her clit snapped Evans's attention away from the blonde. Kennedy approached her. As he got nearer, she could hear the bee buzz as the tingle grew stronger. By the time he stood before her, she bucked and jerked as little shudders wracked her body.

He smiled, baring perfect teeth. "I like responsive women." He lifted her left breast in his hand, bouncing the weight a little. "Interesting. A bit larger than the right one." He ran his thumb across the nipple. "Nice."

Evans gasped as he scraped his fingernails lightly across the sensitive underside of her breast.

"What are you called?"

It took her a moment to order her thoughts. "Bliss6."

"Well, Bliss6, I will make sure you enjoy yourself tonight. If you please me, I'll give you a two thousand credit tip. What do you think of that?"

"You are very generous, my lord."

He chuckled and stroked the sides of her breasts. His fingers were warm and gentle. "I chose well. You learn quickly. Only my household pets call me that. You may address me as Master. Do you understand?"

"Yes, Master."

"And my favorite attendant is to be addressed as Mistress."

"Yes, Master."

He pinched both her nipples, hard. Evans flinched at the sharp pain.

"That was a command, not a question. Only speak if you are asked a question. Did Dominique5 instruct you?"

"She did, Master."

"That's better." He turned and stepped away. The buzzing in her crotch subsided a little, then more as he took another step. "My dear, when you have a moment, please assess the worth of Bliss6."

Mistress finished buckling a strap on the suspended woman, and stepped back. The attendant now wore a leather harness around her torso. It left her breasts raised and bare but for a pair nipple clamps connected by a thin gleaming chain, and spread her shaven labia to reveal another clamp on her clit.

Evans tried to shift her position to bring Angel into view. Why was this guy ignoring the girl?

Something to do with dominance. Evans's stomach clenched. She contemplated the effort needed to subdue the unbound attendants. With Master and Mistress both free, and the way Mistress handled that whip, Evans knew she'd never make it to Angel before they subdued her.

"I believe she's ready, my lord."

"She looks good." Master walked around the woman, examining her closely. Then he strolled to Angel and stroked a hand over her bowed head. Angel leaned into his leg as much as she could. "This one looks fine as well."

He went back to the chained woman and tugged on her bonds. She moaned. "Nice and ready," he said.

"What do you have in mind for our novice?"

He looked across the room at her. "I haven't decided. Let her wait for a little while." His deep voice still caused Evans to tremble inside, even when he was far enough away that he didn't trigger the vibrator strapped to her.

Mistress approached Evans. "I saw you watching me," she said softly. "You have a nice lift to your breasts when you work out." She ran the whip handle over Evans's neck and down her side, skirting her breast. "Soft. Not a single piercing. Totally unimproved." Amazement sounded in her velvety voice. "Charming nonetheless. The master seems taken with you. If you play your cards right, Bliss6, you could become a regular attendant for Master's visits."

Sweet Sol, not if I can help it, Evans thought. And not with Angel, either. She contemplated at least three of the ways she knew to disable a man... or a woman.

Mistress left Evans, went to where Angel knelt, and lifted her chin.

Angel looked like the proverbial zombie. Her eyes were glazed, her lips parted, her jaw slack.

Anger seethed through Evans. These people had far too many credits. Why didn't they work on the UV issue instead of catering to their libidos?

Kennedy came to stand behind Evans. His body radiated heat. Cloth rustled softly before bare flesh pressed against her back. He thrust his hard cock between her legs, rubbing back and forth below the vibrator. His hands trailed heat across her skin as he massaged her lightly, learning her contours.

"You entice me," he whispered in her ear. She struggled not to stiffen in his arms. "You are unusual. So natural, so artless, a sensual delight." Sensations roared through her, as he cupped her breasts. The vibrator going full tilt made it hard for her to think.

"Now, I shall give pleasure to those who prefer a man, and we will watch Mistress as she enjoys pleasuring those who want a woman's touch. I plan to save you, the best, for last."

Evans met Grace8's eyes and shivered at the jealousy she saw there. Cloud9 might solicit her conversation, but this woman never would. When Grace8's eyes flicked back to Master, Evans understood. Grace8 was no longer the favored one. She'd bet her last pay that Grace8 was usually the best saved for last.

Evans would have given anything not to be best. She would have given more to be somewhere, anywhere, else.

She watched as Grace8 stepped up onto another set of blocks and put her hands through the straps hanging above.

Mistress held up a soft puffball and looked to Master in inquiry. He moved Evans forward, away from him. Cold air washed over Evans, colder this time because of his withdrawn heat. Stepping around her, he took the cluster of feathers from Mistress and smiled.

"Yes. I want to hear her cry out her delight."

He brushed the feather lightly over one of Grace8's nipples, and she did open her mouth, throw back her head, and cry out. She also kicked and thrashed and cracked Master in the head with her knee. He stumbled back, knocking Mistress aside. The only thing for him to grab to regain his balance was Evans.

She reeled under his weight, straight into the path of one of the silver-blonde's feet. It caught her squarely in the crotch. The blow drove the butterfly upwards, grinding against her clit.

Evans screamed.

So did Mistress, who rolled on the floor, cradling her arm against her ribcage and knocking Angel to one side.

Evans forced herself to her knees, eyes blurred with tears of pain. She headed for Angel.

Guards boiled into the room. One scooped Angel up and shouldered his way out the door. It took the guards several minutes to sort out the chaos.

Mistress was loaded onto a stretcher and wheeled out, her arm at an odd angle. Grace8, groaning and retching, was placed on another. One of the guards grabbed the puffball. Evans only had a moment to see him stuff it into his uniform jacket before they took her away.

Master himself helped Evans up from where she had doubled over in pain. He cradled her gently against his chest. As if from a distance, she heard him say, "Tomorrow, my pet, you will find a nice bonus for your trouble. We will meet again, perhaps next week. If you please me then, I will consider adding you to my household." He handed her over to one of the guards.

Evans shuddered. *That would really screw the mission.* The guards escorted her to the cubicle next door.

She hobbled in to find Heaven4 waiting for her. With little sympathy, the older woman helped her up onto the massage table, inspected the damage and gave her a long, icy blast of the numbing spray. "That'll take about forty hours to wear off. Fake it until then. You're not bad enough to take off the rota."

Evans insisted on having a medical professional evaluate her. She limped to the infirmary, a silent guard at her back.

To her relief, a woman with the tag *Miller* on her crisp, white tunic was on duty and not the cold Jennel. Evans saw a look of sympathy on the young med-aide's face when she examined her.

"I think the S-11 spray was just the thing, although you will still feel it when the spray's effects begin to diminish. Here's a little something to take the edge off if you're still uncomfortable when that happens." She dropped a sealed pouch about an inch square into Evan's palm. "Have you had a disease check lately?"

Evans nodded. "After my last encounter, yesterday… or the day before. I think." Her mind was so hazy, she couldn't remember the time.

"Well, if you can't remember, I'd better do it. We won't need you," the woman said to the guard.

There was something about Miller's manner that told Evans she craved conversation.

The exam room had a small desk in one corner, a wall comm unit, the cabinet from which Miller had taken the anesthetic pouch, and a door in each wall. As she slid her feet into the examining table's stirrups, Evans whispered. "Can we be heard?"

"No. There's a regulation about eavesdropping on non-paying clients. Doctors wouldn't allow it. Not after the malpractice and privacy revolutions in '56 and '61."

"I guess not." Evans relaxed as the med-aide probed and checked her inside and out for any sign of disease.

"Clean and sweet," Miller declared.

Evans thought about the implications of Kennedy's words. Many clients had unlimited wealth. *Shit.* What if one of them buys Angel?

She strove to keep the concern out of her voice. "That guest said that if I please him next week, he will add me to his household. Can he do that?"

"Attendants sometimes choose to leave The Palace, when their contracted term of service is up," the med-aide replied.

Evans relaxed against the table once more.

Miller looked up from her datapad. "Of course, a few of our attendants are here to work off significant debt. Any of those may be purchased and criminals, of course, can have their time purchased. So, if you're one of those, yes, he can purchase you, with or without your permission."

Double shit. Then she'd better work fast.

There was a possibility Miller didn't really know if they were being monitored, but Evans had to take the chance if she was going to get results on this catastrophic assignment.

"The young girl in that scenario was injured. Will you be treating her?"

Miller cocked her head to one side. "Probably. If she was hurt, they'll bring her in when I'm done with you."

"I think her name is Angel."

"Angel?" The med-aide paused as she helped Evans into her robe. "You mean one of the Angels? There must be dozen or more."

Shit. Evans remembered she was Bliss6 to this woman. "No, I mean that's her real name. She looks childish, but she's really twenty." Evans held her hand to her chest.

A shuttered look came over the woman's face. "We don't have any underage attendants here."

"I think there are. And I really need to speak to her. We're friends," she lied.

Miller licked her lips and glanced around. She walked to the examining table and the stretch of poly that covered it. Slowly, she used her fingertip to write a few words.

Nothing to be done.

Give her a message? Evans wrote with painstaking slowness.

The med-aide shook her head.

Someone wailed in the background. A disembodied voice said, "Miller, I need your assistance. Stat."

At the same time, the guard who'd stolen the dildo poked his head in the door. "You've got an assignment. Let's go."

Evans cringed at the thought of servicing some guest while she had a numb crotch. Then she brightened. Maybe it would improve the experience. Feel nothing inside. Feel nothing outside.

And now, she knew Angel was here. She'd met a sympathetic med-aide and she knew one guard who was corrupt. All in all, that was more progress in an hour than she'd made in weeks.

"May I come back later, if I'm still sore?" she asked Miller while the guard hovered.

"Absolutely. Any time, if they deem it necessary." No need to say who "they" were.

Double shit. She couldn't even use her own discretion to seek medical help.

She made a big deal about fastening her robe and peered over Miller's shoulder as she exited through a door opposite the one where the impatient guard stood, hoping for a glimpse of Angel Martinez.

All Evans saw was another short corridor with several doors, but she added it to her mental map anyway. Who knew what scrap of information might prove useful? This infirmary was only about fifty feet from the maintenance stairs she'd seen earlier.

On the short walk to her next appointment, she ignored the silent guard and thought about the Angel Martinez she'd seen in the fetish scenario, who was very different from the young Angel Martinez she'd seen in the family vids. Yes, the girl had appeared drugged, but what if it was more of an addiction to the experience than to drugs The Palace had administered?

Her appointment was in a chamber stenciled with a crescent moon. A chamber for straight fucking.

Evans drew in a deep breath, placed her robe over a hook, and took her place on the soft bed. The room's color shifted to a golden glow. She rolled to her side, strategically drawing up one knee and arranging her hair in a tantalizing pose that exposed only the rise of her breast and cast her gaze down — just as she'd been taught to do.

The door clicked open, the guest slid his card into the slot.

"Look at me."

Her guest was Link. Lovely, wonderful, gorgeous Link.

He dropped his robe.

She even thought she detected a quiver in her very numb crotch as he stretched out beside her.

* * * * *

Link knew she was faking her orgasm. She couldn't fake her nipples tightening or the rosy blush she got across her breasts during a climax. Right now, those signs were absent.

He was pretty low in credits again. He was down to a simple face-to-face screw. No frills. Timed. He'd almost chosen fellatio by itself, but he wanted to be in her, to be able to touch her and kiss her. He wanted a real, mind-numbing orgasm for both of them, not a faked climax.

"That seemed less than genuine," he said and climbed from the bed.

* * * * *

The two attendants came for her at about the time the spray wore off. They escorted her to a guest cubicle in an area she'd not visited before. One glance told her it was bare except for an examining table.

Dr. Owen, the very elderly physician who'd done her med checks, greeted her with orders to climb up on the table and spread her legs.

Wondering what was going on, she did as he directed.

He parted her lips and examined her clit. She gasped at his touch. *Damn.* The spray had worn off, and time hadn't done much to heal her.

"A guest get a little rough?" he asked. There was a tremor in his hands.

"Yes. Very rough."

He shook his leonine mane of white hair and clicked his tongue against his large teeth. "Well, you seem on the road to healing now. I'm done with you, but you're to report to Block L."

She went to Block L, an area she remembered from her induction. She'd been trained here. When a set of double doors slid open at her approach, she knew she was being monitored even without an escort.

In Block L she stood at attention before a beautifully carved desk of what looked like mahogany. Link would love its age and the soft patina of the leather top. She focused on the painting in an elaborate, gilded frame—the Rape of the Satyr—over the mantel while a tall woman with very improved breasts chastised her. Was that a thoroughly modern dildo being inserted into the half-man half-goat's ass? She looked down at her hands.

"Attend me," the woman said sharply. "Your numerous lapses of manners are not mitigated by the compliments of one of our most prized guests. An attendant must be perfect at all times. Your ridiculously fake orgasm with your morning client has been noted. You will have to work on it. Immediately. Before someone else selects you."

Oh, Link. She felt the heat rush up her cheeks. The one man she really had never faked anything with, not her emotions, her love, her joys, nor her sorrows, had gone on record condemning her.

"Lie down on my couch and pretend you're aroused." The woman indicated a long, black satin-covered bench. "Take it from the top and all the way to the orgasm."

Evans remained in place. How could they expect that of her? By herself? In front of this cold woman? Her temper got the best of her. "I can't. I'm still sore as hell. I'm no good at faking stuff and I was numb, damn it."

The woman stood even taller. Her short spiky hair quivered with indignation. "Are you refusing?"

"You bet I am."

The woman pressed a button on the desk's raised keypad. "You're free to go."

Back in her cell, Evans wondered at the ease with which she'd been let off the hook, both for faking the orgasm and for losing her temper.

Chapter 10

ဢ

The next morning, Evans saw she'd not been let off any hook. Instead, she was firmly impaled on it. The screen detailing her duties for the day was filled with entries. Usually, only one or two clients a day wanted an over-thirty, unimproved attendant.

Today, it looked like she'd be getting a client once every hour.

Every one of them was coded with a Q. She asked for an explanation of the Q.

Her disembodied companion thanked her for her question. "The Q designation is a training code. You will not be receiving any guests today. As is noted on your schedule, you will remain in chamber 82. There, staff members who have volunteered to assist in your reeducation will be given free access to you. They are instructed to stimulate you to orgasm while you, in turn, will stimulate them.

"The better the quality of your vocal and physical reactions to the stimulation, the shorter the training period. Some of our volunteers may be disappointed by the cancellation of their appointments if your reeducation goes well. So, enjoy each orgasm. Or enjoy the simulation if you are unable to enjoy the real thing."

Chamber 82 was empty except for a bed in the center of the room and a large monitoring screen that showed the list of appointments. Evans was shaking with rage when the first volunteer arrived. It was the man who mopped the floors in the cafeteria. He was a gentle soul with the thought processes of a child.

He pulled out his cock and shoved his hand beneath her robe.

This was her punishment? She slapped the man's groping hand. He yelped and danced away from her, banging on the door when she stuck out her tongue. When it clicked open, he disappeared through it as if he were on fire.

The next volunteer was Grace8. She glided into the cell, opening her robe to reveal her very improved breasts.

She whispered. "You think you're hot. You're never taking my place again. I want you on your knees, your face in my crotch. Now. And lick nice."

Evans wrapped her robe around herself more tightly. *Saturn's rings*. She raised one hand and clenched her fist. "Don't touch me, or you'll be licking the empty spaces where your teeth used to be."

The door clicked open again. This time, two men stood in the entry. "Go back to your chamber, Grace8," one said.

The woman hugged her robe close and sauntered off with a backward sneer. The two men entered Evans's cell and shut the door.

"You're not being very cooperative," the taller of the two said. He licked his lips.

Fear slicked Evans's palms. "I don't deserve this punishment. I've done everything required. I can't help it if Heaven4 numbed my crotch. Did the client complain?"

"He remarked that you'd faked an orgasm. You know all encounters are recorded for quality assurance."

"But did he complain? Did he put in an official, written complaint?"

"No," the second man said. "But he expressed displeasure. So you need to be re-educated."

"The guest made an observation, nothing more. I won't accept 'reeducation' when I don't need it."

"Then you'll force us to take other action."

"What action? At least let me know what my options are." Were they going to beat her? She could disable them before they took a step, but then, where would she be?

"Options?" He indicated the list of clients still showing on the screen, "If you won't accept the retraining, then you will be punished. A counselor will decide on what is appropriate."

She looked at the monitoring screen and the twenty odd employees who'd be doing whatever they wanted, playing with her all day, and she chose the counselor's punishment.

Hopefully, it would be peeling pseudo-potatoes for a month. Even a beating might be better.

* * * * *

Link couldn't find Evans in the scores of attendants. He slapped his hand on the view screen and howled. A real, honest-to-God, primal scream.

Someone had bought Evans. Someone had gotten to her first. Someone had taken her home and was able to fuck her anytime, anywhere. He punched the wall at the thought.

When he regained control, he looked at himself in the mirror. "I've become a fucking nutcase."

His third attempt to find Evans among the unimproved women available for his pleasure was interrupted by a message from General Richter. Link swore when he saw that his leave on Earth was being curtailed.

He was to report to the launch site for pre-flight exams, Tuesday of the next rota. That meant he had little time left for hanging out in brothels. Once he started pre-flight exams, he'd be too busy at the base for any play time from now until ignition.

He activated the card and made a quick choice. A blonde beauty. Improved. Back massage only. Maybe somehow he could find out what had happened to Evans.

At the brothel desk, he again used a quaint pen to sign-in. As he handed the antique back to the receptionist, he asked him, "What happened to G752H? I didn't see her on the roster."

"Oh, I'm so sorry, sir. We can't give out that information. But usually it just means an attendant is on leave." The young man touched Link's hand in an intimate way and leaned near. "Everyone needs a little respite from their job now and then, even those who *love* their work."

Link stepped back from the receptionist's beaming smile and minty breath and took the familiar slideway to the section where massages were administered.

All around him, men and women moved about as they would at any hotel. There was nothing to suggest what went on behind the closed doors.

The blonde masseuse was a treat, her hands talented, but he could think only of Evans, of how *her* hands felt on him. As he contemplated the waste of his credits on this empty experience, the usual voice informed him of upgrades.

He started at the words that followed.

"We have a special event taking place in our quadrangle today. For one hundred credits, you can watch a foolhardy woman sunning herself. Not a sight for the squeamish, but you might enjoy it," finished the voice. "The event begins in ten minutes. Simply say 'Special Event' and your wish is our command."

Link wondered at the cheap price on the voyeurism and then realized the woman in the quad would not be a volunteer. He imagined spectators would see some poor soul grovel and beg to be let in from the sun's blistering rays.

The thought sickened him. He'd seen the scars resulting from UV badges being ignored. The only place to safely hang out in the sun was north of here. Far, far north. Polar bear land. Or what was once polar bear land.

Evans. Sweet, unavailable, Evans.

He said, "Special Event," in a rush and thought he could hear the credits evaporate in voyeurism, but something in his gut told him exactly where he would find Evans.

He snatched his robe from the attendant and despite her obvious displeasure at being deserted, he stormed out of the chamber. He dressed in moments and found a guide waiting to escort him to his assigned window for the special event.

* * * * *

Evans would not let them drag her to the center of the green sward. She strode between two of The Palace guards with the demeanor of her military rank though she was naked. A third man attached a cuff to her ankle and secured the long attached chain to a ring protruding from the grass. Fully protected themselves in long pants, long sleeves, hats, and UV glasses, they ignored her nudity.

She refused to beg.

They left her there, in the center of the grassy area surrounded by lush gardens with no shelter and nothing to drink. The heady scent of flowers filled the space. The grass beneath her feet was soft and lush. She presumed it was watered each night, or it would be dead straw.

The beat of the sun's rays on her bare skin heated her rapidly. She became woozy in only a few minutes. After a brief moment of surprise that it all affected her so quickly, she realized the drugs they fed her must enhance the effect of the sun.

Above her loomed blank windows. Stories and stories of them. She bowed her head to shield her face.

How many sick souls stared down at her? How many of them wanted to see her beg and scream to be let in? How many of them hoped she'd resist, so they could watch her skin redden, then blister?

Fuck you all.

She sat on the grass and curled inward, making herself as small as possible.

Chapter 11

ဆ

Link felt the bile rise in his throat. He left the window and ran along the slideway to the reception area. He grabbed the young man by his glittering tunic. "Show me to the management."

The woman who ushered him into her quiet, windowless office was every bit as attractive as the attendants but she didn't do a thing for his libido. He waited until she had taken her seat, but only barely.

The instant her bottom hit the cushion, he leaned toward her, balling his fists on the desk. "I want the torture of that woman stopped."

The woman folded her hands in front of her and considered him for a moment. "I'm sorry. We don't interfere in the pleasures of our guests or counteract the wishes of our attendants."

"Wishes? She'd have to be mad to opt for a 'sunning,' as you call it."

The woman took a deep breath and glanced at a data screen on a small console by the desk. "But she did, Sir, I assure you. And I'm afraid that you really don't have enough credits to lodge a protest. You are one of our, shall we say, less profitable customers. Your name does not even appear on our list. I assume you obtained your card by purchasing it from a member in need. How you got it is immaterial to us, but only as long as you abide by our rules. Should you abuse the privileges that accompany membership, we can and will revoke your card."

Link could barely contain his fury. This administrator had the audacity to sit here, as cool as you please, lecturing him on proper behavior, while Evans was roasting alive.

"How am I abusing the membership by demanding you stop the sadistic treatment of an attendant?"

"You are abusing the membership by curtailing the pleasure of others." The woman played with a thick gold ring on her thumb. "Many enjoy the suffering of others. It's a fact of life. Should we — both the management and the attendant — choose to provide them with the entertainment they desire, it is not your concern."

Link took a deep breath. He had no idea how to get into the quadrangle. The minutes Evans had already spent there made his skin break out in a sweat. Who knew how much longer she would last?

Computations for permanent damage from UV exposure ran through his head, tumbling about with calculations of how much profit The Palace was making from her agony. He set the thoughts aside and strove for control. It was his turn to take a deep breath.

The woman spoke before he could renew his protest. "In fact, sir, you cannot protest actions that arose from your own complaints of the attendant's poor service."

"What the hell are you talking about?"

"I have it here," she tapped her screen with a long fingernail polished a dark green, "that you indicated your displeasure at her less than genuine orgasm."

His words came back to him, along with his irritation that she'd faked a climax.

A deep anger welled up inside him. "I wasn't displeased. No woman can control some of the physical indications of orgasm. And that attendant has several."

He paused, realizing he might be giving away too much of his history with Evans. "Or she did when I purchased her services for a shower scenario.

"Sweet Sol," he swore. "I wasn't complaining. I merely commented." He shot to his feet. "It was NOT a complaint! I'll sign a testament to that effect, an affidavit, whatever you want. How do I get her off the hook?"

The woman gave him a smile as cold as the quadrangle must be hot. "Purchase only, I'm afraid."

"Ah. I see. She's a pain in the ass and you'd like to get rid of her." That he could readily imagine. He'd bet she'd been a pain in the ass. Evans in a subservient position never had seemed right to him. "So, I can solve your problem by taking her off your hands. How much?"

The woman sat up straighter. Her fingertips danced across her keypad.

Within moments, he'd taken out a second mortgage on the old family home in Maine, and signed over a vintage PF he'd planned to restore when he retired.

The woman accompanied him to a door far from the front reception desk. "They will bring her through here. I've ordered a public ground vehicle for you. Best wishes."

She held out her hand, took his, and shook it as if they were sealing a bargain on a new PF, not the sale of human flesh.

Link listened to the click of her heels until she crossed into the carpeted area of the hallway. He wondered how the hell people like her slept at night. He'd never struck a woman in anger, but her lies and corporate extortion had brought him closer to decking her than he liked to admit.

What was taking them so long to get Evans out here?

He paced. Images formed in his head of her condition, half roasted in a garden that looked like paradise but was really a hell.

He thought of her unable to walk, comatose, or perhaps already dead. No, he wouldn't permit himself to consider it.

A set of doors slid open.

Evans stood in the portal. Her skin was fiery red, blistered across her nose and high cheekbones. Her eyes were wide and staring. She walked slowly, planting each bare foot carefully before shifting her weight, as though every inch of her body pained her. He could only assume it did. Her long robe whispered along the floor as she followed a guard past him to a door hidden in a trompe l'oeil painting on a far wall.

The guard said something and it slid open. They walked through a short corridor to another set of doors, double-width this time. These opened into the alley, where a public ground vehicle awaited them. This was where they put out the trash, Link saw as he followed her out. Banks of rubbish containers lined the alley.

He refused to let the intended insult get under his skin. He had her. She was safe now.

Evans moaned as she eased herself into the embrace of the soft seats.

"Med Center," Link barked, sitting beside her, not daring to touch her. He couldn't take his eyes off her reddened skin, her dazed eyes. "Hurry!"

A lone tear ran down her blistered cheek.

* * * * *

"She'll be fine, but there will be some scarring on both shoulders and one patch on her hip. Those areas are too deeply burned to heal without leaving a mark. Sorry." The physician, not much older than Evans, skimmed his fingers over his wrist pad. "Too bad she was under the influence of drugs. Whatever it was, it made her skin hypersensitive. It cooked her a little faster. And I'm sure she felt it more keenly."

The young doctor saluted Link and Brad and dashed away.

"What are you planning to do?" Brad asked.

"Find out why she was working off her prison sentence in that place, first. Then when she's healed, I'm going to... I don't know."

And he didn't. She'd refused to look at him from the moment they entered the hospital. Now, she lay a few feet away, silent, slathered in some vitamin compound goo guaranteed to help the burn heal in half the usual time, with minimal scarring.

Link eased the door closed behind him and went to her bedside. He wanted to hold her hand, but she was greased everywhere. "It's amazing, isn't it, that they haven't really come up with something easier than this since the early '30s?"

She ignored him.

He walked around the bed to where she faced. A bouquet of flowers had spilled a few petals on her bedside table. Their scent filled the room and reminded him of the flowers that had surrounded her in the garden.

What a stupid gift. He could be such an asshole.

"Evans."

"Shut up, Link. Just shut up."

"I'm sorry I said you were faking. I had no idea—"

"Shut up and go away."

Evans was a little surprised when Link obeyed her and a bit more surprised when he didn't return. She was bowled over when the hospital said she could not leave until he collected her.

* * * * *

She sat on an uncomfortable chair in the hospital lobby a week later, feeling healed and a touch greasy when Link strolled in.

He wore his dress uniform and he looked so good her eyes ached. Or maybe she was still experiencing withdrawal from the drugs.

The black tunic of a colonel fit him well. He'd chosen the loose, flowing trousers designed for social events, not military exercises. The small row of colored ribbons on his chest denoted combat and bravery under fire. So, she'd been right about the heat weapon scars on his ribs.

He moved like a cat. A decorated, military cat.

Arrogant bastard.

"Let's go." He held out his hand.

She ignored it and walked at his side, her hands tucked into her pockets, knowing what she had to say should not be said in public. The instant they were in his room at the headquarters hotel, she rounded on him. "You bastard. You arrogant son of a bitch."

Link unfastened his tunic and hung it up. Beneath, he wore a snug fitting shirt that hugged every muscle.

She refused to be seduced although she couldn't help looking. Lots of men were in great physical condition. Every one of them would look sexy in military garb. So what if he did? One of many, she reminded herself, and most of the others were not such bastards.

"Why am I a bastard?" he asked, sitting in a chair and propping his feet on a low ornamental table.

"You bought me. How dare you!"

"It was the only way I could save you, you ungrateful bitch."

"Bitch?" For a moment the room tipped.

Then he was there, hands on her shoulders, holding her, bruising her tender skin. She gasped and he loosened his grip.

"I'm sorry. I was angry. I don't really think you're a bitch."

"No," she said, slipping from his grasp, still dizzy, still under some aftereffect of the drugs. Who knew what the ones they'd given her in the hospital had done to her when they'd mixed with the dregs of the ones from The Palace. "No, you probably didn't really mean to call me a bitch. Pole princess is more likely."

"Sit down and listen," he said.

He brought her something fizzy in a glass and she drank it without really tasting it. Her stomach churned. "I can't listen, Link. I'm too angry. How dare you *buy* me!"

"I told you. I had no choice. And what the hell made you embezzle the base funds? Were you nuts or what?"

"I needed a new dress." She finished off the drink, clunked the glass on the table, and rose. "I'm leaving."

"Oh no, you're not. I own you. For seven more years. That's how long you have on your sentence."

This was the worst of all possible situations. She sighed and dropped onto the bed, her mind working furiously. Could she confide in Link? That went against every bit of training she'd ever had. *Trust no one.* Breaking that edict would get her into even more trouble than she was in already. As soon as the thought occurred to her, she rejected it. She'd trust Cadet Link Taylor of their Academy days with more than her life, but she couldn't be sure Colonel Link Taylor was the same man.

He'd have to leave sometime, to go to the base at least, and then she'd get through to Homeland Security. They'd help her disappear.

Shit. No, they wouldn't. She'd failed in her mission. They'd probably strip her rank or something. Worse, she'd have broken the heart of a worried father.

And if The Palace realized a HS agent had infiltrated their operation, Angel Martinez might disappear forever.

Evans fumed. How could she have let her temper make her lose sight of her mission? Given a choice between The Palace's reeducation process and having to face the Department Chief with her failure, the prospect of having strangers paw her wasn't so bad. She took a deep breath.

"You have to return me, Link."

"What?" He stared at her.

She stared back. His pewter eyes were almost black. She forced herself to hold a steady gaze with him. "You have to return me. I want back, Link. I loved my job."

His face flushed. "Too bad."

"What do you mean, too bad?"

He went to a security pouch and drew out a sheaf of papers. Very impressive papers, watermarked and stamped with official seals. He tossed them to her. She let them flutter to her lap.

"This is your sales contract, Evans. Read clause seven, line eight. Over thirty-five, unimproved. Not returnable. No refund."

Chapter 12

🔊

Double shit, Evans thought. No mission, no chance at redemption. No way out. Well, at least in Link's custody she'd be better off than in a court-martial.

"Seven years is a long time, Link."

"Not as long as we spent apart."

He stood and stretched, and she permitted herself to drink in the way the shirt clung to his body.

"You survived those years, you'll survive these."

"What are you going to do with me when you're back on-station? You can't very well keep me in your little officer's cubby, like a pet." He started, and she looked closely at him. "Are you on leave? On duty? Why are you in New Virginia? I can't imagine you taking a ground assignment."

"I'm on an extended leave, to get my finances in order."

She hardened her expression and injected ice into her tone. "Then you shouldn't have been wasting them on an expensive brothel. Or strained them buying me."

He said nothing.

"How did you get a membership card to The Palace, anyway?"

"I found it in a junk shop."

It was such a Link Taylor kind of answer. And she knew instinctively from her intimacy with him in the past that it was the truth.

She also knew it was all the answer she'd get.

"You'll forgive me if I don't trust you not to run off the minute I turn my back." Link turned away to rummage in a closet. He came out with a duffel, set it on the bed and began to sort through the contents.

"What are you going to do, tie me up?"

His expression was answer enough. She didn't need to see the riot restraints in his hands as he straightened.

* * * * *

He was gone for hours. Time enough for her to become stiff and more furious with every minute.

The tender skin on her wrists and ankles soon hurt like hell. Her struggles to free herself hadn't done her any good; these were the cuffs that ratcheted tighter with resistance.

And thoughts of mission failure ensured her brain hurt as well. She had to come up with a Plan B to rescue Angel now that working as an insider was no longer an option.

She'd managed to wriggle her way toward the foot of the bed. The comm unit was in plain sight across the room. It should respond to voice commands, but Link had been smart enough to set a password so she couldn't activate it. The tether he'd fastened to her wrists and the headboard kept her on the bed.

By the time she heard the door swish open, she was sore and pissed and ready for a fight.

When he stepped into sight, he held a bag from the base clothing boutique as well as a bulging bag from her favorite bath and beauty shop. He hated shopping, loathed it. And he'd been at it a while.

His thoughtfulness wasn't enough to deflate her anger. She hoped he'd thought of it simply to please her, but she suspected it was a calculated move.

"We'll get you some more things in a few days." He set the bags down by the closet. "Where I go, you go. I've arranged for larger quarters on Mars. It's something I could have done long ago, when I took over command of the station, but there seemed no need. You'll find the place rather comfortable."

He removed her gag and tossed it through the doorway into the bathing chamber sink. "General Richter took the news that I'd acquired a servant rather well, under the circumstances." Her wrist and ankle restraints followed. "You'll have restrictions because of your criminal record, but I'm sure you're used to that."

She tried to swing at him but her stiff muscles wouldn't obey her commands. She couldn't clench her fingers into a fist. Her hand just flopped toward him in a pitiful motion. The pain of the circulation returning to her extremities made her cry out.

"You didn't have to pull on them," he said. "You of all people should know that just tightens their grip."

Evans glared at him and kept her mouth shut. Anything she could say right now would only make her captivity worse.

Link flipped her onto her belly and straddled her. His big hands worked the cramps from her shoulders. His touch was gentle on her tender skin. She shivered and tried not to moan in delight. She failed and found herself mewing like a kitten. Stars and stripes, she didn't want to respond like this. That she did just made her madder.

She'd given many massages in The Palace, but hadn't had one like this in years. Ten years, to be exact. The man had talented hands, for sure. He hadn't lost any of his technique in space.

"I have better news, too. There's some holdup with the supplies for the transport, so departure has been set back two weeks." He moved on to her upper arms, building heat as he went. "I don't trust you here, so don't bother to unpack. We're going on a little trip."

She barely heard his words. She was too engrossed in the feel of his fingers as he shifted his attention to her back, beginning below her shoulders and making his way down, loosening the tension as he went. Each push shifted her slightly on the textured spread, rasping her sensitive skin a little. Not enough to be painful, just enough to be enticing. Her mews turned to soft moans.

He spanned her waist with his hands, then kneaded the globes of her ass. By the time he reached her calves, there were no cramps and no tension left in her. She was almost purring between the moans.

Then he smacked her bottom and pulled away. "Get changed and we'll be on our way."

She sat up in the cold left by his retreat and tried to recapture her anger. "What?"

"Weren't you listening? We're going on a trip," he said over his shoulder. She watched as he pulled a case out and began stuffing clothing into it. Casual clothing.

Saturn's rings. Her oath to Secretary Martinez forbid her telling Link the truth. She had to stay right here. She had to get back into The Palace.

"Where to?" she asked, trying to keep her voice calm.

"Some place far away, where I won't have to watch you every minute. A place we can relax together."

She climbed slowly from the bed. Despite the lingering discomfort in her shoulders, she smiled at his broad back. She knew where he was taking her. They'd been there before.

And when he was nice and relaxed, she'd steal his vehicle and head right back to New Virginia.

* * * * *

Link eased down on the controls and the rented PF swooped low over the pine forest. Off to their right, the sunlight glinted off the waves of the Atlantic Ocean. They passed over a number of homes, tucked into clearings or perched on the cliffs. Efficient domes, tiny cottages, sprawling mansions, representing every level of wealth and social status.

He watched Evans lean forward, pressing her forehead to the window. He knew she was trying to see everything. The

Maine coast hadn't been this developed ten years ago, when they'd had their last long weekend at the Taylor family cabin.

God, how many times had he'd dreamed about that weekend in the long nights since? More than he was comfortable admitting.

The old cabin looked the same as he lowered the PF to the landing pad. As the structure blocked the view of the sea, just before the wheels touched down, he heard Evans sigh.

He knew the feeling.

From the time he was a tiny child, this place had meant comfort and family. His grandmother always spent her summers here, welcoming her children and grandchildren. Over the intervening years, the family's habits had altered with the change in climate. Now, he knew, the cabin sat abandoned all summer, when the UV risk was highest.

They would be alone and undisturbed. If his grandmother had worked her magic the way she promised when he called her, they wouldn't even have to go to town for supplies.

He'd have time to clear the air with his new servant. He hadn't beggared himself for the pleasure of her services. He'd done it for her, to save her life.

Now, if he could just make her realize that. He had a week and a half.

No, *they* had a week and a half.

He powered the craft down and locked the controls with a password. The same one he'd used on the comm panel at the hotel.

Venus Rising.

She'd never guess it, and he didn't trust her as far as he could throw the cabin.

"Oh, Link, I'd almost forgotten how beautiful it is up here." Her voice caught in a sad little sound. "I thought I'd never see it again."

Maybe a week and a half would be enough.

* * * * *

Link wandered to the edge of the deck and leaned against the railing. The sun had set over an hour before, but enough ambient light remained for him to see Evans clearly.

"Link?" She touched his back, then leaned as he did, clasping her hands together. "I guess I owe you an apology."

"No. I owe you. I just couldn't stomach you in that place. Being punished like that. How could I know you'd chosen to… " He fell silent.

"Chosen that life deliberately?" She snorted. "Come on. No one chooses that life. I did the crime, so I had to do the time."

He turned and leaned his rump on the deck railing. "Just what was your crime?"

"I'd rather not say."

"The public records say embezzlement."

"Then that's it."

"People don't steal credits to hoard them. You wanted something. Tell me what."

"I told you. A new dress."

He frowned and shrugged. He didn't believe her, but he'd let it go for the moment.

He took her into his arms. She was warm from her nap. "You smell like vanilla cookies."

She tasted of them, too. Her tongue strolled across his lips and he opened his mouth to savor the full flavor of her. "Yum," he whispered.

"I raided the freezer. Did your grandmother make the cookies?"

"Must have. Only a professional cook has the time anymore."

"How is she?" Evans pulled out of his arms.

"Great for well over a hundred. And still in business, if you found cookies in the freezer."

"Come to bed, Link."

His heart began a slow dance in his chest. He rubbed the spot. "Now?"

"Well. Now would be nice."

"Why not right here?" He swept his hand out to indicate the deck.

"A bit hard on the back and knees, don't you think?"

Evans watched a slow smile make its way across Link's face. He flipped open a storage box and pulled out a long, sectioned cushion meant for a hover bench. He dropped it at her feet.

A sudden thrill ran through her, leaving desire in its wake. Desire to feel a real breeze caress her skin, to feel as she had on their camping trips. There was something wanton and wonderful about nakedness in the open air.

She stripped for him, her eyes on his face. *His* eyes were on her hands, following her every move. From the unfastening of the center attachments to the slow peel of her skin suit.

"Fuck me, Link."

He frowned. "Fuck?"

"What else did you have in mind?"

"Making love."

She bit her lip. "I'm not in love."

"It's a figure of speech."

She started when he reached out and skimmed his fingertips across her nipple. A shiver ran through her, from his touch as much as the knowledge that anyone might see them.

"Take off your clothes," she said to him. "You can't imagine what it feels like to be naked out here."

She stretched, knowing it aroused him. His cock bulged against the fabric of his trousers. Her insides went wet with the memory of what he would feel like inside her.

Deep inside.

She took matters into her own hands, pushing his questing fingertips away and reaching for his shirt. To tantalize him, she took her time hanging the shirt over the back of a deck chair. She slid his trousers down, then his underwear off his hips, and finally, slowly, freed his penis.

Moisture gleamed on the tip. She folded his trousers neatly and then bent over to tongue the drop of moisture.

"Unimproved. Just like I want it," she whispered against his warm skin.

"Evans," he moaned, grasping her head and threading his fingers through her hair. "Wrap your lips around me."

"Later." She danced away and placed his trousers over the back of a second chair.

When she tried to turn around, he was behind her, hands on her hips. He pressed behind her, shifting his cock across her cheeks.

"Link. Be patient."

"I can't be. I want you. Now."

He thrust his knee between her legs and within the space of a heartbeat, he was in her.

"Oh, Link," she said, the air suddenly tight in her chest.

"You can talk to me here," he said, his mouth by her ear. "You don't have to wait until I tell you to."

"W-what should I say?" The words barely made it past her lips as he cupped her breasts, gently rolling the nipples between his fingertips. His hips shifted, thrusting his penis a touch deeper.

She moaned.

"That's not talking." He pulled a few inches from her and then slid slowly back in. "Talk to me."

"I can't stand it. Move faster."

"No." Again, he drew out a scant few inches, then slid in slowly.

She leaned forward, gripping the back of the deck chair. The air was cold. Or her body was suddenly burning hot. "Please, Link. Now."

"Now, what?"

He moved his hands to her hips and stroked up and down her sides.

"Now what?" he repeated.

"In... me. Deeper," she said on a moan.

He slipped and slid his penis in and out with agonizing slowness. "Speak up, Evans. I can't hear you."

She pressed her hand between her thighs, against her clitoris. He reached forward and pulled her hand away, trapping it against her back.

"No playing with yourself. If you want touching, say so."

She wriggled back, pressing her buttocks against him.

"Okay, Link," she whispered. "Rub my clit."

"Please?"

"Please, damn it."

His fingertips found her. He was practiced, skilled, sliding his penis in and out, in rhythm to his stroking hand. "What now?" he asked.

"Down. Down."

"Down? Go down on you? Is that what you want?"

"No. NO. Lay me down. But don't... uh. Uh."

"Don't what?" He licked her shoulder, then feathered a kiss where her skin was scarred from the sun.

"Don't stop."

She felt his grin, but couldn't wipe it off his face. She was too close to nirvana to care if he smiled or not. He lowered her skillfully to her knees, his cock still buried deep, his fingertips never breaking their rhythm.

"Spread your legs."

And she obeyed him, sliding her knees out. He kept his hand on her clit, his other on her hip. He moved more quickly. She felt his testicles slap against her and moaned.

"Link. I'm going to come. I don't want to come."

"Okay." He jerked out of her and stood up.

For a moment, she remained on her knees, frozen in place, unable to believe he was gone, the freshening breeze whipping through her legs, bathing her wet crotch. She shivered and groaned.

"Link, you bastard." She rolled over to her back.

"I said talk to me, not order me around. I don't want fuck talk. I want to know what's going through that criminal mind of yours."

His cock was as stiff as the fireplace poker inside with the rest of the tools.

He wrapped his hand around it. "I can jerk off and get the same result as fucking you. A quick orgasm. I want something else. The mind fuck."

"Women want the mind fuck, Link, not men." She raised her knees and squeezed them together. "Men only want the orgasm. Fast and however it happens. They don't really care. If a hotel maid offered to suck your dick, it would probably be just fine with you."

"I've never gotten head from a maid. What I do have is you. And you used to mind fuck me all the time. I used to come in my uniform just by listening to you whisper in my ear."

She dropped her knees to the side and wrapped her arms around her waist. The sky was almost purple. A star stood off the horizon. The scent of pine filled the air. Real pine, from real trees.

Quietly, without thought, she said, "I love the scent of you, Link. I used to close my eyes those first few months you were gone and it was your scent I conjured up. The way your hair smells."

"Shampoo."

"And the way your neck smells when I lick it. And the spot behind your balls."

"Shit." He stretched out, face to face with her. He slid the hair behind her ear. "What does a man smell like behind his balls? Do I want to know?"

"Warm." She drew her thumb along his cheek. "Warm and aroused. It made me feel all frantic and slick inside to think about what I was doing to you to know what you smell like there."

"More." He kissed her mouth.

"And if I was really lonely," suddenly her eyes burned with tears, "if I was really lonely, I'd close my eyes and touch myself."

He put his fingertips between her thighs and she squeezed against his hand. "I'd think of the touch of your tongue on my clit. The feel of your fingers inside me. I'd imagine touching you here." She ran the ball of her thumb over the head of his penis and it came away wet. "I'd do this in my mind." She sucked the end of her thumb. He moaned. "I'd remember the taste of your semen. The slick, thickness as you came in my mouth."

He rolled her over and entered her in one motion, driving deep. He locked his mouth on hers and groaned through his climax.

She came a moment later, a quick, sharp, frantic pulse of sensation. Not a full, grinding, need-to-scream-out-loud climax, but another kind.

The small kind, one that she knew would be followed really soon by something more shattering if he kept making love even after every drop of his come was spent.

He laced his finger in hers. He licked her nipples, her throat, across her lips.

"I loved you, Evans. I fucking loved you. Shit," he whispered by her ear. "I think I still love you."

He kissed down the middle of her body and then parted her nether lips. His tongue was agile, his breath warm. She planted her feet on his shoulders and braced herself for the second shock wave, the one that would come in a few moments. He pushed two fingers inside her and she rode the motion of his hand.

Her cries echoed through the pine trees. She wanted to shriek again, but he covered her mouth with his and drank in her sounds. She pushed against his hand as he encouraged her to another orgasm.

She came three times with him. The little one. Then two stronger ones. Her insides burned and her clit was numb when he was done.

"I'll need a deep soak to recover from that." She pulled out of his arms and stood up, stretching and indulging in the freedom of standing in the open air, now in the dark night, where no one could see her.

"That's it? I tell you I think I love you, and all you can say is you'll need a soak in my bathtub."

"What else were you looking for? You wanted your mind fucked. I guess I did a good job. It's what I do."

He jerked as if she'd slapped him. She saw the confusion flit across his face, then wipe away as if he'd passed a hand over his face. His face went stone cold and expressionless.

"There's a whirlpool tub in the big bedroom. But you know where it is, don't you?"

He stood up and approached the deck door. It slid open silently to admit him. In moments, he'd disappeared into the dark recesses of the house.

She remained where she was, her palms on the railing, making sure her body was arranged with her legs slightly apart. She knew without looking that he was in there, in the darkness, watching her. She reveled in the knowledge that he cared enough to say he loved her. But she also knew he'd ship out again and forget her for the next ten years of his life, back on Mars.

This time, she wouldn't humiliate herself by begging him to stay. Even now, so many years later, she cringed inside, had to wrap her arms about her waist in a protective gesture against the memory of that last-minute, final breakdown while he'd been making love to her in the ship-out center.

Thank heaven the couple in the next room had hammered on the wall because Link had fucked her so forcefully against the wall. And they'd laughed.

And the moment had been saved.

But she still cringed to remember how the tears had run down her face, how she'd been begging him to stay, how she'd kept repeating those three words.

I love you. Love you. Love you, to the rhythm of his thrusts into her and the banging against the wall.

She'd been called to sick bay and her bruises examined during her training in the Homeland Security squad. Some grunt had seen the bruises in the locker room.

Homeland Security didn't want any abused partners in the squads. They wanted recruits with their minds on their jobs, recruits without baggage.

She'd frankly confessed to the enthusiastic fucking. They'd nodded and okayed her. But that night, she'd stripped in the bathroom and looked at the marks of his fingers on her buttocks, hips, breasts. For the first of many times, she relived the way she'd gotten those marks.

Not the way she'd become bruised during a few sessions with guests at The Palace. No, these bruises were simple marks from Link's passion. From holding too tight, from squeezing her when his orgasm overcame him.

The marks had faded quickly, along with any possibility she'd ever see him again.

With a sigh, she realized she was cold. The tub would help a bit and if she made the water really hot, the dripping sweat would camouflage the tears if she couldn't hold them inside.

Chapter 13

℥

Link heard the water thunder into the old tub. He belted his robe and went in search of a few cookies of his own.

His grandmother ran a successful restaurant in town. Even turning a hundred and ten hadn't slowed her down. Thankfully, she rarely visited the old homestead. She preferred her completely automated flat in town.

He rummaged in the deep freezer and found what he wanted. Cookies. Vanilla sugar cookies. Peanut butter. Maybe even with real peanuts in them, if he knew his grandmother and her black market dealings. He saw chocolate and knew that would be synth, but still, it would taste good to a domer who spent his time off-planet. Earth-bought synth was always better than the tasteless stuff that made it to the outposts.

He pulled all the cookie packages out and scattered them on the counter like decks of cards.

Next, he rummaged around some more and whistled softly. "Good ol' Granny. I really owe you for this. My providing angel." He pulled out several box-shaped packages that were labeled with tantalizing words in her quaint script. Words like *meatloaf* and *spaghetti*.

"I've died and gone to heaven."

He shoved one of the packages of spaghetti into the old cooker and in a few minutes removed a steaming, mouth-watering serving of pasta covered with what looked like real tomato sauce. While he transferred it to a proper bowl, he took a moment to savor the aroma, breathing in the steam before he smiled to himself and headed for the master bath.

She lay back, eyes closed. Her head rested on a folded towel, her long dark hair fanned out across it. He realized he didn't mind it now. The long hair suited her classic features.

He eased the door open and came up behind her. He knelt on the fluffy rug, stifling a groan as his knees protested the position.

But anything for love, he thought. And seduction.

He plucked a strand of spaghetti from the plate and dangled it over her partially parted lips. Lightly, he dangled a strand until it grazed her mouth.

She licked her lips, then her eyes flew open. She rounded on him. "Pasta?"

"God bless Grandma." He smiled at her flushed face. *And breasts.*

The room was steamy. Sweat dripped on her skin. "Lean back."

She did as he bid and he said, "Close your eyes, or no food."

Obediently, she shut her eyes, but her mouth opened like a baby bird's awaiting a worm.

He laughed at the picture she made, dragged a footstool close to the tub to spare his knees, and sat beside her. One strand at a time, he fed her the spaghetti. He played with her, tempting her with a touch to her lips, then pulling the pasta away to drip sauce across her breasts.

She played along. It took a long time to feed her. She had sauce on her cheeks, her chest and her lips when he was finished.

He set the plate down and began to savor the sauce while he licked her clean. One drop at a time, starting with her chest, lapping up the goodness and ending with her mouth.

"Mind fuck me, Link."

So now she wanted to play games.

He stood up and shed his robe. He climbed into the tub and shoved at her legs until she had them pressed close together and he was standing with his feet on either side of her hips.

"Okay, Evans. Here's your mind fuck. When I was lying in my bunk, hurtling through space—the first time—I went to sleep with these thoughts. I remembered this tub. Standing just like this, over you. I thought about how you were, lying back just as you are now, and how I'd told you to suck me. That's exactly how I said it, didn't I?"

He winked. She winked back.

"I believe I told you a good soldier takes orders from her superior. We argued over just who was the superior back then. But there's no question today, Evans. Now, comply with the order just as you eventually did that day." He fisted his penis. "Suck it."

She sat up with a grin and reached for him. He watched as the head of his cock disappeared between her lips.

Her mouth was silky, wet, warm. He groaned.

"Harder," he ordered and she complied.

"Deeper," he said and she gulped him in.

"More tongue," he demanded and she stroked him.

"Use your teeth… gently," he said. She raised the stakes and dragged her teeth up and down his shaft.

"Swallow it," he just managed to gasp as he shot his hot come into her mouth.

He sat down in the tub and planted his big feet by her shoulders.

"You did pretty good, Evans. You obeyed orders just fine. But your technique hasn't progressed much in ten years."

"And you have no idea how to fuck with a woman's mind." She shook her head.

He reached out and hooked his hand behind her head. He jerked her forward and kissed her hard, thrusting his tongue into her mouth, tasting his come on her, sliding his own tongue into the residue.

He broke it off, practically shoving her back against the tub. "Is that what you think? I don't know how to read a woman's mind and produce the kind of reaction you produced in me?"

"No. I think you can't." She watched him lean back and clasp his hands behind his head. Water beaded in the hair under his arm. She wanted to reach out and stroke the soft tufts, knowing how he would shiver and drop his arms, trapping her fingers.

But she remained where she was, in the tub, his physical presence dominating her just by his sheer size.

The water was dangerously close to the tub lip. He shifted and some slopped over.

"I like tasting my come in your mouth." He said it quietly, his eyes closed, his head lolling back on his hands. "I like feeling your tongue on my penis. And if you rub my balls, I can feel it in the soles of my feet. I never understood that. How can rubbing my balls make my feet ache?"

He gave a short, low laugh. The sound curled her toes.

"Do you remember the first time we camped out? How I took those drugs to keep from ejaculating since we'd be in a sleeping bag?"

"You got a rash. And vomited."

Link opened his eyes and nodded. He sat up. "That's why I'm unimproved as well, Evans. I'm one of the two percent of the population that can't tolerate sperm suppression drugs. Or the erectile enhancers."

"So, are there dozens of little Link Taylors running around somewhere?"

He shook his head and leaned back again, this time folding his hands over his belly. "I've never screwed a woman who wasn't taking care of herself."

"If this is how you romance a woman, you're failing."

"Are you wet inside?" he asked, eyes still closed.

"Dry as a bone." She knew she was still wet from their deck wrestle.

"I'll take care of that. Okay. Where was I? Ah, yes. The camping trip. I know I was sick and I blew it for you, but I had great plans. I intended to make you howl at the moon. A little like you just did out on the deck."

Superior shithead, she wanted to tell him with scorn, but instead, she said, "I howled because I worked you up so well, you performed really well. Without my mind fuck, as you called it, it would have just been a run of the mill screw."

"I remember telling you that I'd make you come once for every shooting star we saw. Remember it was the Leonids that time? The meteor shower in November?"

"I remember." She wished she hadn't said it. She needed to put him in his place. "And we know how impossible that would be. They may have discovered how to keep you guys from making wet spots, and science may be able to keep you stiff for a certain amount of time, but they haven't figured out how to increase the number of times you can get it up."

He smiled, but kept his eyes closed. "I only wanted to do it twice. Once before I asked you to marry me and once after."

"Link." She sat up and pressed her hand to her pounding heart. Typical of his love of all things old, he'd used the antiquated word for a life partnership. "You were going to ask me to marry you?"

"Yeah. Stupid idea. I was headed for Mars and you were headed for Homeland Security. What made you drop out, by the way?"

"Drop out?" she mouthed the words and realized they'd shifted focus, to the here and now. She tried to remember her cover story. If she screwed it up in one little detail, Link would zero in on it like a targeting laser. "Oh. I didn't drop out. They threw me out. Drugs. I got hooked on drugs."

He surged to a sitting position. Water sloshed over the side of the tub in a tidal wave. He grabbed her shoulders. "Drugs? Is that why you embezzled the base funds? And how the hell did you get involved with drugs?"

She looked down so he couldn't see the lie in her eyes. She looked at the dark hair encircling his penis and slipped her fingers into the thick thatch and stroked him.

"Old story. I pieced it together much later. I got somebody else's drink at a party, one somebody'd boosted with their drug of choice. I was hooked and ordering up a storm with the base supplier before I knew what hit me."

He lifted her chin on his hand and examined her face. Not for lies. For signs of drug addiction.

"What was the drug?"

"Nine-oh-two. One of the virtual ones. I was spinning after you in space, Link, trying to reach you in my mind."

"Shit." He kissed her and enveloped her in a bone-crushing embrace. "I should have insisted you sign on for the Mars study. You'd have been safe with me."

"No, I'd have slit your throat the first time you fucked someone else. And there were other someones, weren't there?" She placed a finger over his lips. "No, don't answer that. What you and I have done in the interim has nothing to do with now. With us here. And you are such a miserable mind fuck."

He cupped her face. "Kiss me and consider yourself mind fucked anyway."

He rose and plucked her out of the water. Scattering droplets everywhere, he carried her in his arms to the huge bed and dumped her on it. She squealed. "I'm wet. This bedspread is silk."

"Enjoy." He gripped her ankles and dragged her to the foot of the bed. He buried his face between her thighs. She would be raw, she figured, but she'd been worse off before — and this was Link, who'd planned to ask her to marry him.

It was her last coherent thought. His tongue was magic, his hands finding all the right places... between her legs, the gentle swell of her belly, her breasts.

Just when she thought she couldn't stand any more, he stopped, standing up and wiping his face with the robe she'd hung on the bedpost. He jerked the bedspread down and with a gesture indicated she was to get beneath the blankets.

"I want to make love to you, face to face. Like a pair of ancient missionaries."

He reached out to a touch pad near the bed, and skimmed his fingertips across it in a motion that was almost a caress. He didn't smile, but his eyes softened.

"And I want to do it beneath the stars."

The roof curled open like a giant iris. A billion stars appeared, spread across the black background of space. Some bright, some faint, glittering with every color imaginable.

"You see this every day," she whispered. "I can barely see a few hundred in the city."

He lay down beside her and rolled on top of her. "Watch the stars, Evans. Keep your eyes open while I love you and enjoy what you see. It may be the only way I can make you see stars and I accept that – for now."

She guided him between her thighs and the feel of him sliding into her was so familiar, so perfect, she wanted to weep.

She kept her eyes on the heavens as he'd directed, but drew up her legs and lifted her hips to meet each of his thrusts. He went deeply into her, his face buried against her hair.

His breath gusted harshly on her. Every now and then he moaned.

The stars blurred a bit as his hard strokes broke into an arrhythmic thrusting. She felt the spurt of his seed. He must have known she'd not come, because he put his hand between them and touched her.

The stars spun.

Her breath burned out of her chest and she gasped for air. Her nails bit into his buttocks and she ground against his fingers, prolonging the nearly painful climax.

He stroked her gently from breast to mid-thigh, running his hands on her as if smoothing in some silky cream.

"I used to masturbate to thoughts of you, Evans. You in the shower, washing between your thighs. You with your head back, mouth open, gasping when you came. I needed that. The memories. The first woman I slept with after you, I pretended she was you. Shit, Evans. I've been mentally replacing every woman I've fucked with you in my head."

"I win," she said and took his lower lip, a full, sensual lip, between her teeth. "You're a complete loser. That was a terrible way to end a fuck… telling me about other women you've been with. You're impossible."

Ignoring the words, he focused on the softness in her tone. She hadn't minded at all. Her hand found him. Her fingers were easy on him, cupping his balls and kneading them as if he were made of something tender, something fragile.

He shifted around so he could kneel over her in the classic 69 position.

Her bottom was the perfect fit for his palms as he slid his hands under her and raised her butt so he could taste and smell her.

She was drenched with his come. Tasting it on her mouth was titillating, but here, between her thighs, here her taste and scent mixed with his and made a primordial soup he had to lap with his tongue and dip into with his fingertips. He pressed against her knee, flattening her leg to the bed. He licked her with the patience of a cat, then lightly touched a kiss to the mole on her inner thigh.

"Venus, rising," he said and returned to the slick joy of her swollen clit.

She began to weep. Her body shook. Her thighs quivered.

He released her and cradled her in his arms. "Tell me," he said, wiping away the tears.

"My crotch is raw. You're going to kill me with sex."

He laughed. "Here I thought I'd moved you to tears. What a jerk I am."

He shifted her to her side and curled his body around hers. "Okay. I can take a hint. You're sore. I'll give you a few hours to recover. Maybe you can get back into the tub later and soak that twat. I'll be needing it ready for action very soon."

She pinched his arm that lay around her middle. "That's it. You're a hopeless cave man. Twat. Where did you hear that word?"

"From the same guy on my team who said you were a cock jockey — or was it pole princess?" He yawned.

She felt and heard his breathing shift to the rhythm of a sleeping man.

Cock Jockey.

Pole Princess.

She'd called herself that. Even if it was an undercover assignment, those few words reminded her that he thought she was a professional whore, one in the life because she was working off the penalty for embezzlement.

Tears did run down her face at that thought. She had no need to cover them with the excuse he was chewing her raw. No, now he was asleep. She could weep for real.

Weep because he'd done something from their first time together under the stars.

He'd been in the same position, head between her thighs, mingling his saliva with her juices and his come. Then, too, he'd pressed her knee back, kissed her mole, and said. "This is my small personal mark. Venus, rising."

From that moment, whenever he found her clitoris engorged, he'd say, "I see Venus is rising."

* * * * *

Link worked the muscles of his upper body. He liked the old free weights, the ones only useful here on earth, where they worked against the pull of real gravity. He counted so he didn't focus on Evans.

She wanted a mind fuck. He wasn't giving her one. If he did, he'd start babbling about loving her. And he couldn't reconcile this stranger with the one he had loved ten years ago.

This woman inhabited Evans's skin, but her head inside was all wrong. His Evans would never have succumbed to drugs even if she had started off the victim of some screw-up. No, his Evans would have trotted over to the base infirmary and checked in for help. Nor would she have agreed to work off her time in a brothel sucking dick and for all he knew rimming some guy's asshole.

That thought made him drop the weight bar with a crash onto its support.

He took the steps three at a time and tore through the house. He jerked the blankets off her.

She sat up, lips puffy, hair tousled. There was a bruise on her hip... maybe from his fingers.

"What is it?" she asked, reaching for his pillow and putting it in front of her. Sheltering herself.

"I have a question." It came out sharp and hard.

"What is it?" She put out a hand, but he ignored it.

"I want to know just how far your duties took you in The Palace."

"I don't understand."

"Just tell me all the acts they required of you."

"Link—"

"Come on. I want details. Am I swapping spit with someone who's had her tongue up ten guys' assholes?"

Her face, still a bit rosy from her punishment, went pale.

"Why are you asking me that? What I've done is none of your business. I would never ask you such a thing. How do I know you and some cunt captain haven't been plowing each other's assholes? And it is none of my business. What you've done, what I've done, since we last saw each other, doesn't matter."

"It matters to me. I've had fun, I'll admit that. But it's been the kind of fun any guy has on a station off-planet. What you've done as a –" he broke off.

"Pole princess? Say it, Link. You said it last night. I'm a pole princess, a cock jockey. I'm a whore!"

He stood there in silence for a moment. "This is ridiculous." He scrubbed his hands over his face. "Sorry. I knew what you were when I bought you."

She rose from the bed, dropped the pillow, and took up her robe. After she belted it, she went to his case and threw it open.

His throat felt a bit tight as she rifled the contents and found the papers on her purchase. Her hair slid from her shoulder and concealed her face as she read the pages. It took a long time, but he didn't move.

"Well," she said, softly. The papers fluttered from her fingertips to the floor. She kept her gaze on them, head bowed. "I see I'm required to answer any and all questions you put to me. I'm also required to perform any service you deem appropriate." When she turned, her hand went to the throat of her robe and she held it closed. Her face was set. He couldn't read her expression. "What would you like to know? How can I be of service?"

"Forget it, Evans. Forget I asked. Forget those papers."

"I can't. You fucking *own* me."

"As far as I'm concerned you can walk out of here any time you like."

"Right now, if I like?"

"Yeah." *Shit*. How could he say that? What would he do if she left? "No. I'm a fucking liar. I don't want you to go." He walked to where she stood and wrapped his hands in the lapels of her robe. "I'm suddenly understanding your drug thing. I'm addicted to you. I can't get enough of you."

He pulled her close by the cloth he crushed in his hands. "It's too sunny outside right now, but we can go into the woods."

"I can't."

"Why not?" Her gaze was still shuttered, private, hiding her thoughts.

"I'm too sore."

He scooped her into his arms. The tub heated and filled in only a few moments. Those moments he passed by kissing her. Her lips. Brows. Cheeks. The silky skin of her shoulder, her fingertips, her lips again.

The water was too hot for his taste, but just right for a sore body. She yelped a bit when he lifted her and lowered her into it.

Then he left her alone. For an hour. He used that time to whip up breakfast. God bless Grandma, he thought again as he threw cheese omelets into the cooker along with something bearing the intriguing label, *blueberry muffins*. Grandma must've been out in the woods hunting wild berries again. He couldn't wait to watch Evans's reaction to what his providing angel did with muffins.

Then another memory intruded. Wild blueberry stains on Evans's shirt. From his fingers, from touching her.

If he was an asshole with words, maybe he could do better wooing her with food. And memories.

Chapter 14
🔊

Evans opened her eyes when Link elbowed his way into the bathroom. He had a huge tray, wide enough to straddle the tub. Tantalizing aromas wafted from the covered dishes.

"Is this real food, Link?"

"Yep. More Grandma gifts. She really knows how to stock a pantry."

Her hands were steady as she dug into the real egg omelet. The berries in the muffins were real, too.

"Heavenly. Please thank your grandmother for me, will you?"

"Maybe you'll get to thank her yourself."

"I don't think I'm going to be here that long." She shoved the tray aside and stood up. He didn't reach for her, but he did study her as she dried off and donned her robe.

He followed her into the bedroom.

She dropped the robe and climbed back between the sheets. He must have changed the bed while their breakfast was cooking, for the sheets were fresh, if rather amateurish in their installation. The smooth cotton was cool on her tub-warmed skin.

He stretched out beside her. Would she ever have her fill of looking at him? His body was so beautiful, inviting her to touch. Nevertheless, she resisted.

His penis lay flaccid against his thigh. She drew up the sheets and covered them both to the chin. Then she rolled over and stared at the wall.

It was time to go. Somehow she had to break away and contact headquarters.

To report the complete devastation of her mission to rescue Angel Martinez. Every moment in Link's bed was a betrayal of that mission. Every moment brought them closer to Angel's twenty-first birthday, and that would put the poor girl beyond their reach. Evans had seen just what Angel was caught up in. She couldn't do that to any parent. She certainly couldn't do that to a man she'd come to admire and respect.

Link's hand stroked her hair. He said, "I remember once we climbed down the rocks to the beach. The water used to be cold here, according to my grandmother. Down in the sixty-degree range. But it was only chilly, if I recall. Maybe in the mid-eighties. The day had been really hot, so we didn't mind the cold."

She nodded to let him know she remembered too, but she kept her gaze on the wall.

"We swam and then made love on a towel. You kept yelping about getting sand in your crotch. And I teased you." His fingers stroked her hair. "That day, you said something that really stayed with me. You said I had something no other man had. You didn't know what it was. An invisible chemical that I gave off and only your sensors could pick up. You said whatever it was, it was like a leash from you to me. And all I had to do was tug the leash and you'd come to me. Not come, come. But... you know what I mean."

She nodded. Her throat constricted. *I'm a fucking security operative, level twelve, and I can't stop crying.* Her voice sounded reasonably normal when she said, "I said a lot of things. And they proved the chemical thing a century or two ago. I just smell good to you at some unconscious level. It's all bullshit."

"I'll ignore that." He tugged a lock of her hair, then smoothed it on her shoulder in a soft caress. "Anyway, I think you were wrong. I think the leash is there... you were right about that, but it works the other way. You tug and I come to you." He kissed her shoulder. "I'd go anywhere you asked me to. Do just about any damn thing. I'd give up space for you, give up my command. Give it all up."

She rolled to her back. He had a growth of stubble on his face. Men who were allergic to sperm suppressors couldn't take the drugs that eliminated beards, either. She skimmed a finger down the line of dark hairs sprouting along his jaw.

He turned his head and captured her fingers between his teeth. She felt his tongue sweep over them and then he let go.

"I would give it up to know I was going to wake up every morning and find you by my side. Right here. Well," he bent and kissed her shoulder again. "Not right here. This place is going."

"Why?"

"I mortgaged it again to buy you. The payments are too high for me to keep up."

She thrust her fingers into his hair and drew his head down. The kiss was slow and gentle. He'd mind fucked her all right. He loved this place. Loved it.

To sell it for her… to take her away from The Palace.

She remembered a song, a revival tune, from a couple hundred years ago, something about a slow hand. He had slow hands.

Very slow hands.

"What am I going to do with you?" he whispered.

She could not allow him to mesmerize her, keep her so enthralled she lost sight of her mission.

"I have to go, Link. Back to New Virginia. It's really important. Can you take me?" She knew by the terms of the sales agreement with The Palace, she could not go anywhere without his permission.

"I'm not done with you yet," he said and entwined his fingers with hers.

He stretched her arms out and kissed her. She felt a quiver of anticipation from deep inside, but forced herself to speak. "I have to get back, Link."

"Later. Later." His mouth roamed her throat and shoulders. His hips shifted his erection against her belly. When his knee moved between her thighs, she moaned in anticipation.

With their hands linked, there was no way to guide him where they both wanted him to go. She lifted her legs and locked her ankles across the small of his back. He probed, missed, shifted, laughed a gust of warm air against her throat when he could not put himself in her.

She tugged one hand free and slid it down his flank, then to his penis. She guided him home and put her hand back in his.

Their hips undulated in a familiar rhythm. Just as she felt the quivering rise of her climax, he put his lips to her ear.

"I'd go anywhere, stay earthside, to be with you," he whispered.

She wailed and churned her hips as her climax overtook her. He groaned and joined her. When they lay limp, limbs entwined, hands still locked, skin sweaty and damp wherever they touched, he said it again, softly, by her ear.

"Anywhere, Evans. Anywhere."

* * * * *

Evans stood ramrod straight before her boss. The Undersecretary of Homeland Security, Eric Samuels, paced and ranted. His aide, Mark Jordan, sat like a statue with his recorder, ready to take notes.

She tried to block out most of Samuel's tirade, but it was difficult when she knew it was all true.

Link thought she was shopping for new clothes. She *was* wearing a new, plain rose-pink suit, but she was no longer in the Skyhigh Mall. She had signaled Samuels from a public panel in the rest room and Jordan had picked her up at the back entrance.

"What is Colonel Taylor going to think when he finds you missing?"

"I don't know. It'll be unfit for human ears, if I know Link."

Samuels sighed. "We're back to where we were before you entered The Palace. And Angel is still missing."

Evans leaned forward. "I am sorry. I had no idea Link had a card. We put that membership list through a fine sieve and I know his name wasn't on it. He told me he picked up someone else's card in a junk shop. No one had any reason to anticipate that. Those cards are worth a large fortune."

Samuels tapped his fingertips together. "There isn't any answer but infiltration. There just isn't, and we're running out of time. If the legal age of majority is raised, it would give us four more years, but the Councilors are particularly fractious right now, and unlikely to pass any bills during this session. Nothing is going to change before Angel's birthday. And I can't let Secretary Martinez know the mission fell apart."

A few moments later, Samuels lifted his dark eyes to hers. There was a sheen of perspiration on his coffee-colored skin. "I have an idea," he said.

He turned to his aide. "Jordan, pick up Colonel Taylor at the Capital Mall. He'll be fairly easy to spot. Look for a man with steam pouring out of his ears."

They waited in Samuel's office. She paced in front of the wall of windows that overlooked one of the parks. There were no pedestrians to watch in the midday sun, but the wide avenues were filled with vehicles and the air with PFs.

She smoothed her suit over her hips and touched the tight knot of hair at the base of her neck. A buzz sounded at the office door. Her heart thudded in her chest. Her stomach churned. With military precision, she turned and stood at attention.

Link walked into the office, saw her and, with barely a sign he knew her beyond a slight inclination of his head, shook hands with Samuels when introduced by Jordan.

"Please sit, Colonel." Samuels indicated a comfortable chair by his desk.

Evans remained standing.

"You have complicated matters considerably, Colonel Taylor."

Link raised one eyebrow but said nothing. He remained silent while Samuels explained the part Evans was playing and her mission. He remained silent through the Undersecretary's description of his idea for another infiltration of The Palace.

Link sat for a moment, his mind working to reorganize the events of the past few weeks, recasting them in light of Eric Samuels' revelations. All this was more than he had ever suspected, although Evans on a mission for Homeland Security made sense. Evans addicted to drugs, stealing to get drugs, never had.

He felt like a fool. Looking back, it all made sense, except for his addiction to Evans. *Shit*. How could he have behaved like an animal in rut?

"With all due respect, sir," Link said, "I do not see how sending us together into The Palace as clients will help your investigation. Didn't you say other guests had tried and failed?"

"From Lieutenant Colonel Evans's report, we now realize the effort was underfunded. Using the sudden wealth you've acquired through inheritance or a lottery win to indulge your interest in sexual experimentation is the perfect cover. We'll make sure you have enough credits to get wherever you need to be."

"Once we find her, why not just buy her like I bought Evans?" Link asked.

"Unfortunately, by law, Angel didn't enter The Palace as a debtor or a convict. So she has no contract for purchase. She won't be for sale."

Link thought it would have been too easy, and it was.

"We'll take care of your new good fortune, leak it carefully so it doesn't make a splash but gets to the right ears. Our intelligence indicates that it's not uncommon for personal servants to accompany their owners to these appointments."

Jordan shifted in his chair, as though he wasn't entirely comfortable with the discussion. Link wondered how many daughters the man had at home.

"Sexual experimentation is what you need to undertake, because Lieutenant Colonel Evans here has informed us that the only place she's actually seen Angel Martinez is in one fetish scenario." Samuels flashed a glance back at Evans before he continued. "Those clients are served in a different area of the building from where Evans was based. And that area is probably restricted to those guests with exceptional wealth. It's likely that those guests, who are wealthy and powerful and thus motivated to keep quiet, are offered the underage attendants. Just having the wealth to access the next level of menus should help you get to Angel."

The thought of what the staff at The Palace had done to Evans made him sweat. What they might do to Angel made him just sick.

Samuels must have paid attention in those classes about reading interrogation subjects' faces. At that moment, he said, "We're almost out of time. When Angel turns twenty-one, she's beyond our reach."

When Link looked up and met his eyes, Samuels said quietly, "It's taken more than a year to track her to The Palace."

Link stood. "If General Richter agrees to loan me to your division, I'll do it—provided several conditions are met."

Everyone visibly relaxed. "Whatever you want, we can work it out."

"Fine. I want the money back that I paid for Evans's contract. Find the antique PF I sold and return it to me. Once this is over, Evans gets promoted to full colonel. Whether or not we're successful." He ignored Evans's indrawn breath behind him, focusing on the man behind the desk.

Link had paid attention in those classes, too. He watched as Jordan made several notations on a panel display. Samuels looked relieved, and he apparently had expected more in the way of demands. Link searched his plan and wondered just what he'd missed.

Samuel rose. "Is that all, Colonel?"

"Yes, sir."

"Don't you want to be in charge?"

"No, sir, I believe Evans and I will be fine with whatever you choose to give us in terms of backup. Frankly, I don't expect to need it. Between her knowledge of the facility and our combined skills, we should be in and out of there on our own just fine."

"If you will excuse us, I will go and see about these arrangements." Samuel and his assistant stepped outside, closing the door behind them.

Link lost no time. He grabbed Evans by the shoulders and shook her. "What the hell were you doing, not telling me about your mission?"

"Link, you know I couldn't tell anyone. I was under orders. Covert ops, deep cover."

"Not from me," he growled.

"Yes, even from you. Especially from you." She freed herself with a sudden move and stepped back. Her chin set, she glared at him. "Just how did you get into The Palace? We checked those membership lists against every database we could think of, and no one came up who might have blown my cover. Then, one week into my mission, you show up for a hand job. From me."

"I bought that card for five credits. I had no idea you were there until I saw you on the attendant roster." He hated the defensive note in his voice.

"Just like that?" She snorted. "Link, I'm not the only one who's worked this case. Two other agents have spent thousands of credits—and precious time—getting membership cards and appointments, and they both came up empty. Until I went in, we had no idea there were hidden menus, where one might expect the illegal stuff to be available. It was just a fluke that I found out about it. That was right before you complicated things and bought me."

"So it's all my fault?"

Before Evans could answer, the door opened. Eric Samuels and Mark Jordan returned.

All smiles, the men shook Link's hand. "The general was very sympathetic to the Director's situation. Welcome to the team, Colonel. And congratulations on your giant MegaSweeps win."

* * * * *

Evans ran her finger along Link's hand. He ignored her and walked faster. She had to run to catch him. At his hotel room door, she grabbed his arm. "Link. We have to talk about this."

"No, we don't." He slapped his palm over the door identity pad and it swung open.

She just managed to slip through before the door whispered shut. Link jerked his hand through the fastenings of his uniform tunic and pulled it off, throwing it across the bed. "Can't even slam a damn door."

"Would that vent some of your anger?" she asked.

He turned, military fashion, and faced her. "Anger? Why would I be angry? Because you lied to me over and over again, or because you're happy to fuck for your country?"

"Did you like me better when you thought I was fucking for fun? Or when you thought I was fucking for drugs?" Heat ran through her, flaming her cheeks, she was sure. Her head throbbed and her veins pulsed.

He strode across the room and cupped her face. "I liked you better when you were just a grunt like the rest of us." His kiss was as hard and angry as his tone.

She didn't want to make love to a man so angry he might have no control. But she wanted to make love to him. His fingers tightened when she set her hands on his waist.

"Be angry, Link. Be as angry as you like. But remember, we don't always choose the path we walk."

With a maneuver learned at the academy, she slipped from his grasp and went to the wall of UV-tempered glass. The curtains were closed, and she touched the wall control that swept them aside. A bright object gleamed near the horizon.

"Venus is rising," she said softly. Her insides clenched when he sighed.

When he encircled her waist from behind and set his mouth on her throat, she knew the anger had gone out of him as quickly as it had come. She planted her hands on the glass after he'd stripped her.

He took her from behind, not quickly or even very skillfully, but each thrust of his hips sent him so deep within her she groaned aloud. The window fogged from the heat of her breath, the glass grew slick from the sweat of her hands.

Then he boosted her into his arms, still impaled on his cock, and pressed her face down on the bed. His hands were hot on her hips as he shifted and settled himself.

"Stop," she said and he froze over her. "That's enough. Let me up."

Instantly, he withdrew and she rolled over, drawing in her knees. "This is stupid. You're angry, you feel betrayed and yet, you're still happy to jam me."

A smile twisted his mouth. He set his palms on her knees and pulled. "Why should I deprive myself?"

He was powerfully strong, but she had great thigh muscles and held fast against his efforts to spread her legs. "You should deprive yourself until you've figured out why you're so angry."

"What are you, a psychiatrist as well as a pole—"

She flipped quickly out of his grip, rolled and came to her feet on the opposite side of the bed. "Don't say it."

"I'm sorry for that." He ran his hands through his thick, dark hair and sat down on the edge of the bed, his back to her.

Evans shrugged into and belted the robe she found in his closet. "We have to work together, Link, so we have to resolve this thing between us."

Suddenly, she felt as vulnerable as she had the day he'd left her. He had such power to hurt her. No matter how many years had passed, she could not deny the power he held over her. The power she gave him.

Their gazes met, locked, then his slid away. He rose, stretched, ardor gone, and headed for the shower. She heard the water, felt the liquid heat of desire. Should she join him?

Link found her asleep in the chair, legs tucked beneath her. He stroked her hair from her cheek and thought of their hard words in the Secretary's office. But wasn't what she'd been doing, in the name of her country, the same as if she'd chosen that profession deliberately? She'd fucked who knows how many men because her country had asked her. No matter the mission—rescuing an imprisoned AOA—still, she had sucked and fucked whoever The Palace assigned to her.

What if Jack Elliston from base communications had taken leave at the same time and hung out with him? Jack's father had enough credits to send him to The Palace for a bit of sex play. For all Link knew, he'd been a guest there before. What if they had gone together, and Jack had found Evans on the list of attendants? Link covered his face with his hands.

Now, they had assigned him to the mission. His cock stirred at the thought of going there again, only this time with Evans and almost unlimited funds. Of course, the other operatives had failed to find Angel Martinez that way. Maybe because they never got to the reputed "hidden" menus of fetishes, quirks, and illegals, the one he'd never seen but Evans said existed.

Link went to the comm panel and activated The Palace card.

"Welcome," the hostess said. Did he detect a touch more enthusiasm in her tone now he had megacredits in his account from his phony MegaSweeps win?

"Menus," he said softly, mindful of Evans, still asleep or at least pretending to be so.

He read through the menus with growing frustration, slapping his hand on the screen, rejecting whatever he saw. Nothing even smacked of fetish stuff.

"Stop playing, we need to search every menu tree for Angel's face," Evans said from behind him.

The search was fruitless. Angel was not among those attendants available to the new, rich Link Taylor. "Why not do as Intel recommended. Go for multiple partners and work our way into more involved scenarios from there?"

"Shut up." He let the screen go blank. "If you're so hot for multiple partners, I'll get Brad up here."

"Your friend?" She held the lapels together at her throat. Her grin was toothy and broad. "I'd like that. I've always wondered if I could handle two men at a time."

He tried and failed to keep a straight face. "I cry uncle."

"Good. Now. Let's see if we can set aside our hostilities and get to work."

"Yeah, good idea. Work. I can handle work."

"The twosome is probably a good idea. You could take me in with you. I *am* your possession now, and you could ask for another partner."

His eyes widened. "Screw someone in front of you?"

"Ah... I think I'd actually be one of the screwees."

Something low in his belly tightened. Whether with dread or anticipation, he couldn't tell. "Shit, Evans, I can't handle this."

"No, the women handle *it*."

Link grinned and his cheeks flushed.

She felt something inside her relax. As much as she was appalled by the idea of making love to Link with another woman in the room, another woman participating, touching him, she knew it was possibly the only way to get to Angel now that he'd trashed her chances of working alone.

Although she balked at the thought, she knew the partner they should order was Grace8.

At least Evans knew Grace8 had contact with Angel. Surely, Grace8 knew about all the hidden menus.

Evans watched him walk to the communications console. He was a cowboy, or maybe a knight. It might be hundreds of years past those eras, but still, the need to ride in and rescue the fair maiden had not been eradicated. She felt more than a twinge of acid bubble in her stomach when he went back to the communication console and activated his card. Whatever happened, she was along for the ride.

"Done," he said.

"What is?" she asked, her insides as tight as they'd been the first time she heard her assignment—find Angel Martinez by entering The Palace as a prisoner.

"I did the deed. We go tonight at nine, you and me. I picked a partner for us. The youngest brunette I could find."

"Shit, Link, I had someone specific in mind. I should have told you I knew a woman who'd been in at least one scenario with Angel." She wasn't about to tell Link what that scenario had involved… or that she'd been there.

"Too late. I'm sorry. I wasn't thinking like an investigator. We are partners and I should have consulted you first. I can be such an asshole."

Evans looked over the appointment, then went through all the menus, searching for his choice. The hair on her arms stood up. The attendant Link had reserved was Grace8. Her hair was dark, but it was definitely Grace8.

She wondered at this connection they had. She was in his arms in less than a heartbeat, her mouth as hard on his as his had been on hers but a few hours before.

"Make love to me, Link."

But he pulled her arms from around his neck and shook his head. "If I'm going to get it up tonight, I shouldn't be messing about now. I'm *unimproved*, remember?"

"You could take one of the milder erectile... never mind."

"Even the milder drugs affect me, so I can't play any games. Tempting as it might be."

There was a touch of acid in his tone that she couldn't account for. Then she thought he might still suspect she had accepted the job in the brothel because she was drawn to it.

The room felt cold. "Where's the heat control?"

He flipped her the room's control device. When she caught it in mid-air, he said, "We're only fucking when the job says fuck. Is that understood?"

She nodded and skimmed the ball of her thumb across the control button. The curtains billowed out from the vent that supplied the heat, drawing her eye to the window.

Venus stood high above the horizon.

Her own Venus throbbed, aching for his touch. But she would not ask again.

Chapter 15
හ

Link drew on a loose black tunic and trousers. He was almost painfully aware of Evans behind him, pulling on a bronze fabric tube that slid like liquid down her curves. The gown fit her like skin from chin to ankle. His cock stirred, so he tried to tame his need for her with a touch of ice. "Move it, Evans. And that's an order."

"Actually, since you're on loan I think I outrank you on this mission, Link, so I'll give the orders."

He bowed and threw open the door.

When Link's newly leased, luxury PF slid to a halt in front of The Palace, Evans gulped. Her insides went hot. Her palms were damp as she smoothed the wrinkles out of the gown chosen by the Department. As thin as the fabric was, she thought the rapid pounding of her heart might be visible. It was one thing to work inside, unseen by the public, and quite another to walk in boldly through the front door.

No, that wasn't why her heart was racing. She had to be honest with herself. It was one thing to perform sexual acts with no one to see but the paying customer, another to do them before the man you loved.

She sighed. "This love stuff is for the birds," she muttered as they entered The Palace.

This time, against all her inclination to lead, she forced her eyes down and followed Link at a respectful distance, their footsteps producing whispers of sound on the thick carpet.

It was a new product, a pliable digitized crystal fiber whose color shifted to complement whatever lighting scheme the brothel had chosen that night. The rug looked like a glittering array of stars on an indigo sky. Just what she needed, reminders underfoot that Link was earthbound... exactly where he didn't want to be. He might never get back to Mars if she screwed this up.

Then she mentally slapped herself. Angel Martinez would miss a happy, healthy life if the mission failed — something far more important than the possibility of losing a planetary posting or a promotion.

Keep the mission in mind, Evans, she rebuked herself. You have to find Angel and convince her to give up this life and go home. And if she's here against her will, break her out.

The stars beneath their feet reminded her that, despite the vastness of the cosmos, one small person still mattered.

The check-in process was new to her since she'd only seen the operations from the opposite side of the door, so to speak. There was nothing to indicate that The Palace was anything but a very elegant hotel catering to the discriminating tastes of a wealthy clientele — one that valued privacy.

They approached a sweeping counter behind which stood a woman. The expansive surface was real wood, polished to a soft sheen. On the wall behind the receptionist was a painting Evans wished she could examine at close quarters.

Link had instilled a love of antiquities in her by dragging her to museums. At first, she'd gone unwillingly, teasingly laughed through his lessons. Later, she knew he had opened a window to another time and world for her.

This painting looked like a genuine Desmond. In a real wooden frame. Desmond had been one of the few artists to escape the conflagration that ended the first Mars expedition over 150 years ago.

His work would be priceless. Of course, cynic that she was, this could be a rather good copy in a rather good ersatz wood frame.

Link placed a strategic elbow in her ribs, drawing her back to their mission.

The beautiful receptionist greeted Link with what Evans thought was a touch too much enthusiasm. She was not an attendant. Her hair was tinted a pale green and stood out from her head in short spikes. Evans felt a stab of envy. How she missed her easy-care military coif.

The hostess escorted Link to the lift, touching him way too often. Her hand lingered, stroking his sleeve when the doors slid apart. Evans was ignored and just made it into the lift before the doors closed. The slight twinge in her stomach was the only indication they were rising to a fuck-fest who knew how many stories overhead. Or was it just indigestion and nervous anticipation, and they were actually dropping hundreds of feet down into some pit, to be fed to alligators? She wondered briefly if there were any alligators still around to eat them.

Link wrapped an arm around her waist, palmed her breast and licked her cheek. "Like the dress," he said. By her ear, he whispered, "Love what's in it."

His thumb rubbed over her nipple, peaking it against the fabric. She shivered. Something inside her started to produce a scalding liquid. An urge to squeeze her thighs together to keep that fluid from escaping and dribbling down into a giant puddle on the lift floor made her swallow a giggle. Shit, what was happening to her? A lieutenant colonel, unable to keep her mind on the mission. She no longer had the drugs to blame for her flights of fancy.

The doors slid open. A man, as handsome as Ms. Green-hair had been lovely, stepped forward and bowed. "I am your host for this visit. Please accompany me, sir." He didn't even glance her way.

They were in a section of The Palace she'd never seen. Here, as with the reception area, one's impression was only of a fine hotel. The guests must not be permitted to realize what lay on the attendants' side of the walls. A prison. She began mapping their progress, counting doors and paces between turns in the corridor.

The young man escorted them to a chamber fitted with nothing except a wide bed covered by slick golden sheets. She knew that color was more a trick of lighting than anything else.

To her intense embarrassment, the young man began to undress Link. The man was as free with his hands as the receptionist had been as he drew off Link's tunic, and was way too solicitous about hanging the damn thing in a closet. She marked where the doors were, for they were so perfectly crafted, they disappeared into the walls when he closed them.

When Link was stark naked, the young man approached her, but Link held up his hand. "No thanks, I would like our attendant to do the honors."

The young man bowed and left them alone after holding out one of The Palace's signature robes for Link to slip into.

Link watched Evans pace the room. The bronze gown shimmered over every curve. It might as well be paint, the way it revealed every detail beneath. Her nipples were tight, the mounds of her buttocks sleek, their cleft clearly defined. "Settle down. You've been here before—"

A disembodied voice interrupted him.

"Welcome to our couples area. Where *we* aim to please. Since this is your first selection among the delights of multiple partners, we wish to offer a few suggestions to enhance your pleasure."

Link schooled his features into politeness and thought there could be few greater pleasures than watching Evans pace a room clothed only in a liquid metal gown.

"Please indicate to your attendant what 'safe' word you will be using to end any activity that makes you uncomfortable. In addition, if you wish to upgrade, this chamber is voice activated and you have merely to say 'upgrade' and your wishes will be granted."

And debited, Evans thought.

The door swung open after a click Evans knew well. Grace8, eyes downcast, entered the room. A Grace8 whose hair was now brunette.

"You may look at us," Link said.

Grace8's eyes widened a touch when she saw Evans, but Evans did her best to pretend all was well. She could never tell Link of the emotions boiling inside her. She had a dozen reasons Link and another woman in bed would disturb her mightily. She hadn't included in her list this flaming heat of anger and jealousy she felt.

To lie with a straight face was a skill she'd learned early and made good use of during various missions over the years. Now, she would be lying with her hands, her mouth... all of her body.

"Our safe word is *Venus,*" Link said. Evans felt the intensity of his gaze upon her.

"Why don't you take off your robe," Link said to Grace8 and Evans wanted to kick him in the shins for being so quick to get the attendant involved.

Grace8's now dark hair fell over her shoulders like a sheet of ebony and her pubic mound was shaved and decorated with elaborate artwork. The body art was a golden design that gave the impression of entwining snakes sliding from the slit of her labia. Evans wondered if these same snakes also adorned Cloud9.

Grace8 might have changed her hair color, but she was golden everywhere else. A dusting of glittery powder, one applied with a base that ensured it would remain on the attendant and not rub off on the client, graced the aureoles of her pierced nipples. In addition, she wore a gold ring through one of her labia and Evans knew it was situated to increase the friction against a man's cock as he fucked her.

The young woman stood facing Link with her hands crossed behind her back. The stance put her breasts forward.

Evans remembered what she'd said about her nipple enhancement and controlled a shudder.

"What are you waiting for?" Link asked. "You may speak."

"Shall I help your partner undress?" Grace8 asked.

"By all means." He crossed his arms over his chest.

As Grace8 approached her, Link turned away. Evans took the opportunity to whisper as she moved close. "My partner really wants a scenario like that last one we were in. He's looking for a submissive like that young girl."

"In your dreams," Grace8 whispered back, her hand slipping down Evans's front to deliver a sharp tug to her nipple.

Evans realized by the evil look on Grace8's face that she'd made a mistake.

Link found the only way to still the flush of nervousness that roiled his stomach was action, so he went to the bed and pulled back the top sheet, flipping it to the floor so all that remained was the wide acreage of the mattress. He figured it would be made of some substance guaranteed to enhance sex acts. The management certainly took their job of catering to wealthy hedonists seriously.

Then, there was nothing left to do but watch. He sat down and tried to appear as if having two women at his disposal was an ordinary event. Or at least, that it was something he couldn't wait to get involved in, rather than something he dreaded.

How many times had Brad and he talked about this fantasy? They'd talked about having one twat in their face and another on their erection. Or, Brad's favorite, screwing one woman from behind while watching her lick the bejeebers out of the other woman's crotch.

Right now, to his horror, he realized he felt as jealous of this dark beauty as he would be if it were Brad doing the honors. She was mauling Evans.

It might be okay when your heart wasn't involved and your brain fried with jealousy.

And he was so hard he might explode on contact. How would Evans react to his arousal? His penis had hardened watching her pace. She'd never believe it wasn't from the big boobs of the attendant.

Brad, a breast man, would be fainting with lust right now if he were here. Link couldn't help analyzing all the consequences and seeing them in a list.

Evans angry.

Evans wet from someone else's ministrations.

Evans kicking his balls if he got off with another woman.

Evans having no reaction.

Evans not caring.

The last thought brought him back to the here and now. What if Evans didn't give a shit about his reaction to this woman?

It was imperative he examine Evans for clues to her thoughts and feelings. He knew her so well. He'd know when she was angry... hurt. Happy. Maybe.

Now that he knew she was an undercover HS agent, that must mean the whole covert package... lying, faking, lying, faking. He couldn't imagine having his life depend on making no false moves, no mistakes, giving no trust. There was no way he wanted a career undercover. Give him a standup fight any day.

Shit, what if I screw this up?

The attendant stood behind Evans. She stroked her hands from Evans's shoulders, down her arms, then to her breasts, peeling the gown as she went. He frowned. He didn't like the submissive way Evans was behaving.

Her nipples were hard already, but the attendant tugged and stroked them before smoothing the gown to her hips.

His cock took notice of the rosy nipples that he knew the taste and shape of. He also noted that this strip was for his benefit, rather than for Evans's pleasure. He realized that there might be three people in the room, but only he was a paying client. Evans was an appendage for his pleasure, so he knew without being told that anything done to Evans would only be done if it was thought to please him.

It stirred him, watching another woman disrobe this woman he loved, watching the fluid fabric sliding over Evans's slim hips. His cock was hard as a landing strut when the woman moved to Evans's side and eased the gown an inch at a time down her thighs. The woman licked Evans's hip.

His body clenched. He'd come the instant Evans climbed on board.

Shit. What if the attendant climbed on his penis? He sat up straighter and said, "What's your name?"

"I'm called Grace8," the woman said. "Would you like me to please your partner?"

"Ah. That is. I've never done this."

The ever-watchful god of the brothel said, "The attendant is yours to command. Ask anything of her, save violence, and it will be performed."

Link realized those two words, *save violence*, meant they'd not gotten deep enough into the menus.

"We have an upgrade today that would include your host's participation in the pleasure for no extra cost."

Link remembered the eager young man who'd helped him disrobe. If he couldn't get a grip on the idea of some other woman sitting on his cock while Evans was around to do the honors, how was he going to handle some other guy's cock competing for space? He ignored the voice.

Then he almost swallowed his tongue. Grace8 was licking Evan's nipples. Evans glared at him over the attendant's head. He grinned and kissed the air at her. And she smiled. A sound like a snort of laughter came from her throat.

Suddenly, all his self-consciousness washed away like footprints on the beach in Maine. He centered himself on the bed. "Bring 'er here, Grace8. Bring 'er here."

Grace8 put her arm through Evans's and led her to stand before him.

"Now, here's what I want, ladies—my servant on board and you, Grace8, you see that there aren't any erogenous zones left lonely while we're at it. And that's any erogenous zones on her or on me."

He unbelted his robe and spread it open. Grace8 helped Evans onto his erection, but not before giving it a long, leisurely stroke. Evans shot him a look that would blister a heat shield.

"That's perfect, ladies," he just managed to say as he arched into the heated silk of Evan's body.

She planted her hands on his shoulders, nails biting to tell him her true feelings. They served as a sharp counterpoint to the attendant's wet lips busy on his balls.

Then Grace8's fingertips left him to tease Evans's clit. Evans's eyes went wide. The urge to laugh as she fought the arousal took the smooth rhythm from his strokes.

The ever watchful god said, "We have a special offer today. Your attendant will be happy to offer you a second hour of her time for half the credits. Simply extend your session by saying, 'Upgrade.'"

Link fought the urge to do so. This woman wasn't Angel Martinez. They needed to dig deeper, not play games.

He had only a few moments left. Evans had her head back, eyes closed, the stretch of her neck drawing his hand. He wrapped his fingers about her throat and caressed the smooth skin, eyes closed.

He lifted his knees and Evans tipped forward. He jerked his cock in and out of her, moaning. The attendant kept her hands and mouth busy on whatever spot she could reach, but he was only tangentially aware of her touch, his entire being focused on the hot clasp of Evan's body, the moist puff of her panting breath against his cheek, the stifled moans from deep in her chest — a Grade A, unimproved chest.

Evans imagined herself alone in Link's arms. It took little to block out Grace8. All that mattered was the feel of his rock-hard biceps, his damned uncomfortable, rock-hard chest, and the equally granite length of his penis stroking into her.

Then Grace8 scratched Evans's clitoris so hard she cried out with the pain. It was a needle hot pain. Deliberate.

Link would never know. Grace8 had chosen the exact moment he'd stiffened under her, his body racked by the spasms of orgasm.

At the first moment his arms relaxed, she tore from his grasp, rolling away from Grace8's sharp nails.

Curled on her side, a hand pressed between her thighs, Evans watched Grace8 lick Link's balls and penis as a cat licks cream from a bowl. The soft sigh of a door opening in the wall told her it was wash-up time. She pictured the bathing cloths, the pouch to seal them in.

She imagined them sliding down a chute to a busy compacting facility, somewhere in the bowels of the building. Just the place for Grace8's stupid wig, too. It was a touch off-center on her forehead now from all her toils between Link's thighs. Under the wig, Grace8 now had a shaved head.

Grace8 performed the cleansing process on Link. To avoid the sight of those sharp nails caressing as they cleaned, Evans pulled on her gown.

Link never took his eyes off her. What was he thinking? What was he feeling?

Evans knew from the cafeteria discussions among the attendants that most of them would avoid clients who didn't take sperm suppressors. It was such a rarity, however, to copulate with a man who still spilled real semen, that some of the attendants found it very arousing.

Grace8 appeared to be one of those.

And the scratch? It was a message.

About what? Maybe for supplanting her in the fetish scenario. Or was it simply an exercise of power?

Evans felt her heart sink. There was no way Grace8 would help her find Angel or anything else.

Grace8 stroked the cleansing cloth on Link as if leaving even one cell of his semen behind might get her sentenced to a tethered sunning in the garden outside. Evans was sure this sensual bathing was to remind the client that other delights existed for him.

"We have a special chamber," said the brothel voice, "fitted for a group bathing experience. If you like the sensual delights of water, we have an offer good for one week that will be sure to delight you. Two Palace attendants for the price of one."

"Where do I sign up?" Link said.

"Simply say, 'Partner bath.'"

"Partner bath."

Evans nodded approval. She made it as professional a nod as she could muster.

While Grace8 held Link's robe for him, she gave Evans a satisfied smirk. Evans rubbed her cheek with her middle finger.

Chapter 16
ॐ

Outside, when Link and Evans had gained the privacy of his PF, she turned to him. "You enjoyed that too much."

He shrugged and bit on his lip to keep from laughing at her indignant tone of voice. "Was her eyesight unimproved or was she just trying to see inside my ass?"

"Very funny. I know her. She's the attendant I wanted to talk to. We must have a psychic connection."

"You didn't look like you were trying to get anything out of her."

"Believe me, I tried. She wasn't cooperative."

"She was certainly all over us. I think I'll pick her next time… next time I need my pipes plumbed."

"Not funny."

Link ruffled her hair. "I'm teasing."

"She scratched my clit."

He lost his smile. "Say again."

"She scraped my clit, hard, with her nails. It not only hurt, it also ended any hope I'll feel any fun for at least a few hours."

"Well, scrape or no scrape, when we go for the tub fun, I won't be picking her. We can't choose the same person twice—"

"Right. That would be a waste of time. We need to pick a younger looking woman each time."

They sat in silence for a few moments then Link said, "Grace8 was way too intense. The only thing that kept her from eating my balls whole was probably some rule The Palace has about cannibalism."

"I'll eat your balls whole if you like."

It was said in jest, but the silence that fell between them was filled with something heavy and hot. He let the PF drift into a cul-de-sac formed by three office complexes. It was dark and silent now that commerce had shut its doors for the day.

"Cameras," she said softly when he took her hand and rubbed his thumb across her palm.

"So they'll get an eye full."

With a punch of his index finger on a button, the PF's seats tilted back.

Evans felt the same heat she imagined was filling Link's cock. Her insides felt as warm as syrup. The wetness was not just his semen but her own juices as well.

His groan was low and guttural when she tore his trousers open and pushed them over his hips. They struggled in the small space to get him naked from the waist down.

The scent of him was warm and fragrant, luckily mixed not with that of another woman's body, but with the neutral one of the cleansing cloths. She slipped onto her knees between his. He propped a foot up on the PF's seat and let his thighs fall apart.

"Evans." He gasped when she drew one of his testicles into her mouth. "I'm gonna die."

"No, that's one thing I can guarantee. You're too alive."

"You know what I really want?" he whispered, his hands restless on her hair as she stroked his balls with her tongue, suckling them, drawing them alternately into her mouth.

One of her bare shoulders lifted in question.

"I want the mind fuck."

He was moist with sweat and her saliva and she used it to stroke the smooth skin behind his balls, rubbing him gently.

"The mind fuck, Evans. I want it."

She rose over him and straddled his lap, and stood his penis gently against her sore clit.

"Taste yourself on my lips." She ducked her head and lapped at his mouth. "This is your taste. And I love it."

She bit his lower lip, fuller now, she was sure, with his arousal. His tongue followed hers, his teeth suckling her lip as she had his.

"This is what I want from you," she said, and wrapped her hands around his penis, stiff between their bellies.

Slowly, she stroked him. "If I close my eyes," and she did, to emphasize her point, "I feel more. I can almost feel the blood rushing through these veins." She teased her fingertips up and down the swollen blood vessels on his shaft. "I feel the stretch of your skin here." She skimmed her palm across the engorged head of his cock.

He groaned and thrust a few times into her hand.

She smiled inside. And wished her clit was capable of responding.

"I feel the silk of your come." She swirled her thumb across the drops that oozed from the head of his cock, then opened her eyes.

His were wide open, his lips slightly parted. She drew her thumb back and forth on his lower lip and said, "I like to keep my eyes open. That way I can see yours. Eyes don't lie, Link. They tell the truth."

"What truth?" He whispered, lifting his hands from her hips to cup her face in his large palms.

The truth that you might love me as much as I love you.

But she didn't say it. It was too late as Link came with a groan.

She felt the hot flow of his come across her hands. She raised them and licked the semen as Grace8 had.

"This is what I love. Your taste." She licked her fingertips, then drew them deep into her mouth. He arched and bucked beneath her when she sealed her mouth over his, slicking his tongue with his seed, driving her tongue deep into his mouth.

Link gasped for air when Evans drew back. His chest was tight. "I think I'm having a coronary, right here. Now. In a dark alley, far from help. They'll find me in the morning, my pants around my ankles, my balls shriveled to marbles."

"Marbles cannot change from soft and warm to hard and warm."

When she giggled, he felt all the tension seep out of his body. He slapped her bare bottom. "You weren't taking this very seriously, were you? I was busy going mad with desire, mentally fucked and sucked, and you were just teasing me."

No, I wasn't, but it's best you think so. She felt the burn of tears behind her eyes.

He put her on her back in the tiny space, doing as she had, kneeling between her thighs. "We both know I'm an amateur in the mind-fuck game, so I'll just do what I know best."

She held him off with her hands planted on his shoulders. "No. Don't. It still hurts."

"I'll be gentle."

He touched the tip of his tongue to her swollen clit. "Why didn't you have lip jewelry?"

"Tacky," she said and jammed her heels against the control panel. "If you're unimproved, you have to be completely natural. Nothing enhancing your –"

"Beauty. You are beautiful, Sara."

"Sara?"

He blew warm air on her clit, not quite touching it with his lips, and slid a finger into her.

When he felt her body relax and her hands changed from fending to caressing, he lifted his head. "I think it's time I admitted who you are to me. You're not that cadet from ten years ago." He kissed her inner thigh.

"You're not some brothel pole princess." He drew his cheek, now a touch rough from the reemergence of whiskers, across the tender inside of her knee. "You're the woman I love."

She looked for sincerity in his gaze, and saw it.

"You did it, Link. You finally… mind-fucked me."

He puffed warm, moist air on her clit a second time. She writhed her hips and moaned. When he licked her lightly, she came. Her cry filled the small PF's space, throbbing around them.

In the utter, heavy silence that followed her sharp cries, he said. "So, Sara, what do you say? Be Evans on duty and Sara in my arms — in private, where no one can see us, or hear us, or care what we do or think."

Evans felt a shiver of something that was not sexual. A shrink would probably say it was fear. She shifted out of his embrace and pulled the airy gown down her body like a shield.

He was going back to Mars. Without her. And soon.

"That was a fabulous mind fuck, Link. But let's keep it casual, shall we?"

He withdrew with a jerk, his gaze still locked on her face. "Sure. If that's what you want."

"That's what I want."

The ride back to the hotel seemed ten times longer than necessary. She couldn't remember which parking entrance they used, or how they reached his room.

He said nothing, stripping and taking a shower. A small chime from the communication center drew her there. She saw that it was a message from the management.

Link was way over his officer's allotment of water and would be charged a 100% surcharge on all future showers.

"Well, he certainly won't care. He's rich as a LaGrangian smuggler, now." She frowned when she realized she'd been speaking to a message screen.

When he came from the bathroom, toweling off, she noticed he made no effort to don a robe or otherwise cover himself. And she knew why when he bent over to flick back the bed covers. Grace8 had marked him, sucking a nice love bruise on his left cheek.

She told herself she didn't care. But in the shower, taking her time, knowing he was being charged usury rates for the water, she knew she did care. Grace8's hands had been all over Link.

But that shouldn't matter. The mission mattered. Angel Martinez mattered. But Evans faced the fact that Grace8 wasn't about to be a conduit of anything but Link's sperm.

The lights were dim when she stepped back into the room. Link lay on his stomach, face to the bank of windows, curtains open. The suck mark stood out starkly against the Mars-pale skin of his buttocks.

She went to the window and looked up at the sky.

Venus had moved out of sight. There was nothing to see now but the moon and city glow.

She slid into bed beside him and listened to the sound of his deep breathing. Tomorrow or the next day, they would try again. This time with two attendants in a bathing chamber.

It was smart of him to do the upgrade. It didn't look suspicious and it allowed them to pick two attendants at once.

Great... twice the torture.

Chapter 17
ℬ

Link ate a large serving of the real bacon he could now afford, using his fingers and not his fork. Evans ate almost nothing, waiting impatiently, pulling the plate out from under his hands as he picked up the last greasy slice. She packed the dishes into the discard recess while he wiped his fingers on a gleaming white napkin that bore the hotel's embroidered logo. There were more changes here than she'd expected when they moved from the headquarters hotel into a commercial, luxury one.

She activated the card and asked over her shoulder, "We're looking for young, aren't we?"

Link finished wiping his mouth. "Yep. We need to pick the youngest we can find."

Evans nodded. And younger still the next time. And so on, until they reached the other menus, the exclusive ones she was sure existed. The one that featured girls who should be at home, learning how to apply makeup or mulling over the body improvements they could opt for when they turned 21 and were legally permitted to make their own decisions.

* * * * *

The enforced wait for their appointment was agony. She and Link moved around each other as if there was an invisible shield between them, preventing touch. They ate and slept.

Watching him sleep was a choice torture. He usually lay on his stomach, stark naked, Grace8's suck mark vivid on his ass despite the low light.

He moved restlessly, muttering unintelligible phrases from time to time. She grew tired of sitting in a chair watching endless infocasts she could neither care about nor concentrate on.

"Come to bed," he said near dawn.

She could hear no edge in his voice. Instead, it had a husky tone that touched something deep inside her. She knelt by the head of the bed, her face inches from his.

They stared at each other for a while. His eyes were dark and unreadable.

He touched her hair. "I liked it better short."

She shrugged.

"What's that? The I-don't-care-a-damn-about-anything shrug?" He gripped a handful of hair.

"Link—"

He pulled. She climbed on the bed and straddled him. "Let go."

"Maybe." He thrust both hands into her hair and held her head. Then he pushed her face toward his groin.

"Shit, Link. Stop it." She wrenched away, breaking his hold smoothly, rolling to her feet.

He surged from the bed. "See how easy it is."

"Easy? What the hell are you talking about?" Her scalp stung where he'd pulled her hair.

"Easy to get away from a man. Not to brag, but I'm pretty strong and you broke my grip."

"What's your point?" She knew what was coming. She wrapped her arms around her waist.

"Why didn't you fight the clients? Why did you—"

"Just suck them off like I did you?"

He sat down heavily on the edge of the bed. "I can't wrap my mind around it. I see you in my mind's eye giving head to some guy who's fat and ugly. Or taking some guy up your ass—"

"Stop it, Link. This is completely non-productive."

"Is it?"

She knelt before him. "Yes, it is. I know you don't approve of what I did. I know you think it's somehow way beyond the call of duty, but... maybe you should think of it this way—"

"It *is* way beyond—"

"Shhh." She touched his lips. "What if the Secretary had sent me to the Uron Conference six years ago? I was on the list of available operatives."

"The Uron Conference." He grimaced and shook his head.

"You know what happened there. You know what history will say about Uron. A flare-up of the corporate wars. A minor blip in peace. But I know you have the clearance to know the truth."

His gaze held hers. He did know, but she continued anyway.

"Seven Homeland Security operatives died there. Three were dismembered during torture. They died doing their duty, and they knew the odds were terrible when they went in. But they saved lives—fifty of the Uron employees, to be exact. I'd have been there if I hadn't been delayed during a debriefing in Hawaii."

"Shit, Evans." He pulled her in close, wrapped his arms around her.

She shoved at his chest, resisted the siren song of his embrace. "I could not have refused the Uron Conference assignment any more than I could the one at The Palace."

She entwined her fingers in his, but had to bow her head to avoid his eyes.

"Is it dishonorable to follow orders? Even if you do something others might deem objectionable? That's what we do, Link, we follow orders. At Uron, I'd have killed people for my country. At The Palace, I just fucked them."

He turned her hand over. She had a small scar across the pad of her thumb, more evidence that she was unimproved. He traced it and thought about what she'd said.

"I'm a miserable fuck."

At last, she smiled. A real smile. "No, you're a good fuck... maybe a little set in your ways—"

"Set in my ways?" He grinned. "I'll show you set in my ways. Stand up."

She arched a brow, but did as he asked. He had to get them back to a comfort level. A level he could take. They'd moved off it and he needed to find it again.

Link pulled her to the center of the room and then walked slowly around her, sweeping his gaze up and down her body. Although the room was filled with grays in the dawn light, he was pretty sure he detected a pale pink glow on her cheeks.

He licked a fingertip and touched her nipple. She shifted her hips. He licked his finger again and stroked the other.

"Kiss?" he asked, leaning forward so only their breath touched. When she parted her lips, he parted her other lips, dipping a fingertip into her. Her insides were satin smooth, warm, and lushly wet. Her fragrance floated around him. Enticed him.

Their kiss became a tangle of tongues. He thrust a second finger into her. She moaned and pressed down on him, gripping his wrist.

"Don't touch. Stand still," he ordered and she obeyed.

Her long hair flowed across her breasts. He lifted her and she wrapped her legs around his waist.

"No," he whispered as she reached for his cock. "I wouldn't want to seem set in my ways."

"I lied," she gasped as he took her earlobe and bit on it.

"Too late."

He walked to the bed and threw her on it.

She lay there, legs spread, her surprise easy to see in the half light.

"Try to get away."

She cocked her head and considered him. Then she bolted. He caught her ankle. She twisted. But he hung on, locking his fingers around the slender ankle and dragging her close.

She fought. Used tactics he knew well and knew how to counter. They bounced off furniture, sweating, panting. She slipped his grasp, then he slipped hers.

Finally, she lay on her back, panting, and he held her, ankles firmly locked in his fists.

"Okay. Now what?" she asked.

Inch by slow inch, he dragged her toward him, pulling her up until her legs draped over his shoulders and he had only to bend his head to lap at her fragrant center.

"Link," she gasped when he tongued her clit.

She crossed her ankles behind his head and curled up to grip his forearms.

Then she fell back, stretched in a long, enticing flow of sweet, toned muscles. Her belly quivered. She covered her face with her hands and moaned when he nuzzled her clit again. He thrust his tongue into her and she almost crushed his head as her thighs tightened.

He spread her nether lips and teased her clit until she came. Then he let her slide into an upside-down heap on the bed.

She flopped to her side and glared at him. "So what did you prove? You're stronger than me?"

"No. I proved I'm not set in my ways." Her gaze shifted to his penis. "Hey, some things never change."

"Thank our lucky star." She pointed.

Venus stood just at the horizon. And he stood painfully at attention. She smiled and turned around, going up on her knees.

He slid into her from behind. It was quick. Just two quick, hard pushes into her slick passage and he felt the uncontrollable shift from conscious to unconscious rhythm. The climax came from deep within him and left him breathless, buried inside her.

Chapter 18
ഇ

Evans entered the bathing chamber first. Link had selected a forest milieu from a menu at the same time he'd reserved the attendants. Angel had not been among them, though they had all looked like what Link had termed "jail bait".

The chamber was scented like the deep woods, the lighting muted, a wide pool of dark water ringed with what looked like real rocks. She felt as if she'd stepped into a clearing in the forest. The two attendants sitting with their legs dangling in the pool looked like forest fairies and a lot like Angel. The girls were slight and dark, with elfin features. Evans felt big, gawky, awkward.

Real ferns and flowers decorated the verge of the pool as well as the attendants' hair. Their naked pussies, quite visible with their spread thighs, enhanced their appearance of being childish. Although both the attendants were young, it was clear neither one was below the legal age of 21. As she got closer, she decided the one with the darker hair might even be pushing thirty.

Link shucked his robe and draped it over a stack of artfully placed boulders. Evans wrapped her arms around her waist, but Link bumped her with his hip and she stumbled into the pool.

The attendants were superbly trained. They didn't laugh and both even managed to keep their eyes downcast.

She hoped Link would be true to his word and get this over with as quickly as possible. They needed to look further for Angel.

And if she admitted it, just the thought of another woman's hands on Link made her blood boil.

How ironic. Once more, she was here on a mission, thinking of The Palace's sexual activities as a task. She wanted to get on with it, complete their mission, not just for Angel and her family. She'd much rather have Link all to herself, she thought, as Link stepped down into the water.

Evans found that for some reason, the licking and stroking the elves lavished on Link bothered her not a whit compared to the tiniest touch of Grace8's fingertip to his nipple. In fact, as Evans wiggled her feet in the heavenly warm water, she contemplated the consequences of biting off one of Grace8's slim fingers for the audacity of making Link's nipple tighten.

Link held out a hand. "Come here," he said and she had to obey.

Evans settled within the circle of his arm and watched as one elf held her breath and went underwater to suck his cock.

Link crossed his eyes. Evans pressed her face against his shoulder to keep from laughing.

"We have a special offer available to those who like water play. Your attendants are skilled in all water sports. They have the equipment at hand to please you any way you choose. Imagine the joy of knowing you're clean both inside and out."

Red flared across Link's cheekbones.

"Simply say, 'Upgrade to water sports.'"

Link pantomimed fastening his lips closed with a key. She took the lobe of his ear between her teeth and bit gently. While he sought her mouth, she went for some space on his cock. She failed to outmaneuver the eager elves, so she shrugged out of his embrace and worked her elbows until she had made a place for herself between the two, in front of him.

She dipped down in the warm water until her chin kissed the surface and put her hands firmly on his thighs. As the elves caressed his cock, she slid her hands up the insides of his thighs to his balls.

She blew some bubbles across the surface of the water. Sweat ran down his chest and one of the elves leaned to sweep the drops off with her tongue.

Evans saw his gaze move to the young woman, so she took the opportunity to palm his balls. She squeezed. When he gasped, she eased the pressure.

The next time his gaze went to an elf, she squeezed again.

He kissed the air in her direction before boosting himself out of the water to sit on the edge. Water sluiced down his well-honed body.

Evans found herself gulping for air, floundering beneath the water. The elves had shoved her quite blatantly aside—and under. Blowing water from her nose, she stifled an urge to dish out the same treatment. But she had a role to play in this farce, and it did not include assertive behavior. Much as she'd like to dunk an elf or two.

The elves were oblivious to her. One held Link's cock ready while the other prepared to climb astride his lap.

To Evans's utter amazement, Link blocked her efforts with an extended arm.

"Not yet. I want my partner pleasured. And I want to watch."

She shot him a look she hoped would shrivel his gonads when the elves swept her up into their strong little arms, pulling her out of the water to lay her on the smooth stone edge of the pool.

One elf parted Evan's thighs while the other licked her nipples.

Link knelt behind her and lifted her head onto his lap. He smoothed her cheeks, her eyelids, her lips with his fingertips while the elves teased and pleasured her.

"Make her come," he ordered the attendants.

To her intense embarrassment, they redoubled their soft touches and light kisses. She closed her eyes so she could not see

Link's watchful eyes looking down on hers. She closed her eyes to feel the caresses more intensely, to hurry the rising climax. Her fingers itched to touch him, but all she could reach were the elves or his wandering hands.

She wanted to feel his cock inside her, not their fingers. The yearning for him to fill her added to the tension building inside. Frustration swamped her, almost overpowering the effect of the elves and their adept little tongues and hands.

But if pressed, she'd have to say the pleasure was superb when it came.

* * * * *

A young blonde woman, with startlingly beautiful eyes, came into the changing room just as they entered from another door. She hastened forward, took Link's robe, then helped him dress.

Evans took a moment to recognize her. It was Cloud9 with the reddish tint gone from her hair. After all the time she'd spent in this prison and the brief time she'd been free, it amazed Evans how long it took her to recall some things and people. Was it because of all the drugs they'd fed her?

"May I offer you a drink, sir?" Cloud9 pushed a recessed door and it swung open to reveal a tray with two glasses. One was tall, frosty, and pale green. The other was a deep purple and steamed. "The Emerald Elixir is said to restore vigor to those unable to take advantage of erectile enhancers."

"The other?" Link asked.

"It is meant to soothe. We do not recommend it if you are personally piloting a PF."

"Do you have something for my partner?" he asked, taking the green drink.

"What do you require for her?" Cloud9 asked.

Evans opened her mouth, but Link spoke first. "I would like her to have something for the rather extensive irritation between her thighs. On our last visit, the attendant deliberately scratched my partner. Today's attendants were quite gentle, but their play has undoubtedly caused her further discomfort."

Cloud9 bowed and withdrew.

Link took a long swallow of his drink and watched Evans over the glass's rim. She dropped her gaze and remained still, sitting on one of the dressing room's benches, her robe demurely closed over her knees.

She kept her features still and hid her joy. Link did care, more than she'd expected. Then she sobered. Would Grace8 be punished as she had been by his complaint?

Of course, Grace8 probably didn't have her own defiant genes. Grace8 wanted the success The Palace offered and would never refuse the retraining process, regardless of who was given time with her. She'd undoubtedly do her best to enjoy it.

Within a few moments, Cloud9 returned. Evans stole a peek. There were two items on her tray. One was the spray Evans knew well. The other was a substance that looked like whipped cream in a silver bowl.

"What do you have there?" Link asked.

"This spray will numb the area and aid healing. If the chafing is severe, we recommend the cream. It seals and heals more serious damage."

"Oh, I think she's pretty damaged. Seal and heal." He swept out a hand and she bowed and set the tray on the bench beside Evans.

Evans slid away when Cloud9 reached for her robe. "I'll tend to myself," she said.

Perhaps Link heard the urgency in her voice, for he nodded. "Leave it. We'll take care of the problem ourselves."

The door sighed softly and shut with a click. Evans knew that did not mean they were in any way private.

She pushed the tray away. "I'll take care of the *problem* at home."

Link went down on one knee and plucked her robe open over her knees. "I think not. Let's see what's what, shall we?"

"No." She shoved at his hands.

A voice said, "Do you need assistance with your personal attendant? Help is but a step away."

"Thank you, but no thank you," Link said. But he mouthed, *And fuck you.*

"Cream or spray?" he asked aloud. He took one of her hands. His thumb stroked gently back and forth over the back, soothing her. His touch communicated what he could not say.

A throb pounded in her forehead. "I've never had the cream. The spray numbs you for hours. You can't feel anything. I wouldn't be able to have a climax for a long time."

She saw understanding cross his face as he realized why she'd faked her orgasm with him.

"Then let's try the cream. Why don't you slide to the edge of the bench?"

He dipped his fingers into the whipped goo. She spread her thighs and leaned back, doing as he'd asked, sliding her bottom to the edge of the bench so he had complete access to her crotch.

The cream was warm. The scent of vanilla filled the air. Her skin warmed as he massaged between her thighs. His touch continued to be as gentle as she knew he could be sometimes.

"Sorry I asked them to give you two climaxes. I guess that was too much." He kissed the inside of her thigh. "Do you feel numb?" he asked, meeting her gaze.

The gray of his eyes reminded her of a stormy sea just as it looked off the coast of his summer home.

"A little, but not cold like the spray, more of a warm numb."

He stood up and held out his hand. "Let's go. I'm hungry and maybe you can cook me up a real steak, bloody on the inside, charred on the outside."

So much for tender and caring.

"As you wish." The three words reminded them she was an attendant in this place. His partner only for sex acts. And at home, society would assume she tended to his other needs equally as assiduously.

* * * * *

At the hotel, she was halfway to the closet to hang up her dress—one Link had purchased through his personal shopper that morning—a soft green, backless, strapless thing, long and silky against her body, when a strong pulse of heat flashed between her thighs.

She gasped and clutched her groin at the stab of pain that followed. "Oh."

"What is it?" he asked, laying a hand on her shoulder.

The pain flared again. "Link. Help me."

She fell to her knees, pain radiating like fire from where he'd smoothed the cream.

"Sara?" He wrapped his arms around her shoulders. "What the hell?"

The pain coursed and flashed like hot knives. Grace8's scrape was a fleabite compared to this agony.

"I think Cloud9 gave me more... than just cream." She moaned. "I think it was... Grace8's revenge."

The room spun. Sweat slicked her skin. Link wavered before her. The room grew hot. Hot as the skin between her thighs.

The pain escalated, spread, entered her belly, ran down her legs.

She couldn't tolerate it. Couldn't fight it.

The room tilted into darkness.

Chapter 19

Link watched Evans as she lay like the dead. The base physician leaned over her.

"And you say you don't know what was in the cream?" the gray-haired civilian swabbed Evans between the thighs. Whatever it was that caused the pain and rendered her unconscious, it did not show on her skin. Even the chafing was gone. She looked healed.

"No, I don't. It was white and felt a bit warm as I... rubbed it on."

The physician grunted and pulled the covers up to Evans's waist. "I don't see how a cream rubbed here," he tapped her groin area, "could cause this reaction, unless she's allergic to one of the ingredients. Even then, I'd expect the reaction would be topical or at least show some sign on the skin there as well."

"Do something."

"Young man, I am not a miracle worker. She's out cold. Now, her blood pressure is fine, her samples when run through diagnostics say she's fine. Let her sleep it off. I'm sure it has nothing to do with the cream."

He bustled out of the room with an officious bow.

Link called Eric Samuels of Homeland Security and demanded the Secretary Martinez's personal physician, then he sat on the edge of the bed and held Evans's hand.

While he waited, he watched her. She moaned once. It was a raw sound of extreme pain. And he couldn't rouse her.

His throat was dry. What if something happened to her? What if this mission ended with death?

He almost tore the door from its jamb flinging it open when the physician arrived.

The Secretary's physician spent a good half hour analyzing the diagnostics streaming across his hand-held unit.

He tut-tutted. "Drugs. I'd have said R89-17, but somehow the readings aren't quite right—skewed a touch to the alkaline. Whatever it is, it's very similar. Something new. And whatever it is, she must be hypersensitive for such an intense reaction."

"What the hell's R89-16?"

"17. It's a drug often used to stimulate sexual responsiveness in women who are, shall we say, a touch cold in their responses to their partner."

"Shit. They said it was to soothe chafed skin –"

The man waved him off, punching another series of commands into his unit. Readouts flickered across the screen. "Sure. Sure. The drug needs a delivery system, so they put it in with something that *will* heal. Yes, indeed, that's it. Right there, as I suspected."

The doctor slid his diagnostic unit into his pocket. He pursed his lips. "Look, it's none of my business what you and she are up to. But I suggest that next time, when she proves cold to your advances, seek partner counseling instead."

Link nodded and stifled an urge to shove the doctor's gadget down his throat.

At the door the doctor turned. "Oh, and get some rest."

"Why?"

"If this drug is a derivative of R89-17, when she's slept off the worst of it, she'll still have a high level of it in her system. She'll be insatiable."

* * * * *

Evans opened her eyes. Her irises were so wide they looked black. *The better to find his cock in the dark,* he thought as she reached across the small space separating them on the bed.

"Fuck me," she demanded, her voice low, raspy. Her hands were sweaty as she fumbled, touching him here and there.

Before he could evade her, she'd rolled atop him, her hands between their groins, gripping his cock roughly through the cloth of his trousers. Shameless soldier, it obeyed her touch.

She sank her teeth into his shoulder.

"I should have worn armor," he said half in jest. He might as well have saved his breath, for she gave no indication he'd spoken.

She ripped at his trousers, barely getting them past his balls before climbing astride his erection. She kissed his cheek, his shoulder, his throat, licking and moaning his name.

She rode him, jerking up and down on his shaft, panting.

It wasn't getting done.

Her moans became wails.

"Take it easy." Gripping her with both hands, he tried to slow the frantic slam of her hips. He flipped her over.

She cried out in alarm when he pulled out of her. He clamped a hand over her mouth. "I'm not going anywhere."

The words were useless. She either couldn't or wouldn't hear.

She pressed her hand between her thighs, rolling side to side, knees drawn up.

Link gripped her knees and pushed them back against her chest and slid into her. She wailed as if in pain each time he thrust his cock deep into her.

"Shhh," he said over and over, trying his best to satisfy her, moving his hips for her, drawing out, spreading her legs, putting his mouth to her, then repeating it all again.

A scent swirled around them, the vanilla he remembered from applying the cream, only now she exuded it from every pore.

It was heady, almost toxic in how it drew him to want to taste and smell her. He laved her from clit to throat and watched her writhe and tug on her nipples until they stood out from her chest like rivets on a bulkhead.

She came four times before his cock fell, a soldier defeated by her onslaught. He used his fingers and mouth on her instead.

"Make me come. Make me come," she begged, even after the sixth and seventh climaxes.

So he did.

Finally, after he'd lost track of the number of orgasms that had convulsed her body, she began to quiver with spasms that had nothing to do with sexual tension.

He scooped her into his arms. Luckily, he had the presence of mind to heave the bathroom chair into the shower before stepping in.

She remained in his arms, still, limp as a washrag in his lap, the warm water jetting on low over them.

"What?" she finally said, pushing off his chest.

Water ran between her breasts, pooled in her lap. She shifted her thighs apart a touch and arched as the water trickled there.

"The cream from The Palace was R89 something or other. You're sensitive to its ingredients. It's also something that made you insatiable."

"I think it was revenge from Grace8."

"Why don't you tell me about her?"

"She was really pissed when I supplanted her as the favored attendant for one client."

"Whoops," Link said. "You supplanted her twice. I abandoned her massage for your sunning event. And I complained about her scratching you."

"And she and Cloud9 are inseparable. And Cloud9 has more freedom than most attendants. She could pull something like this off."

Link kissed Evans's hair. "Are you feeling any better?"

"I feel like my brain is filled with that stuff we packed our weapons in." She rubbed her stomach. "And my insides feel greased." Her head drooped to his shoulder. She touched a set of scratches on his chest. "Did I hurt you?"

"You should see my butt."

Her cheeks pinked and he could not resist touching them as he said, "Fucked out, sucked over, exhausted."

Evans leaned against his chest and let his strong body renew her own. He held her gently, as if she were a fragile treasure.

She shared his exhaustion but didn't want to sleep. She didn't want to face the dreams she'd had. Dreams of smothering. Of something clinging to her face and her desperate efforts to claw it off. And finding her limbs frozen. But the smothering had been the worst. That must have been how she'd scratched Link. Embarrassment filled her. She shifted in his embrace.

"I'm hungry." She slithered from his arms, grabbed a towel, and scooted from the bathroom.

He rose with a groan and dropped the water ten degrees. It puckered his skin and pounded on his head. The scratches she'd touched were deep. So were the ones on his ass.

"I ordered us whole lobsters," she called from the bedroom.

"Thank God Homeland Security is footing this bill. Whole lobsters must cost as much as —"

"Three sessions at The Palace with underage girls. Come look," she said from the bathroom doorway.

Wrapping a towel around his hips, he followed her back to the touch screen.

"I thought I'd explore while I waited. I've been looking over the attendants. Only the young ones. When you enlarge them, some aren't so young, but others are. And when I went to the menu again, this is what I found—new stuff."

It was definitely a new menu on the screen. "Look at the prices." He whistled. For an amount just under one year's salary, he could enter a realm called, *Hidden Delights*.

"Hidden because you have to prove yourself to get in and you have to be dripping bucks."

"Speaking of dripping." He touched her arm. Water dripped off her hair, down her shoulders and arms.

"I'm too hot to care."

When he raised his eyebrows she said, "Not that kind of hot. Hot deep in my stomach like I'm sick, hot."

He enveloped her in a light embrace and held her so her back nestled against his chest.

"Look," she said again and touched the gilded letters announcing the Hidden Delights.

A woman appeared. She was so beautiful, almost a caricature of beauty, that Evans thought she must be a virtual composite. Her lips were very full, her eyes as black as onyx, her hair a startling contrast of silver blonde. She wore a gossamer robe that showed every inch of her lush body. Her breasts were very large and high, her nipples an impossible blush pink. Silver jewelry graced her thumbs as well as pierced her nipples, her navel, and when she spoke, her tongue.

"Welcome to the hidden delights offered by The Palace. We are pleased to serve you. Your balance and frequent patronage permits you to take advantage of the most exclusive pleasures. Your searches also tell us you are looking for something beyond the usual, that you have a special reverence for youth. If that is so, please continue."

The woman stood a moment, frozen. Link reached around Evans and tapped one of the woman's breasts. She smiled as if he'd actually reached in and touched her.

"We are pleased to serve you." As the nymph spoke, she parted the robe to touch the silver rings that graced her nipples, hooking her fingers through them and tugging. A visible shudder ran across her skin. "Hmmm. So delicious," she said. "As are all of our available pleasures. But we ask you to choose wisely."

"I wonder why?" Link said.

As if she had heard him, the woman said, "The hidden delights can be addictive."

"I'll just bet," Evans snorted.

"This might be it," Link said by her ear.

She reached out and touched a kaleidoscope of words, each framed in silver rings as glittery as those on the woman's body.

The twirling rings halted. Each word now stood in an orderly row of silver circles. Perfectly readable. And selectable.

"You choose," Link said, his arms tightening around her waist.

"No. You pick."

"Coward."

But he didn't reach past her to pick. Instead, he said, "Off."

The screen went blank.

"What the hell?" she pulled from his arms. "What if we can't get back there?"

"Oh, believe me, we'll get back there. I just think we need to talk about this first."

"Talk about what? We have to find Angel. We know she's there. Each day of delay is one day closer—"

"And you. You might be closer to something just as grim. Do you think Grace8 and Cloud9 are going to stop at a little aphrodisiac revenge?"

"Personally, I think it was just Grace8 wreaking havoc on my sex life, but we can be extra cautious about anything we ingest or apply while we're there."

"I hope it's that simple." He paced the room then settled next to her on the bed. If Evans could handle it, who the hell was he to act the coward?

"So, what will you pick?" Evans asked.

They sat in their damp towels and stared at their feet.

Finally, Link said, "We have to pick Young and Foolish."

Evans sighed. "You're right. It was the only menu option that pretty much guarantees we'll find what you call jail bait."

"Yeah." He stretched out his legs and crossed his feet at the ankles and put his hands behind his head. He stared up at the ceiling.

She knew he was avoiding her gaze. And avoiding thoughts of what other options might need to be explored if Young and Foolish didn't produce Angel Martinez.

A shiver ran down her spine at the last option on the menu. *Partner Pain.* Had it been her imagination that the silver ring around the words had reflected the light like the hard glint of a knife blade?

"Link. Do it. Get that menu back and make the choice before I get cold feet."

He did as she ordered. Evans snapped her fingers through the preliminaries.

Silver Girl appeared, along with her tantalizing menus. Tantalizing if you lived on the edge. Frankly, he liked his sex firmly in the middle of ordinary.

He rose immediately. Before she could call out to him to stop, he'd returned to the screen.

"Come over here." He held out his hand.

She entwined her fingers with his and watched as he touched *Young and Foolish.*

"Welcome," said a voice, high and breathy and sounding like it came from a child, not a woman.

The very young female, if she was young, who bid them welcome to this part of The Palace menus was veiled like a concubine in a sultan's harem.

"That covers the legalities," Link said.

"We have many willing attendants who are just too foolish for their own good. Enjoy," the greeter said and faded away to be replaced by a screen full of thumbnail photos.

"So many," Evans said, squeezing Link's hand.

"Find her."

Evans moved closer and scrutinized each face. She knew Angel had undergone the hair treatment, just as she had. The memory of Angel tied with the lavender ribbons made Evans shiver.

She touched thumbnail after thumbnail. At about the eighteenth touch, she gasped. "Angel," she whispered.

It was Angel Martinez. Her hair might be a dark smooth mane, instead of the riot of curls showing in the last photo taken before she'd disappeared, but there was no doubt. It was their quarry.

"A beautiful girl," Link said.

"Choose her."

Link went through the motions. When the room printer spit out his appointment, he fought the need to touch the hard copy with his fingertips, disgusted at what he'd agreed to.

Angel Martinez looked much younger than twenty.

* * * * *

"Here's the best plan. I'll wear something really concealing but sexy, so it isn't suspicious, and when we have Angel with us, we'll somehow convince her to leave in my place."

Link took her hand. "I can't agree to this. Even if I have Homeland Security standing by to take Angel and then enter with writs or whatever to bust the place wide open, it might be too late to save you from something that will make your sunburn seem tame."

"I'm prepared to do this. It's the only way. You saw how many doors we need to pass through. The cameras. The attendants. We'll never get out if we don't use subterfuge and as far as I'm concerned, KISS is still the smartest plan. Keep It Simple Sweetheart."

Evans pulled her hand away and went to the desk. She read the details of the appointment over again and kept her back to him. It was necessary he not read the truth in her eyes.

There would be no cavalry arriving to bust her out. No one would be slapping any writs of search on that glossy marble reception desk.

She'd lied to Link. She'd lied because without his help, she knew she would not get back into The Palace. Without his help, she'd never redeem herself.

When she'd been assigned this mission, it had been made very clear to her that Angel Martinez's presence in the brothel must never be revealed, nor any hint of it breathed anywhere, at any time, to anyone.

It would compromise the Secretary's position. He'd be ineffective, subject to blackmail.

No, getting out was something she'd have to manage on her own, but not until Link had Angel safely away.

"Help me buy a suitable outfit," she said with false brightness.

"Shop?"

"Yes, and don't look at me as if I've asked you to donate your right ball to a sperm bank. Let's go spend some of the government's credits."

* * * * *

Link stood like a statue as the women of Haute Boutique fluttered around Evans. Only those who could afford designs straight off the runway shopped here. The carpet was thick and the women who browsed at the racks expensively scented.

Evans pretended she was a regular. Link looked as if someone had nailed his feet to the floor. Each time a woman passed him, they gave him a once over. Each time, he pretended he was a synth mannequin.

For the first time, Evans realized how truly impressive a man Link had become. His years in SpaceFleet Command had matured him well. His height, fine shape, and military bearing turned every woman's eye. Yet there was also something aloof about him that made the patrons give him a wide berth. She bet she was the only one who could detect that bit of panic beneath the reserve in his expression.

Evans realized Link probably only used a personal shopper. He had no idea of the joys of making one's own choices. With a small smile, Evans thought she could predict the state of Link's closet. All the same general colors. Everything would go together, so he wouldn't have to make too many choices, just reach in and grab.

"I think I'm ready," she said.

"Thank God. Let's go." Link pointed to the front door.

"No, this way." She pointed to the rear of the shop. "I meant I'm ready to try things on. Follow me."

Like a man on the way to meet his executioner, Link followed her with heavy steps to the plush chamber arrayed with her choices.

"You may leave us," Evans said to the personal assistant. The young man mewed a disappointed sound before he left them alone.

With one eye on Link, Evans began to strip. She took everything off and pulled a red silk caftan over her head. Link sat rigidly upright on a small stool, his eyes fixed on a spot just above her navel. She dipped into a curtsey. "So, how's this?"

His gaze flicked up and down. He shrugged. "It's okay."

"I don't want okay. I want sexy but concealing. Help me."

A shudder ran through his body. "I hate these places. They smell funny."

"And a museum doesn't? It's just a mingling of expensive perfumes. Usually perfume is meant to entice."

"I'm not enticed. I have a headache."

What was the matter with him? She knelt on the carpet before him and planted her hands over his where they lay on his knees. "Look at me, Link."

His pupils were dilated, the whites of his eyes threaded with red. Sweat beaded on his forehead and across his upper lip.

"Did you take anything?"

"Green drink."

"That was back at The Palace." She turned his hand over and skimmed her fingertips across his cold, clammy palm. "You must be having a delayed reaction to something they gave you." He wasn't sick with something conventional; all off-planet officers were inoculated with everything the pharmaceutical industry could produce. She snapped her fingers in front of his face. "Link, look at me."

His hands quivered. He licked his lips. "I don't think... I have to get out of here."

She slipped her arm beneath his and helped him up. "Wait." She propped him against the wall. His face looked stiff and his gaze turned inward.

She threw on her clothes. With a quick glance about, she chose a black dress with a matching cape. The hood would conceal her hair and maybe her face. It was also obvious. Too obvious, but she couldn't worry about that now. Not with Link looking the way he did.

Link walked beside her with a slow, shambling gait. She steered him to the door with a shove of her hip and practically carried him to the PF.

The hotel staff carried him to their room.

"Drunk," she said to the two men who usually hoisted nothing more weighty than a few designer bags.

"Looks sick to me," the older of the porters said, stepping back from the bed and wiping his hands. "Sure it's not sickness? Wasn't he on Mars? Do they have weird diseases there or something?"

"Don't worry," Evans said, kissing Link's forehead. "I would be the last person to touch him if he was sick. He just has no head for liquor."

Once the porters were gone, she summoned the same physician who'd treated her. The civilian Angel's father had sent, not the base physician. Link moaned and thrashed on the bed, lost in some nightmare.

The physician spent some time examining him before administering an injection. "This is remarkably similar to your problem. Diagnostics say he's taken a drug to restore sexual vigor, but the results are off-kilter, just as yours were. And if he's allergic to all the sperm suppressors, this will really fry his nuts."

"Is that why he looks so uncomfortable?" Evans perched beside Link and held his hand while the doctor's injection worked through his system.

"I'd say what he's experiencing is akin to having fire ants gnawing on his testicles."

Link moaned and thrashed, scraping his heels against the mattress. His eyes opened, the whites deeply veined in red.

"Can he hear me?"

"Oh, sure, he just won't feel much like answering."

The doctor slid his diagnostic unit into his pocket and headed for the door.

"Will he... like me... want to... when he's better."

"Oh, yes. Be ready. You might want to order in a lubricant or you'll have trouble sitting for a few days. Whatever you do, keep away from that cream!"

Two hours later, Link reared off the mattress, eyes wide, and snatched her into his arms.

"Whoa, lover," she whispered. But just as he had described her actions, he either couldn't or wouldn't hear. So she gave in to it.

He rolled her beneath him and plunged into her. His cock was as hard as her favorite dildo. Just as it would be if drug-enhanced, but she knew more than a simple erectile stimulator had been in his drink.

An earthy scent rose from his skin. She restrained herself from lapping the moisture from his throat and chest. What if the drug could transfer to her that way? His nipples were sharp points against her breasts and each time she slid her fingertips across them, his whole body jerked.

She cupped his buttocks and locked her legs around his hips. The ride was frantic, his climax quick.

The amount of time between his erections was little more than twenty minutes. And between each erection he stroked her, kissed her, his hands wandering, arousing, keeping her on the verge of ecstasy, but never allowing her to fall over the precipice.

"Let me," she said the third time he tried to enter her. This time, she knelt between his thighs and took him into her mouth, drugs be damned. She scraped her teeth up and down his cock, licked his testicles. They were like hot coals against her lips, so hot she wondered how he could tolerate the sensation. His body ran with sweat, every muscle flexed, every tendon straining while she nuzzled him.

His come tasted acrid as it erupted into her mouth. She climbed his body. He was fast asleep.

With a sigh, she ran to the bathroom, spit his come into a cup, then rinsed her mouth for several minutes. She set the cup aside for analysis and went back to bed. She curled beside him and scrutinized every breath she took and each beat of her heart for some sign of Link's drug. After a quarter hour, she laughed at herself and put her arms around his waist.

That proved to be a mistake. He made a guttural sound in his throat, turned and faced her, eyes open, but unseeing. His fist wrapped around his cock. He worked it without any sign it gave him pleasure, so she covered his fingers and slowed his harried motions.

She laved the head of his penis with her tongue. There seemed little point in being fucked raw by him when in less than thirty-six hours they would both need to be fit—or at least appear fit—for a round with Angel Martinez.

His hand fell away, his throat worked. "When will this end?" he asked, his voice hoarse.

"A few hours."

"I'll be dead." He clutched the sheets and spread his legs.

"No, you won't." She stroked the smooth skin of his inner thighs, reveling in the quiver of his muscles to her touch.

"Now." It was all he said.

Whatever he wanted, he indicated it by the impatient push of his hand. She slid to the bottom of the bed and sucked his big toe, licked her way up his leg and feasted on him again. As he neared his climax, she moved up to kiss his mouth, swallowing his moans this time, her hand holding his stiff cock against her belly.

The small amount of semen that erupted was molten hot and sticky, gluing their bellies together. When dawn brightened the sky outside their hotel chamber, he finally fell into a sleep that appeared normal.

She hit the shower and took a basin and wash cloth to the bedside. She bathed him gently, knowing his skin must feel raw as hers had. His skin was still hot. He moaned once and shoved at her hand, but she continued to bathe him, replenishing the cool water as it warmed.

Then she curled at his side and watched his face. How she loved him. Thoughts that something might happen to him in

The Palace made her stomach clench. She couldn't make any mistakes.

None.

Chapter 20

ಬಿ

A ray of sunlight fell across the bed. Link groaned and sat up. His head hadn't ached so much since that first binge when he'd been a cadet, when he'd discovered he had no tolerance for sweet drinks. When he stood the room tipped, but Evans's arm was there, sliding around his waist to steady him.

"Thanks," he said. His mouth tasted like the dust on the soles of his Mars boots. He had to lean against the wall of the shower while she bathed him. It embarrassed him that at any other time, he'd be jumping her bones up against the shower wall, rather than panting from exhaustion while she had her way with him — with a washing cloth.

"Is there anything I can get you?" she asked.

He dropped into a chair after the shower and watched her deftly change the damp bed linens.

"Nothing. I just want to sleep for a year."

"Well, you have about five hours and then you and your equipment have to look perky at The Palace."

Angel. He'd forgotten for a moment. "Can't you get the place shut down for these drug things?"

"On what evidence? We both had acute reactions to something? Pretty flimsy. Who's to say we even got it there?" She shook her head. "Too much time between our visit and the reactions."

"But we have Grace8's hatred of us both. Isn't that enough? You took her place and I ran out on her."

"It's not enough."

She wore a defeated expression that touched him. His Evans wasn't a quitter. He tried another approach.

"If I remember correctly, you said they might be testing drugs, or variations of drugs, on the guests. Why doesn't Homeland Security use that as an excuse to raid the place?"

"I don't know. I'll see what I can do about it."

He watched her spend the next two hours on the communications panel with little effect.

Rapidly she learned that angle wouldn't work to shut the place down. Too many influential people frequented The Palace. She already knew exactly how influential some of The Palace's clients were. No one in the government bureaucracy would take a chance on offending the wealthy and powerful with something as innocuous as illegal drugs, especially since she was talking about drugs most men would pay a hefty sum to get their hands on.

She finally had to explain to Link exactly what they were up against, using an abbreviated account of her encounter with Alexander Kennedy as an example.

There was no help for it. They had to go in again. At least this time they knew they would reach Angel.

* * * * *

Evans followed Link through the corridors of The Palace, her body concealed by her black gown and cape. She hoped she hid her anxiety as well. Today was the culmination of their mission. One way or another, it would be over.

Link still looked exhausted, his eyes bloodshot. But his bearing was erect and she feasted her eyes on him.

She might not ever see him again.

She saw the reluctance in his eyes when a pair of attendants entered the robing chamber to help them undress.

"We don't need any help, thanks. Now or later. I hate all the fawning. Get it?" he said abruptly.

With bows and smiles, the two attendants left with alacrity. Evans realized he wanted to be sure there would be no one helping out when she switched clothing with Angel.

They both hurried, removing their clothing and tossing it onto the hangers without much care. Evans found it hard to swallow. What if something had gone wrong? What if Angel wasn't on the other side of that door?

Together, they stepped into the chamber.

Angel looked so young. Evans felt her stomach lurch. How were they going to do this? How could they get to the end of this session without violating a few dozen of their own personal barriers or standards?

Link set his hand on Angel's bowed head. "Look at me."

The girl raised her face and he cupped her chin and examined her face. When he looked up, Evans met his gaze over Angel's head. She was wearing lavender ribbons tied to her wrists and ankles... with lots of dangling ends... for tying to something, Evans supposed.

"Let's get to it," he said.

"Your attendant wishes to grant your every wish," said a husky woman's voice suddenly. "You'll find everything you need to please the most discriminating tastes at your fingertips."

As the voice spoke, a panel opened and a shelf slid forward. On it lay articles in leather and cloth, pretty standard props for bondage scenarios. She thanked the bondage gods that she could see nothing like the equipment and props from her disastrous session with Grace8 and the Phoenix Freak.

Evans selected a length of deep brown velvet with a gold clasp and put it around her neck. A gold ring lay centered on her throat. Link's hand covered hers as she picked up another length of velvet. He threaded it through the ring and wrapped it around his fist.

As if it were a leash, he led her to the bed.

"Help me tie her down," Link said to Angel.

Angel fumbled through the tray of articles and joined him at the bed. She handed him some velvet covered restraints, one at a time.

Evans felt her heart begin to pound. Yes, there was indeed a difference when someone she loved was involved in bondage with her. Link's hands were cold on her ankles and wrists while he buckled on the velvet cuffs, then tied them to cleverly positioned rings on the metal bedposts.

"I really enjoy this best if someone is watching," Link said with a grin that curved only his beautiful mouth.

Angel climbed on the bed and knelt opposite Link. She spread her knees. Every inch of her body was denuded of hair, enhancing the idea she was not much more than a child. This close, Evans could see the evidence of drugs in her eyes.

"Your attendant is happy to accommodate your every wish. Ask and you will receive."

Link's fingers tightened on Evans's ankle. He leaned across her body and touched his lips to Angel's cheek. "My wish... watch. That's what gets me off. Someone watching every move."

Evans closed her eyes while Link grazed his fingertips along her instep. He'd tightened the velvet bands so she was stretched open, totally open to his kisses and touches. Yet, she was not so tightly confined she could not arch and twist against her bonds. She didn't need to exaggerate her responses to Link's touches and kisses.

He was gentle but persistent in his endeavors. If Angel moved a fraction of an inch, he barked an order at her to remain still. The girl was as much in bondage as Evans was herself, bound by his orders just as she was by the velvet ropes.

Link knelt between Evans's thighs and lifted her hips just a touch, then slid his cock deep inside her. "Tighten my partner's bonds," he said to Angel.

The girl scrambled off the bed and went to each band of velvet, drawing the clasps tighter. Evans arched off the bedcovers, lifted by the bonds, impaled on Link's erection.

He grasped her nipples between his fingertips and tugged them. She felt her insides grow slippery for him, and suddenly realized Angel would describe every moment of this encounter to her debriefer when she was finally home.

Evans began to fight her passion and arousal.

"Come for me," Link ordered, driving deeply into her.

But she couldn't.

She tried, she closed her eyes, but the knowledge that their AOA accomplice watched every move kept her from release.

Link groaned and withdrew.

"See to some soap and water," Link ordered the girl.

She bounded off the bed and went to another panel that opened with cleaning supplies.

Link took the opportunity to lean over and kiss Evans's cheek. "Sorry, if I hurt you," he whispered.

She met his gaze and let him know she was fine with a slow shake of her head.

"Undo her," Link said to Angel, taking the cleansing materials from the girl.

Evans almost laughed when Link washed only one thing, his cock. He was really fitting into his role as a Palace guest.

"Let's get out of here. I'm hungry." He tossed the cloth onto the mattress and put his hand on the back of Angel's neck. "I want you to dress me, little one, and then my partner."

"Your attendant is pleased to be of assistance," said the voice. "If you would like to purchase some of the materials you used today for home pleasure, simply say, purchase and they will be added to your account."

"Purchase."

Angel gathered up the velvet bonds and wrapped them into a neat bundle, securing them with the gold buckle that graced the neck collar. The deft manner in which she did it told Evans customers frequently bought the toys and Angel had often prepared them for transport home.

Link dropped his long arms around Evans and Angel when they stood next to the robing hooks. He mauled them both, kissing and caressing them, turning them, using his robe like wings as Angel took the cue and knelt with Evans to caress him. Hidden. Concealed.

Evans marveled at the easy manner in which Link draped the black velvet cloak across Angel's back.

Evans quickly pulled one of the velvet bands from the neat bundle and shoved it into Angel's mouth, binding it with another to keep the gag in place. Angel stared but didn't struggle. Didn't the girl have any will of her own?

Maybe she thought it was still part of the game. Or maybe the drugs made her docile.

Link kept the girl tight against his body. Hopefully, the concealed cameras would see only two women on their knees pleasuring a customer, one enveloped in a black cloak, one in The Palace's signature robe.

Moments later, Link had dressed in his tunic and trousers, and was hustling Angel away. He did not look back.

Evans had to bite her tongue on the shiver of fear as she remained bent over in the Palace robe, trying to appear as if she were examining something on her leg.

A door opened.

Too soon.

Evans turned away as two strong hands gripped her arms. She looked into the face of one of the guards who had escorted her to her sunning.

"Well, well," said a man's voice at her ear. "You must have missed us to want to stay."

She stamped her foot on the man's instep. He yelped and jumped back.

Moments later, she was through the door, fleeing down the corridor after Link and Angel.

She managed to leap into the lift just as the doors slid closed.

"What?" he said. He had his hand on the back of Angel's neck to keep her head down.

"They're on to us." She rose on tiptoe and whispered at his ear. "When the doors open, just barge straight through whoever appears. I'll push Angel after you. I'm going to create a huge mess. You just keep moving."

"No, we go together."

She opened her mouth to argue, but met his eye and knew it would be fruitless.

Her heart raced as the lift settled softly down, the only indication they'd moved coming from the shift in her stomach.

Link stepped cautiously onto the muted carpet of the lobby. He had Angel in a tight grip. The girl walked between them like a zombie, neither fighting nor cooperating.

Evans tried to look nonchalant as they headed for the doors. Why had the lift worked? Why was this so easy? Where were the guards? What was going on?

"Go," Link said. He propelled Angel straight into her arms.

Evans stumbled over the portal into the sunshine with Angel. Her heart slammed in her chest.

She headed straight for Link's waiting PF.

A strange, gurgling sound made her whip around.

Link stood framed in the glass doorway. He didn't follow. He stood frozen, one foot lifted, making the choking noise. His fingers spread, twitching.

An unseen force blocked the entry. It held him immobile, like a fly caught in a spider web.

"Link," Evans cried, but she knew what she had to do. She grabbed Angel and tossed her into the PF, stepping in after her.

The last she saw of Link, he was still suspended in the entry, one foot poised to step to safety. Behind him stood three men. One lifted a hand and touched Link's ear. His eyes rolled up. As the PF pulled away, he crumpled into the arms of the guards.

* * * * *

Link woke. The chamber in which he found himself was filled with a hazy, amber fog. He took a deep breath and smelled something musty. Sexually musty.

His nose itched. He tried to lift his arms, but they wouldn't move. When he twitched his nose, he realized something light and silky feeling covered his face. It pulled slightly at his skin. That was what caused the amber hue. That was what held the smell.

After he took a moment to orient himself and grow accustomed to the sensation, he knew what it was. A mask. The kind that was sprayed on the face to seal out microbes. Hospitals used them to prevent infection in patients.

Was he ill?

His stomach felt like someone had punched him repeatedly. His testicles ached. He needed to piss.

As if someone had heard him, a matronly woman in a deep blue tunic entered the chamber with a small jug-like thing. She did not speak to him and when he tried to talk, it was nothing but a mumble through the mask.

"Time to urinate, young man," the woman said, manipulating him into the head of the jug.

He relieved himself and tried again to move.

He was frozen on the bed.

"Don't pull a muscle trying to move. You've been given a restraint. Your ear might hurt where they inserted it, but if you relax, you'll be fine. The smell you are probably experiencing is the solidifying agent given off by the liquid mask. As it firms up, covering your face, growing more opaque, it also exudes a small amount of a new drug we're rather proud of. You won't be able to move or talk, but you will be able to feel any and all tactile sensations. You'll be able to have an erection. And a lovely one you're getting right now."

The woman had been stroking his cock. He could feel her hand, but could not move his hips or legs or arms to resist her.

She touched his nipples.

"Ah. A nice reaction here, too. That's lovely. Our patrons will be very pleased."

Patrons?

"How is our new addition, Jennel?" a male voice asked.

Jennel smiled and patted Link's cock. "He's marvelous."

The man moved into Link's view. He was tall and emaciated, with a shock of white hair. Masses of wrinkles creased his face. Those wrinkles had not been carved there by excess smiling. They emphasized his nose and mouth. He must be well over a hundred to look so aged.

The man ran a diagnostic handheld over Link's body. He grunted. "You may go, Jennel."

She bowed and the door whispered closed behind her.

The man stood over Link's groin for a moment, staring down at his cock.

"Do you know why you are here, young man? Why we let those stupid women leave? Oh, we could have stopped them, but you are such a prize, they were of little consequence. We thought we might not see you again, once you made it through the door."

Link strained to make a sound, but nothing came out of his throat.

The man reached out and cupped his balls. "This is what we want from you. You're a rarity. A man who is not on sperm suppressors and never has been."

The man dropped his balls and finally met Link's gaze.

"The mask you are wearing is opaque from here but transparent your way. Patrons who select you will not know what your face looks like, though you will be able to see them.

211

They will avail themselves of your body — on the day of their ovulation. And we here at The Palace who know of your presence in our little private clinic will grow wealthy."

The man smiled and licked his narrow lips. His teeth looked far too large for the rest of him. Link wished the mask obscured the old man's face; he could have made his fortune as a character in those low-budget horror vids, saving the producers the cost of makeup and special effects.

"I'm sure you're asking why? Why me." He pulled out a hand-held diagnostic device much like the one the Secretary's physician had used. "I don't mind telling you. It's not as if you can do anything about it. Personally, I plan to use my share of the wealth you generate for a heart transplant — a black market heart, that is." He touched his chest. "I'm sure you know of the legislation that forbids transplants to those over one hundred. I'm one hundred and twenty."

Link tried to wiggle his toes. Nothing happened.

"As to, 'Why me?' The why you is simple. Science made men happy by making drugs to suppress sperm. At the same time, they also made them happy with erectile enhancers. So, for many generations, we have enjoyed sex whenever it pleased us to have it, and have not had to concern ourselves with birth control. No sperm, no births.

"Women have appreciated that part of the process as well. Some may even enjoy a man's ability to get it up whenever he wants to, no matter his age."

Link felt the man's hand on his wrist. The old ghoul must be a med-aide or a doctor, for he maneuvered his fingertips to take Link's pulse.

"But one must pay the piper, so to speak. And we've been paying dearly. Generations of widespread use of these drugs have had a side effect that the public is kept in the dark about. More and more men, especially those whose fathers and grandfathers used the drugs, now find their bodies unable to produce much sperm. Even once they stop taking the drugs. And the sperm they do produce is often… faulty."

Link wished he could shake off the man's claw-like hand. The moist fingers clutched his wrist so tightly Link didn't think he could have wrenched free even if he had been able to move. His skin crawled.

"We need men like you. You're a healthy, sperm-producing male. High count, active little swimmers. Only with a man like you will women conceive healthy children. Oh, we could do the thing with injections, but that would not involve the women enough." The man leaned his head close to Link's. His breath smelled of something acrid yet vaguely familiar. "Enough to keep them silent about this place. If they actively take part… well. They have reason to remain quiet. We store a little data on each encounter. To the public, the law, their husbands who don't know what they're up to… well, the woman just appears to be involved in a sexual encounter here at a rather high-priced pleasure center."

Link strained to turn his head from the man's offensive breath. It was no use. His muscles refused to respond to his commands.

"And, in truth, many of the clients are women who also wonder what it would be like to couple with a man who is virile without drugs to aid him. Desperation for a child makes them seek our services, curiosity makes them crave this."

The man's claw-like hand moved to palpate Link's belly in a business-like manner. "You had a mild reaction to our new erectile enhancer; it was in the Emerald Elixir you so happily drank for us on one of your visits. Our informants at your hotel have reported that you didn't vomit—one of your less desirable reactions to such stimulants. And I'm sure you can appreciate the problems vomiting might cause you in your present position."

The man put his hand on Link's throat. "If you find yourself unable to respond to a client, you now know we can assist you."

A chill ran through Link. He got it. He didn't need it spelled out.

He was to be a living sperm bank. *Shit.* He hoped he didn't need their assistance. They might be wrong about his reaction. For a moment he felt he was smothering, then he thought of Evans and the panic receded. She had endured far worse.

The man touched his diagnostic handheld. "You are very rare. Our clients will pay millions of credits for the chance to become impregnated by you. Think of it. Not only do you produce phenomenal amounts of motile sperm, you are also a parent's genetic dream." The doctor touched Link's chest. "Handsome. Virile. At the top of height and strength charts. Your genetic profile is clean. Granted, you did have that aunt who wanted to eat her cat, but that could be explained by environmental factors."

Aunt Bess had taken pleasure drugs for over forty years. Auntie had been a hedonist from puberty and was held up to him as an example of what happens when you have too many credits and not enough to do.

"Your first client will arrive in a few moments. She will take one look at your body… well, shall we just say, I'm sure there will be little call for lubricants while you are here." The doctor stroked his shoulder. "We want you to know your privacy is completely protected. The synth mask conceals your features. All you need do is relax and enjoy the orgasms."

When the doctor left, the Med-Aide, Jennel arrived. She asked him if he'd like to relieve himself again before going to work.

"You should feel honored," Jennel said. "The moment we tested your clean-up kits, we knew you were a winner." She shook her finger in his face. "Naughty boy, using someone else's card. Took a while to find out who you were and verify your medical history. We're very grateful you signed your real name to that purchase contract for Bliss6, else our old doc might be waiting forever on a new heart. Now lie back, close your eyes, and rest. Our first client will be arriving in about an hour."

Link lay for more than an hour, trying to discern as much as possible about his situation. He could feel that his legs were spread and the bed, if bed it could be called, was cut in the shape of his body. He knew from relieving himself that a woman could stand between his spread legs. His arms were slightly set away from his body, his palms face up, his head gently elevated so he could see down his body, but not so much that his neck ached.

He could feel and smell. He imagined a thumbnail image of his body on a menu. Some woman touching the screen, selecting him.

A sensation he could not describe flooded through him. Being photographed naked. Being looked over. His stats examined. Being chosen.

Just as he'd chosen G752H.

Chapter 21
ℰↄ

All Link could think of was Evans as he lay there.

Sara.

Even though the old man had said they'd let the women leave, it could be a lie. He closed his eyes, and shut out thoughts of Sara hurt or dead. He had to believe she was safe, or he'd go insane lying here, frozen like a butterfly impaled by a pin in a museum case.

The door opened. Two women entered.

One was from the menu selection screens. He immediately recognized her as the one from the deep menus. Silver Girl.

She came to the head of the bed. The scent of real flowers flowed around her. She touched his cheek and spoke softly near his ear.

"Welcome. We thank you for contributing to the happiness of infertile couples. I will see you enjoy the experience to the maximum allowed by your restraint."

The other woman stood hesitantly at his feet. She was around his age, wasp-thin, her face smooth and perfect, well-enhanced by cosmetic surgery. Her orangish-red hair formed a nimbus of curls about her head. They trembled a little.

Her gaze ate him with ravenous gulps. She kept her arms clasped tightly at her waist, wearing the ubiquitous Palace robe.

The silver beauty dropped her gauzy dress. She climbed astride his body, brushing her small, groomed bush over his belly. She cupped one of her large, lush breasts and stroked the hard nipple back and forth over his. His nipples and his cock rose to attention.

The woman at the foot of the bed, the client, gasped. "He's... great," the woman exclaimed.

The silver vision smiled and licked his nipples and said, "Climb astride whenever it pleases you."

To make room for the client, the attendant slid her body forward so her coiffed crotch was planted on his chest.

He closed his eyes to blot out the vision of the woman's pierced clitoris. Its silver ring was studded with tiny diamonds... or their equivalent.

He groaned when the client grasped his cock. The silvery goddess moved. He made the mistake of opening his eyes. She had turned and centered her crotch over his face. He would smother if she lowered herself. A moment of panic filled him.

But she was not interested in cutting off his air supply. She was helping the client settle on his erection.

The redhead groaned. "Saint's preserve me. This guy is huge. Makes Carl —"

"No names," whispered the attendant, stroking the woman's clit. "Just enjoy. He is magnificent, though." With that she slid her other hand between him and the client and kneaded his balls.

"How long can he last? I mean. You know. He's not on anything, they said. I only get as long as it takes him, they said." The client sank down on him and wriggled in place.

Silver Girl climbed off him and went to a panel in the wall. She opened it and brought out a bottle. She poured a fragrant oil on her hands. "Every man's body has a natural rhythm. But why don't we make it a bit more fun?"

Silver Girl rubbed the oil on the woman's breasts, stroking her nipples, then her clit. The oil warmed when Silver Girl stroked it on his balls. The room began to smell like cinnamon and cloves.

The client began to pant and moan as Silver Girl stroked her.

"I'm gonna come. I'm gonna come," the client gasped, riding him mercilessly. He closed his eyes as Silver Girl climbed astride his face again and pleasured herself inches from his nose, but when he closed his eyes, he felt every slide of the redhead on him. He shut his mind to being used for stud.

Anger filled him. It nestled in his gut. It didn't stop the eruption of his semen or take away the shudder of the climax as it ripped up from his balls, but it did make it distant and cold.

"When will he be available again?" the client whispered as she climbed off him.

"You'll have to check the menus. Now, you are due in the resting chamber. We don't want you to loose any of the goodies you just received."

He heard a door click open. Then he felt a hand on his belly. He hated the way the silver nymph hummed and caressed him as she bathed him clean with some liquid that had a sharp, antiseptic smell.

"I'm sorry this is so stinky," she said. "But we need you germ free for the next client."

He stoked the anger when several hours later the silver nymph led another woman into the room. He didn't see this one. He kept his eyes closed. But he knew Silver Girl from her smell and voice.

This client hung by the door and when welcomed to climb astride him, said, "No. Not yet. I… that is. I'm not ready. I think I'll just… watch."

The nymph said, "I'll just get him ready for when you're *ready*."

She knelt between his thighs. "Enjoy looking at him. He's a treat for the eyes, isn't he?" She licked his balls with a warm, agile tongue. Her fingers were slick with something warm and she had no qualms about sliding them inside him. He felt like he was smothering again, his breath unable to move freely from his lungs as she took him deep in her mouth, licking, teasing the head of his cock.

"Can I do that?" the new client asked.

He felt new hands on him. Rougher. Harder strokes, harder squeezing. He willed himself somewhere else.

One of them nipped his nipples with her teeth. One of them took his balls into her mouth. He groaned within himself. If he could, he'd kill the old man. Maybe rip his aged, rotting heart out of his chest and roast it.

He willed himself impotent. His traitorous cock didn't respond to his commands.

The nymph whispered to the client. "Come, don't be reluctant. Climb on. If you play too long, you may make him come. That would be a waste, now wouldn't it?"

The client touched his erection while Silver Girl said, "Isn't he huge? Hard? Lovely?"

The nymph licked up the column of his throat while the client groaned.

"He is a magnificent specimen. Imagine a son by him." The nymph's voice dropped even lower to a husky whisper. "Imagine all of this inside you. Imagine your climax." The nymph helped the client to climb awkwardly across his hips, holding his cock upright so the woman could sit on him.

He wanted to buck her off, but she shimmied her hips and mewed a sound of satisfaction as she slid down and took him completely.

The nymph rubbed his balls. "I imagine your mate is not so large, or gets so hard. This man is as nature made him. Natural. Unenhanced. Sperm teeming in his seed. Enjoy."

Link closed his mind to the words meant to entice the woman, not him. That was left to her hot tongue, her invasive fingertips.

He came with an inner groan. The woman kept working on him. How could she have missed the eruption? But she rocked and moaned.

He opened his eyes. The nymph had climbed up and put her pussy in his face again. Only this time, she kissed the woman's breasts and rubbed the woman's clit.

"Your husband neglects you here, doesn't he?"

The woman panted and rode his now wilting cock. In a few moments, she probably didn't care if he was hard or soft. She was in the throes of the nymph's ministrations, enjoying a climax, riding the nymph's clever, slick fingertips.

* * * * *

For two days his life was a nightmare routine.

The woman, Jennel, bathed him and saw to his needs. He was hooked to some kind of dripping liquid thing at night. It was something out of the dark ages. Something from history books, seeing a snaking tube attached to his arm. He suspected the fluid contained a drug to make him more compliant. And his sleep was filled with nightmares.

Dreams of an endless maze of corridors and doors. And Evans somewhere behind them. He ran like a rat from hall to hall, opening and closing doors, but never finding her.

He woke each day filled with grief. What had happened to her? To his Sara? Was she safe because as Evans, she knew how to take care of herself?

He remembered the look on her face as she had dropped into the PF. A look of fear for him. Evans afraid? It twisted his gut.

Pain lanced through his body as he strained to move, to break the bond of the device in his ear. He tried to turn his head and brush it off, but nothing happened. Inside, he fought like a madman. Outside, he lay inert. Like the dead.

Except for the parts of him the doctor needed agile and useful.

Clients visited him every few hours. He thought the ones at the end of the day must be getting cheated. How could he have any sperm left? As each day waned, Silver Girl had to work harder to get him to stand at attention. But good soldier that he was, he always did his duty. They saw to it with their clever arsenal of drugs.

The nymph enjoyed her work. And he got to know every tuck and fold of her crotch as she shoved it into his line of vision with boring regularity.

He found he could only leave it all behind if he closed his eyes and focused on Evans… Sara. He wanted to know if she'd gotten safely away. Wanted to know so badly he could not sleep without the wash of chemicals that a woman sprayed near his nose.

She was kind, at least. An attractive young woman, without a hint of satisfaction that he was powerless. Not like the older one, Jennel, who saw to his other needs. Jennel took joy in his helpless state, her expression one that said, *Ah ha. I've got you at my mercy and you'll twist with embarrassment over this for years.*

No, the kindly one did linen changes and saw him to sleep each night. He fought the sleep. Each time it stole over him, it was like a long, slow slide into the dark maze. Endlessly lost, he was powerless there too.

Each morning, he woke to the cruel med-aide standing over him, the old doctor next to her, running his diagnostics.

Finally, Link had a day of respite. Not from worries about Sara, but from being milked repeatedly. The kind med-aide had noted some tiny broken blood vessels on the head of his penis and suggested he be given a rest.

If he'd been capable of speech he would have told her the red marks were from an over-enthusiastic nymph who liked to draw on him with enough power to suck-start a blocked fuel line.

His balls ached as well. The last client had ridden him facing backwards, massaging his balls, leaning over to give him a vertical smile. He didn't even bother to close his eyes anymore.

He watched from outside himself. It was some other man's penis being sucked and stroked.

Only pain brought him to the surface.

Pain... and the powerful orgasms. He couldn't pretend they didn't happen.

Chapter 22
ဢ

Evans sat on the edge of her chair across from Secretary Martinez and tried again.

"He went beyond the call of duty, sir. We can't leave him in there. He could be subjected to UV torture—"

"We've been over this, Colonel. I will agree he did his duty. As he *should*. It would be counter-productive to our program to take any retrieval steps."

Now that your daughter is safe. Colonel Taylor is an expendable asset, sacrificed to keep you safe from blackmail.

The HSS reached into a drawer and pulled out a flimsy. He glanced at it before sliding it across the desk to her. "Your orders and background files. Your flight leaves Friday."

"Yes, sir." She rose, picked up the data sheet, threw him a sketchy salute, and left the office. "Counter-productive," she muttered once the door had sealed behind her. "You mean it would be injurious to you." She tore at a hangnail on her pinky. "And you're sending me to the Asian Confederacy to get me out of your hair."

Back at Link's hotel room, she stood before his open closet and ran her hands over his uniform tunics and off-duty clothes. All as she had suspected, of a general color scheme to limit his choices. She lifted a tunic sleeve and to her intense shame, bent her head and breathed in his scent.

Shame because she was supposed to obey and couldn't. Link Taylor was *not* expendable.

Moments later, fighting tears, she dug in her pack. After all this time, the weapon felt unfamiliar in her hand.

She worked undercover with the weapons of intellect and cunning. She glanced at Link's tunics, hanging with military correctness in neat rows. She hadn't been so cunning.

Angel was home, at least. Or Angel was in a private medical center somewhere, detoxing from the drugs and working out her issues with her family.

Evans went to the firing range and practiced for hours. Her hand-eye coordination was rusty from disuse. Link needed her in the best of shape and although she feared the time he spent in The Palace, she knew she was going in alone and had better be sharp. Very sharp.

While she practiced and improved, she made lists in her head of what she'd need and where she might get it. She had a few contacts who would help her out. With a little digging, she'd undoubtedly find Link had friends, as well. There were those who owed her favors. This was a good reason to call them in. Come to think of it, Link's freedom was the best reason she'd ever have.

The next day, she requested and received three days of leave before her departure.

* * * * *

She knew from her weeks undercover that The Palace was quietest in the morning. Guests didn't as a rule have early-morning demands, and the attendants needed to sleep sometime.

Early on the second day of her leave, she donned her "costume" and loaded her pockets. Reviewing her appearance in the mirror, she had to approve.

The robe she had worn out of The Palace didn't show gathered up beneath her outer clothing. The oversized jacket and shabby leggings wouldn't get a second glance from anyone. She would look like every other worker heading for her job.

Indeed, no one paid her any attention. She exited the public roller a few blocks from The Palace. As she made her way down the street, her eye was drawn to a tiny shop wedged between two huge office buildings. It looked like a mushroom had sprouted in the shadows the towers cast. How could the place survive, with the few pedestrians found at street level?

She quickened her pace, slipping from shadow to shadow as the other workers did to avoid the morning glare. For once, the anonymous swathing of clothing, deep brims, and covered skin served her well.

The Palace loomed above her, its walls of windows turning blind eyes on the world.

"I'm coming, Link," she said aloud.

When she reached the alley she sought, her heart began to thud rapidly in her chest.

The doors where they'd sent her out with Link after her sunning were as wide as she remembered, to allow the passage of rolling rubbish bins.

She waited and was rewarded. Trash must go out. And out it came. The man who dragged the sealed rubbish containers out for pickup wandered to the end of the alley and stared up at the heavy morning air traffic. She slipped into the dark corridor.

Beautiful. Clearly, The Palace staff was not terribly worried about someone trying to get in.

Getting the two of them out would be the problem.

* * * * *

Link woke with a start. The room was empty. He'd had a vivid dream. Evans in a long, dark hallway, the sound of her heart beating so loudly he could hear it here in his cell. The smell of flowers. His heart began to pound.

The door opened and a med-aide entered. It was the young one, the nice one.

"Good morning," she said. "Jennel is busy this morning so I'll take care of you."

He shut his mind off from her efficient tending to his needs. He tried to conjure up his dream, but the woman's voice intruded.

"Stars, your pulse is fast this morning. I'm going to give you a little sniff of vitamins now."

The spray might be vitamins, but it smelled strangely like roses.

She patted his arm, pocketed her spray and shifted her attention to his groin. "Looking back to normal here. The doctor will be in shortly. He'll probably clear you for action."

Get me out of here, Evans.

* * * * *

It took no time at all for Evans to remove her outer garments and stow them behind a crate just inside The Palace's outer doors. For the first time, her long hair was an asset. It helped conceal the mesh of her sensory enhancement helmet. The left earpiece felt odd for a moment until she got it seated properly. She'd probably not need the vision attachment, and it would call attention to her, so she tossed it into a bin of refuse.

She patted the arsenal she'd strapped beneath the robe, making sure nothing had dislodged in transit. The rasp of her hand over the fabric roared in her ear, and she adjusted the volume. Leaning her head against the inner door, she tried to determine if there was anyone on the other side. *Nothing.*

A scrape of a footstep alerted her that the man who had dragged out the trash was returning.

Taking a deep breath, she revisited the map of The Palace she'd built in her head before ducking through an inner door. The waste compacting area was deserted though hardly silent. She further reduced the volume on the helmet to block out the sudden cacophony of noise that buffeted her like a physical blow.

Huge chutes conducted eruptions of refuse from the floors above into large bins that moved along a conveyor belt into a machine that compacted the contents of each bin, sealed it, and deposited neat bundles into the smaller rolling rubbish bins for pickup. Never had she imagined such a volume of trash.

She remembered riding in a maintenance lift when she'd been escorted out with Link, and found it without difficulty.

Have to love technology, she said to herself.

Outside of the maintenance floor, she readjusted the volume of her earpiece while she scanned the lift buttons.

There was one floor that required a code to reach. That had to be where they held Link... if he was still in The Palace. She refused to consider the idea that he might have been moved.

Smiling grimly, she ripped off the cover to the control panel. The robust comm unit she'd tucked against her lower back had four wires that fit into one of the connectors. In a moment, she had the code.

The lift rose smoothly, without any stops at other floors. She hoped the code overrode any calls for service from the unrestricted areas. The Palace executives wouldn't want their secrets revealed to the staff in general. She couldn't see any cameras on the lift, either.

Their paranoia was to her advantage.

Before the lift stopped, she had concealed the comm unit and palmed her dart gun. When the doors slid open, she was in a crouch, sweeping the area with both her eyes and the gun.

A med-aide stood waiting in the hall, intent on her data pad, not even looking up when the lift opened. Evans caught her in the neck just as she stepped toward the lift.

The tranq load worked even faster than she'd expected. Evans barely had time to leap across the six feet to reach the burly woman. Evans dragged her behind a desk, stripped her and donned her uniform. Tucking the woman away in a cupboard, she snatched up the woman's data pad and used it to conceal the dart gun.

Following her mental map, Evans headed toward the area that, in the parts of The Palace she'd been, held the rooms offering the most expensive services. She hoped construction was consistent from floor to floor.

She had to stun four other staff members. None of them were known to her, which reinforced her belief that she was in the right area. She avoided the corridors that could only lead to the prison cells and possible guards who would know her.

The corridor she wanted stretched away from her, with the doors spaced as she expected. Each door was identical, nothing identified any of them.

The little ID plates she'd seen on the other floors were absent. She knew she was definitely on the client side of the hallway as bare and functional gave way to lush flowered carpets and fine wall coverings in shades of gold and copper. Long tables with real flowers were spaced at intervals. Their lush beauty reminded her of the garden outside. Maybe that was where these blooms had come from.

She turned up the volume on the enhancement helmet. She'd have to try one door at a time, to see if she could hear anyone inside. Perhaps fortune would smile on her for once and she'd hear Link's voice.

She moved from door to door, nervous that someone might come, afraid that there might be another floor like this, another forbidden floor not accessible from the maintenance lift. She paced, frightened that she would be out of time. After listening at each door twice and touching each knob to verify it was locked, she stood in the center of the hall.

A wave of dizziness overcame her. The scent of roses spilling from a nearby urn nearby sickened her. Then she realized it was not roses that filled her head, but something medicinal and unpleasant.

Her heart stuttered in her chest. For a moment she felt as if her limbs were frozen. It was hard to breathe. She willed herself to move, but couldn't. Suddenly, she realized she was living her nightmare.

And she knew Link was near. Unable to move. How she knew, she didn't want to examine. In her head she heard his voice.

"That day, you said something that really stayed with me. You said I had something no other man had. You didn't know what it was. An invisible chemical that I gave off and only your sensors could pick up. You said whatever it was, it was like a leash from you to me. And all I had to do was tug the leash and you'd come to me."

Without thought, she walked along the corridor again.

Tug the leash, Link. Speak to me.

The sound of a lift door swishing open filled her ear. It came from the other end of the floor. She stepped up to the table with its fabulous urn of roses and bent her head over the data pad. The voices of the two women who exited the lift sounded clearly through her headset.

"There's no need to be nervous. He doesn't bite."

A woman's tinkling laugh grated through Evans's head.

"I'm paying enough. He'd better not." The guest's voice was peevish. "This had better last longer than the last ride I bought. I'm not a green young girl, you know."

"I can guarantee it. The Palace delivers on its promises." The first woman's voice became soothing.

The sound of a door closing cut off the guest's reply.

Evans stepped back into the center of the corridor and strode anxiously from door to door.

Where are you, Link? Show me.

The door in front of her opened.

Evans froze.

The woman in the doorway did the same. Not just any woman. Miller. Her eyes registered recognition, and fear.

Evans recovered first, pushing the med-aide back into the room.

It wasn't a room, it was another corridor. There were two doors on the left wall, and then another hallway branched off.

"Where is he?" Evans said near Miller's ear.

"Come," Miller whispered. She opened one of the doors and pulled Evans through after her. This was an empty chamber, with a single padded chair and a small cot.

The woman's fingers danced over a comm pad by the door.

"Now we can talk freely. I thought you'd escaped."

"It's a long story. I did, but my partner wasn't so lucky. I came back for him."

"What makes you think he's still here?"

"I know it. I can feel him." The words sounded insane, but Miller only nodded.

Evans stood with her back against the wall by the door, weapon ready, most of her attention focused on the med-aide. The corridor behind them was quiet. She turned down the volume on her headset, so she could converse without being deafened in that ear.

"Relax. I coded this room as being occupied with an on-going medical exam, so we won't be bothered." Miller leaned on the back of the chair. "Is your partner tall, dark, and handsome? Allergic to sperm suppressors?"

"Absolutely. You know where he is?"

"One door behind you," Miller whispered. "I'm amazed you came back, under the circumstances. You know, the chance of you finding this one –"

Evans whirled, ready to retrace her steps and rescue Link. The woman caught her by the arm. "Take me with you. I've had enough of this place."

Evans eyed her for a moment, her thoughts racing. A plan formed. This just might work, with Miller's help. They just might get out alive. All of them.

"Fine. If you don't mind a little acting." Evans placed her gun against Miller's temple. "Do what I say, and I'll get you out with us. Now, talk. What condition is he in?"

* * * * *

Link sighed behind his mask. He ignored the repetitive compliments on the size of his erect cock and his gorgeous body. This patron couldn't stop gasping and touching. The silver nymph smiled and guided her on a tour of the Taylor attractions.

By the time the nymph got down to serious licking and touching, the patron was shoving her aside to climb on. She was tight. Her hot grip almost undid him as she guided him in.

He'd be done in an instant at the rate this woman was riding up and down his shaft. Much longer, and he'd be screaming inside. For the first time, he thanked The Palace for giving him the opaque mask. None of them would ever see the flush of humiliation on his face. Some mercies were small. The mask also prevented the client or this succubus from kissing him. He could disassociate himself from the traitorous appendage between his legs, but a kiss on the mouth would be too much.

The nympho glided in her fragrant cloud up to his chest and bent over him, teasing his nipple with hers. He closed his eyes to it and conjured Sara. He tried to place her on his cock, imagine her hand reaching back to squeeze his testicles.

He even thought he could hear her voice.

"That's enough. Climb down. *Now*."

Sweet Sol, he thought as he opened his eyes. *Evans*.

The client leapt off him as if he had burst into flames.

Evans stood in the doorway, a thoroughly deadly dart gun in her hand. He tried to grin, but couldn't manage it. He settled for a mental cheer.

Evans's gaze swept over the nymph and settled on his groin. "I see we've been a naughty boy while I've been gone."

The nymph sidled along the edge of the room.

"Move," Evans said, "And I'll blow your fake boobs to kingdom cum."

Silver Girl froze. He wondered for a moment why the all-seeing eyes didn't send someone to grab Evans.

Then he thought it might be that The Palace had nothing to do with this little side business. This room might not be hooked up to their surveillance system.

When Evans stepped forward, he saw the woman behind her. The kind med-aide who'd changed his bedding this morning, the one who saw him to sleep each night.

He strained, trying to warn Evans of the danger. No sounds came out.

Evans put her hand on his chest and winked at him. "What is this? Are you hiding from me?"

The med-aide said, "He can hear and see behind that mask, but cannot move."

Silver Girl grinned. "You'll never get him out of here."

"I'll be the judge of that. You keep your mouth shut, or I'll splatter this other nympho's brains all over the wall." Evans held the weapon on the client.

Link wished he could speak. He'd tell her the nympho probably didn't care about the client's fate.

But Silver Girl did care. "Please." She held her hands up. "There's no need for any violence. I'll be good. Don't do anything hasty. Please."

The med-aide stepped around Evans and looked down at him. She took his pulse before she and Evans locked gazes.

"I can get him moving, but not well and not that fast," she said. She reached toward his ear and yanked something out.

Link howled with pain but made no audible sound. *Shit!* The restraint. The old doc had told him removing it would hurt, not that it would feel like she'd pulled out part of his tongue through his ear.

While he felt beads of sweat form on his forehead, the med-aide opened a panel and pulled a couple of items from a cupboard in the wall. Where was Evans? Why wasn't she helping him?

Evans had disappeared. He heard the door click. Had Evans left? The med-aide blocked his view.

Come back, Evans! Don't leave me! A flash of fear shot through him. What if she didn't come back? He worked to control his panic.

Moments later, the med-aide sprayed something over his mask. He felt the webbing grow warm and soften. Just when he thought it would smother him as it relaxed against his nose and mouth, she peeled it off.

"Lovely," the nymph whispered as Link's face was revealed.

"Shut up," Evans snapped, stepping back into his line of vision, dragging an unconscious man wearing a guard's uniform.

The med-aide wiped off the residue of Link's opaque mask and spritzed something cold up his nostrils. He didn't flinch. His fingers didn't even twitch. "This will take a while," she said.

Evans pulled the guard's feet inside the room and eased the door shut.

The woman who'd been sitting on Link's cock cowered against the wall. She wrapped her arms around her knees and whimpered.

"Put on your robe," Evans ordered, using her weapon to wave the woman in the proper direction. "Then help Big Boobs here to strip this guard."

Link's gaze followed Evans around the room. Was he still dreaming? Was she really here?

She came to stand by him, picking up his hand. She looked tough. Ready to use her gun if anyone dared not cooperate. But she leaned over and whispered a kiss across his brow. He breathed in her scent.

She wasn't a dream.

Chapter 23

୧୨

Evans held her gun on the women. With her other hand, she held his in a tight grip. He fought to return the hold, and felt his fingers tremble.

She dropped her gaze to his and squeezed his fingers. "Good boy," she said softly. "How long till he can stand?" she asked the med-aide.

"A few moments, but he hasn't been out of the bed in a few days. He'll be weak."

"The instant he's able, I want him on his feet. Can you put that mask on that guard?"

"Sure."

"Someone will come," Silver Girl said. "They'll catch you."

"Shut up or you'll be looking at your double Ds splattered across the room," Evans said.

A muscle in Link's thigh jumped. He felt a combination of burning and needles and pins sweep from his chest down his body.

Evans held the weapon on the two women and watched them strip the guard while the med-aide massaged Link's limbs. Finally, they helped him to sit.

The instant his back was off the bed, Evans signaled the women. "Lay him out," she gestured at the unconscious guard.

As soon as the guard was settled in Link's former pose, the med-aide shoved the restraint into the man's ear and sprayed something up his nose.

"He'll be as immobile as your partner was in about fifteen minutes."

Evans watched Miller place the soft mask, still hauntingly in the shape of Link's face, over the guard's. The woman sprayed it and molded it and within moments, his features were obliterated, as Link's had been.

"Will he be able to breathe?" Evans asked Miller.

"Indeed. It's completely porous. It just conceals the features, doesn't affect his breathing or vision."

The minutes ticked by with agonizing slowness to Evans as Link sat on the edge of the bed, naked, barely upright. She squeezed his hand and was gratified when he squeezed back. He looked equally pleased though he said nothing.

"Ready or not, Link," she said.

Miller helped her get Link into the guard's uniform. It was not nearly large enough across the shoulders and chest, nor long enough in the arms or legs, but it would have to do.

He stumbled as he straightened, standing up for the first time without help.

The client cowered back as he loomed over her.

"Now, you women have a choice," Evans said, pointing her gun at first at the attendant, then at the client. "Nympho, you probably want to keep your job, right?"

The silver-haired woman grimaced, but nodded.

"Good. Then just pretend you came in here to do whatever it is you do and found this man instead. You could even give the guy a treat and pretend you didn't notice the difference."

Link made a noise in his throat.

Evans grinned. "Okay, so anyone would notice the difference. You'll think of something. If you don't, I promise you I'll be back to tear your implants out through your ass. Is that clear?"

The attendant nodded so hard, her breasts shook.

"As for you," Evans touched her weapon to the chest of the client. "You'll have to leave sometime, won't you? If you make trouble, someone will be outside waiting to make your life miserable. They'll know who you are because I'm wearing a transmitter." Without emotion, she gave a very detailed description of the client as if someone was listening to record the details.

Of course, no one was outside. No one to hear. That made little difference, because she was the only one who knew.

Evans continued. "If I don't get out and you do, you'll regret it. If you're smart, you'll ride this guy's rocket and then leave like nothing is wrong."

The client bobbed her head with enthusiasm and embraced the silver-haired boob princess. Evans suspected they'd be hugging and kissing each other minutes after the door closed. Sheesh, she knew all about how captives could bond to each other, but after only half an hour?

"Where are we going?" Miller asked.

"Out through the trash processing facility. There's an alley and access to two streets. Keeps our options open. Remember, Link," Evans said. "That's where we left when you bought me."

He nodded.

"What do you want me to do?" Miller asked.

"You'll be walking in front of us. If you ever wanted to act in a vid, now's your chance. You get to star in our little drama in real life."

Link made it halfway down the corridor before stumbling against the wall. The med-aide slid an arm under his and he did a creditable job of walking on his own with her assistance.

Evans followed, dart gun trained them, praying each step of the way.

"This is too easy," Link said, his voice raspy.

"Agreed," she said, pushing her weapon more realistically into Miller's back should anyone be watching through the all-seeing eyes.

Instinct raised the hair on the back of Evans's neck as she pushed the button to call the lift. Nothing happened. Even with the headset volume all the way up, she heard nothing to indicate machinery moved behind the lift doors.

"It's not coming," Link said, his voice sounding a touch stronger and booming through her earpiece. One of his hands had a tremor and a muscle beneath his eye twitched.

She herded Link and Miller away. Miller took the lead, letting it appear as though Evans still called the shots. The only good thing about the delay was that it gave Link a little more time to recover his mobility.

Miller led them down stairs and through corridors, moving swiftly and surely. Twice, as they approached very efficient—and deserted—desks, Miller stopped to check the readouts on the comm units before changing direction.

They didn't risk speaking.

They turned a corner and suddenly Evans knew where they were. The next move took them into a part of the clinic she knew well. Once they were shut in the tiny exam room, she let herself relax. When she lowered the dart gun, her hand shook.

The med-aide tapped a complicated code into the comm panel and said, "We can talk freely now."

Link collapsed into a chair. "How do we get out of here?" His speech was thick and slow.

"They know you're here," Miller said. "Whatever you did to the lift operations shut down a few sections of the internal surveillance network. They don't know exactly where you are at the moment, but they're looking. We need a diversion, or we'll never get out the doors." She looked squarely at Evans. "I think I can do it, if you can get to ground level where you came in."

Evans narrowed her eyes. After all of Miller's help, leaving her behind was not an option. "What are you planning?"

"I'll start several fires in the other side of the building. Just small ones, but it will be enough to get their attention away from you two."

"No. You're coming with us. I won't leave you to their wrath."

Link croaked something unintelligible. The med-aide opened a panel, filled a glass with water and handed it to him. They watched him clear his throat and waited.

"Patch the signals from one corridor to another," he finally said.

"How?" Evans asked.

"What do you mean, how?"

"How as in, I don't know how to do that."

He frowned and took her hand. His grip was stronger. For one heartbeat, they stood that way, her hand in his, then he stood up.

"If the powers that be haven't shut our friend here out of the system, we might be able to do a little dance on their codes."

He swayed a bit as he walked to the communication console and sat gingerly before it. They went to his side.

"You're in no shape to dance," Evans said.

Link glared at her. "Since you can't do this, someone has to." He turned to Miller. "I'll need your security codes."

Miller leaned past him and tapped a few keys.

The speed with which Link processed information, with only a few terse questions for Miller, made Evans's eyes cross. No way could she have conjured this magic.

But Link could. He worked efficiently, checking his progress with Miller who guided him with a few codes, letting him access what he needed to get to. The two had their heads together for almost half an hour.

Sweat began to prickle Evans skin. Whatever they were doing, it was a start and stop, try and try again process. Then Link stretched his back and smiled grimly. "We won't need any diversions, and we should all get out in one piece."

"What did you do?" she asked, wanting to wrap her arms around him and just hold him.

"I scrambled the signals from the surveillance cameras. The signals from each floor will be randomly assigned to other floors, changing every ten minutes." He stood up and for the first time, his movements were easy. "I picked up a few stills of our progress so far to throw into the mix, along with some of the menus, active chamber feeds, and guest preference files. Tantalizing glimpses of us will have them running in circles. The surveillance equipment on the route we're taking to the trash compacting area has been disabled. Very destructive, these rogue AIs, don't you know? They cost business billions of credits every year."

"Let's get moving." Evans herded them out the door. "You know where we're going, so you can lead. I'll cover our 'hostage' here, just in case."

She turned toward the end of the corridor, but her earpiece came alive. Someone was coming. *Shit. All the preparations in the world didn't matter if your opponent was lucky.* She hoped it was one of the medical staff but instinct told her it wasn't.

Evans made instead for the door that she suspected hid the stairs. They'd have to scramble, but going down was much quicker than climbing up. When she jerked open the door, relief flooded through her at the sight of the steps.

They'd only taken four steps down when the sounds of heavy boots filled the concrete shaft, echoing around them. From below. Coming up.

Double shit.

Link pulled her back to the landing.

They faced two choices: up, or a large, waist-high, sliding panel in the wall. She chose the panel.

"This way," she said, hooking Miller's arm as her eyes went wide and her head began a negative, fear-filled shake.

Link, good soldier, just followed her to the panel she indicated. He slid it open to reveal a chute. She grinned. As she had hoped, they now had a shortcut to their destination.

Without having to say a word or ask a question, Link gave a nod. Together, they heaved Miller into the chute. Her yelp echoed as she disappeared.

Evans followed, feet first. Link came sliding after her. His greater mass propelled him into her. They skidded along together, buffeting from side to side in the close quarters, slimy stuff speeding their progress, slicking their hands and bodies. Evil odors gagged her.

Their limbs entangled and they fell from the chute into a huge bin, landing like lovers locked in an embrace. Miller squealed and thrashed beneath them.

The thunder of the compacters hammered inside her head. She couldn't change the volume on her headset. It must have been damaged in the wild ride down. She yanked the mesh helmet off and discarded it as Link tossed Miller up and out of the bin.

Then he sagged against the side of the bin. Evans felt as if she was running in a low-grav trainer as she struggled to reach him through the thigh-deep refuse.

"Out," he ordered.

It was clear to her his strength was gone. If he tossed her over the high side, he'd never make it out himself. The thunder of the compacter grew louder. Their bin jerked forward on the unseen track, spilling them both back onto debris she refused to think about.

"Out," he ordered again.

"I outrank you. Get your fabulous hard-ass over. Now."

He shook his head. "You first." He linked his fingers and held out his hands for her to step on. They trembled so hard, the shakes ran up his arms to his shoulders.

"No. You'll never make it," she shouted. "Now, get over the side, soldier."

They stood a moment, the crash of the compacting hammering closer.

"The wall." The compacter was so loud she only saw the words form on his lips.

They turned and attacked the side of the bin as they might have the famous climbing wall in basic training. She felt every muscle in her upper body scream in protest.

She dragged herself up, hooked a foot over the edge and teetered on the lip. Every muscle in Link's arms bulged and quivered as he fought to make it. She reached over and grabbed the neck of his ill-fitting uniform. His weight strained the fabric. It tore, just as they both heaved and he gained the lip.

They fell out together. Miller cowered on the slick poly floor, cradling her wrist.

"Move," Link shouted over the din.

They stumbled into the bright sunlight, Evans first, her dart gun once more locked and loaded. The sudden silence was like a blow.

She dragged Miller along as if she was still a hostage. Link slid along the wall on the other side of the alley.

When they reached the street, she saw why it had been all so easy.

Standing in full UV gear, armed, were a half-dozen Palace guards. They stood grouped in the middle of the street, ready to pick them off.

One guard stepped forward. Her dark full visor concealed her face but not her voice.

"We're only armed with tranq," she said. "There's no reason to make a scene."

Indeed, Evans could see some faces pressed against the glass windows of the building across the street. Several PFs buzzed lower for a look.

The woman raised her weapon and sighted on Link. "He's wanted back. Step away from him and I'll take him down easy."

Evans stepped in front of Link.

Chapter 24
✠

"Shit," Link said and tried to shove her aside.

Thank God his strength is close to done, Evans thought with half her brain. The other half focused on the guard's hands.

"I'm not moving," she said.

"So I'll tranq you first," the guard countered.

Evans looked up as one of a growing number of flyers on the block buzzed a little lower. She had time to register the black insignia of a guest shuttle before it rose again.

"You'll have to," she said. "I'm not giving him up."

Link lifted her bodily and set her to one side. "Let the women go."

"Not likely."

The guards raised their weapons.

One of the buzzing PFs swooped straight down, sweeping its jet wash over the guards. The sudden deep shadow and swirl of air scattered the men like dust from a probe's landing gear.

"Anything I can do to help?" Brad flung the door to Link's PF wide open, the skids hovering an inch from the pavement.

The guards scrambled to their feet as he leapt down.

"Just in time to save your ass. Nice view of it, too, buddy," Brad said to Link as he helped the injured Miller aboard.

"Right on schedule, lieutenant," Evans said with a grin. Link's uniform was split right down the back from collar to inseam. She patted his bare ass as they climbed in behind Brad.

Brad slid into the pilot's seat and began tapping the controls. The flyer rose into the air. She saw the guards running for The Palace entrance. A roller of local police pulled up.

"Go! Go! Go!" Link urged as Brad boosted the flyer.

She settled into Link's embrace, slipping a hand behind him and into the ripped back of his uniform, placing her palm flat against the heat of his skin.

* * * * *

Link didn't quite make it on his own from the PF to the base med center where Brad flew them. They carried him away on a stretcher—just to preserve his dignity, Brad teased, though Evans could read the concern in his eyes as they walked by Link's side.

The Secretary's physician gave her a harassed look when he arrived, but soon returned to reassure her.

"He'll be in lousy shape for a few days. Another strange reading. Looks like the old W54, but also like Q10. Very weird. I suggest you people choose your parties with a little more care. Make sure you always know your host and the other guests, and be careful of what you eat and drink," he advised before he bustled away.

She took a deep breath and had a sudden qualm that she must look like shit, but she eased through the door to Link's room anyway.

He was covered to the chin with a snow-white heat sheet, but his eyes opened when she touched his shoulder.

"You know what the first thing is we're going to do when I get the hell out of here?" he said.

"Make love?" She searched under the warm sheet for his hand. His skin was cold. He had dark smudges around his eyes.

"No. We're getting you enrolled in a fucking electronics course. I can't believe you made lieutenant colonel without knowing how to re-route a simple signal. Or patch in a visual—"

"Shut up," she said and covered his mouth with hers.

Chapter 25

ဆ

Link went through a painful withdrawal from the paralysis drug. He suffered from spasms of cramps in his arms and legs throughout the night.

Evans had upgraded him to a general's level of accommodation back at the headquarters hotel and charged it to Homeland Security. They'd both choked with laughter when she said the word "upgrade" to the hotel receptionist.

But now, she sat beside him as he lolled in the deep pool of steaming water, currents massaging his aching muscles, worried at his continued weakness.

She stripped and put one toe into the hot water. Sweat beaded his face and ran down his chest. The tiled chamber was fragrant with the healing oil the Secretary's physician had supplied.

"This is a bit too hot for me." She sat on the cold tile near his head, her legs in the water.

He leaned over and kissed the mole on her inner thigh. "I won't be long. Just sit here by me."

"Sure. We need you hale and hearty."

"Why? So your boss and mine can ream us out? You'll get lambasted for disobeying a direct order and brandishing—not to mention discharging—a military weapon in civilian territory, and I'll get knocked a rank for blowing a mission for another service."

She stroked the damp hair from his brow. "Do you mind terribly?"

He grinned up at her. "How could I? You saved my life. What's a rank or two?"

"But Mars, Link. You love Mars. Losing a rank might ground you. You'd hate being dirtbound."

He threaded his fingers through hers, turned and rose from the water. He brought her fingers to his lips. "I know only one place I want to be. With you. No matter where that is. I love you enough to follow you wherever you go."

She kissed him. "You're not well enough to go anywhere."

"I think I can get as far as that bureau where they do those old-fashioned life partnership, marriage things. I know I can, if you'll help me along."

"Oh, Link." She slid into the water, into his embrace, oblivious now to the heat of the water.

He kissed the top of her head. "I have to have you tied to me. Officially. Forever. Like the next seventy or eighty years. Maybe longer, if the fates are good to us."

Her breath felt tight in her chest. Tears filled her eyes. She dashed them away. "Must be the steam," she said.

He lifted her chin. "I'm hoping it's tears. Maybe something I've said touched you? Got through the tough woman who broke me out of that hell-hole."

She kissed him hard, tears running down her cheeks. "That was some mind-fuck."

Water beaded his body. One drop hung on his nipple and she touched her tongue to it. It was salty. She buried her face against his chest. "I love you, Link."

He scooped her into his arms and carried her to the bed, heedless of their wet skin or the fine linens. She lay back and reached up to encircle his neck with her arms. She kissed him, dueling his tongue, feasting on his breath.

"I love you, too, Sara," he whispered, tracing her nose and cheeks with his fingertips. "And you have to marry me. What if I'm cast out into the cruel world and have to find love in all the wrong places? What if I accidentally date one of my offspring created in that place? You have to save me from such a fate."

She nuzzled his fingertips. "I'll be happy to save you. But only if you promise to save me."

He shifted his hips against her and she felt his penis, hard and impatient. She spread her legs open and wrapped them around his hips.

A long sigh escaped him as he slid into her. "I'm feeling almost stellar right now."

She smiled and kissed his mouth. He slid his penis deeper and she lifted to him, tightened her inner muscles on him. He groaned.

"Make me come," she whispered.

He increased the tempo of his movements, moaning with each plunge.

"Now. Now. Now. Oh, Sweet Sol," she cried as a rush of sensation sped through her. Then she could not speak as wave after wave of pleasure stole her breath.

She lay back like a limp washrag. The trickle of his come reminded her of why The Palace doctor had wanted him. She touched her fingertips to the slick evidence he was a rarity—a potent man—and touched it to his lips.

He licked her fingers, then gave it back to her with his tongue on hers.

They made love until cramps in his legs stopped them. She then contented herself by giving him a massage.

"I wanted to tear those women apart when I saw them on you," she admitted. "I almost did shoot Princess Big Boobs."

"Don't think about it. And I thought of her as Silver Girl."

His muscles tensed beneath her fingers when she moved her hands from his back to his ass.

"Stop that. You're getting me hard again." He rolled abruptly to his back and wrapped her up in his arms. "What am I supposed to save you from?" he asked.

"From the pain I remember when you left me ten years ago. I couldn't bear to feel that way again. I felt as if someone tore my heart out of my chest. I would wake up every day and scan the Mars reports looking for your name. Then I stopped doing it. It only made it worse."

"Sara." He cupped her face. "Let's just go on from here."

She kissed his lips.

"How did you know I was in that room?" he asked. He ran his hands up and down her back, cupped her bottom.

"You know, it was so strange. I was in the corridor, looking at a slew of blank doors, going insane, sure I'd have to leave without you, and suddenly, I just knew you were close. Remember what you said, about the leash that binds us together? I sensed it. I sensed you. Then a door opened and there was Miller. She knew where you were."

"Good old Miller. Brad's taken quite a liking to her."

Link didn't cramp up the next time she guided his cock into her.

"Make it last, Sara. Move slowly with me."

Her body knew his so well. Each shift of his body, the fullness inside her. His scent, his taste. She licked his throat, followed it with kisses, caressed his nipples, and finally reached down between them and caressed his testicles as he stroked in and out of her.

Then she could do nothing but hold him. She buried her face against his neck and hung on for the ride. Her climax came from deep within her. It came from the soles of her feet, from the palms of her hands, from a burn in her belly and a sudden slam of her heart in her chest.

Her cry of ecstasy was lost in his. He came deep inside her, his body flowing in rhythm with hers.

Epilogue

∞

Brad slapped Link on the back. "I'm glad to see you again."

Link smiled at his friend. Two years at an earthside desk job—the fallout from The Palace incident—hadn't been as bad as he'd expected. It was very different from his other assignments but it kept them together. Sara had left field work for a teaching position at the Academy but planned to retire soon.

"So this is the little guy?" Brad took Link, Jr. from Sara.

"That's him," Link said, trying but failing to conceal a shit-eating grin. He wrapped his arms around Sara and kissed her short, spiky hair.

"You guys did good. Can I steal him tomorrow?"

"Not a chance," Sara said.

"No way." Link plucked his son from Brad's hands and put him back into her arms. She cradled their child close to her breast.

"No," Brad said, laughing. "I mean can I steal Big Link? We need his approval on the architect's plans for the new partner quarters on the Mars station."

"That's fabulous, Link. That means they passed the new orders. You can take us along." Her smile was brighter than a supernova.

Link grinned. Mars *and* Sara. Life didn't get any better. "I wouldn't go anywhere without you. Wait up for me?"

Sara grinned back and waggled her eyebrows. "Only if you'll be up for me."

Brad's cheeks flushed. "You two are a pain in the ass. Don't you get tired of each other?"

"Never," Sara said, moving into Link's embrace.

They headed for the PF. Link smiled and asked, "How's Miller? Are you tired of her yet?"

"Shut up. I know what you're thinking." Brad hunched his shoulders and thrust his hands deeper into his pockets. "I'm a fine one to call you a pain in the ass about Sara. Janet's great. She's relieved that her testimony helped shut down the illegal aspects of The Palace. It seems the corporation didn't know what was going on. There was a rogue doctor running his own show out of the back room. Drug development and testing, sperm sales and even illegal organ transplants.

"Councilor Kennedy's been extremely helpful, even suggesting they establish an Attendants' Board to oversee infractions and punishments, to keep them within reason. Who'd have thought a guy like him, coming from generations of untold wealth, would give a star's twinkle about the little people?"

Who indeed, Link thought. He didn't mention the conversation he'd overheard not long after Sara broke him out, when she finally got Kennedy himself on the comm. She'd been in full dress uniform and when the Councilor first saw Colonel Evans, Link would swear to his dying day that he heard Kennedy's very improved jaw hit the floor.

"So your Janet did a lot of good, besides getting us out of there in one piece," he prompted his friend.

"Oh, yeah. I'm proud of her." Brad didn't have to say the words. Link could hear the bragging in his voice. "She's finishing up her remedial training, to get her up to speed on what she missed while she was in that place. The civilian arm of the corps jumped at the chance to sign her on. Last night, she got orders posting her to the Mars medlab."

Link snorted, barely controlling his laughter at the pleasure in Brad's voice. Sara caught his eye and they both grinned. He'd bet his wife that Brad would talk Janet into a life partnership, and it looked like he'd win. He smiled as he remembered the stakes. They'd both win.

Overhead, the sky was midnight black, no worries about UV rays. One bright star drew his eye.

Not a star. A planet. *Venus.*

He and Sara made a point of looking for it, of making love as it rose in the sky.

He walked more quickly, imaging the evening alone in their quarters, a few candles lit, the curtains open, maybe a few pillows on the floor so they could make love in view of *her*. Or... they'd try to, as long as Link Jr. kept a lid on his hunger.

As they headed toward the tall building housing the Mars Commission, Link asked Brad, "Do you remember walking along here, two years ago?"

"Sure. You went in some old shop."

"So, you do remember."

"Yeah. Lots of junk. Wasn't it along here somewhere?"

Link paused between two buildings. His PF stood between them in the alley.

"Yeah. The shop was here. If I hadn't stopped and gone in, I'd never have met Sara again." He squeezed her hand.

"Here?" Brad said. "The shop wasn't here. It's nothing but an alley. Must have been farther along."

Sara stood on tiptoe and kissed Link's cheek. "He doesn't believe you."

"Love has scrambled your brains," Brad said. "I hope it's not contagious." He headed off down the street, "I'll see you tomorrow," he called over his shoulder.

"He's wrong," Sara said. Link nodded. He knew this was the spot where The Fantasy Shoppe had stood. The shop where he'd bought the card that led him back to Sara.

After they settled Link Jr. in the PF's rear compartment they snuggled close, just as they'd done the night he and Sara had signed their contract to live together and raise a family. He'd told her all about the shop, how he'd gotten the card. How the shop was gone. In return, she'd told him the shop had been here the day she'd gone into The Palace after him. She'd only gotten a glimpse of it, but there was definitely a one-story structure tucked into the now-empty space.

They'd made love right here in his PF and come back twice more to find it still just an alley, as it was tonight. Each time they'd sealed the empty space with a little love, sealed the idea they'd been brought to one another through some force or power they couldn't explain, at the same time they'd sealed a pact with their love.

Link turned to Sara. He parted her thighs. "I see Venus is rising."

The End

Why an electronic book?

We live in the Information Age—an exciting time in the history of human civilization, in which technology rules supreme and continues to progress in leaps and bounds every minute of every day. For a multitude of reasons, more and more avid literary fans are opting to purchase e-books instead of paper books. The question from those not yet initiated into the world of electronic reading is simply: *Why?*

1. *Price.* An electronic title at Ellora's Cave Publishing and Cerridwen Press runs anywhere from 40% to 75% less than the cover price of the exact same title in paperback format. Why? Basic mathematics and cost. It is less expensive to publish an e-book (no paper and printing, no warehousing and shipping) than it is to publish a paperback, so the savings are passed along to the consumer.

2. *Space.* Running out of room in your house for your books? That is one worry you will never have with electronic books. For a low one-time cost, you can purchase a handheld device specifically designed for e-reading. Many e-readers have large, convenient screens for viewing. Better yet, hundreds of titles can be stored within your new library—on a single microchip. There are a variety of e-readers from different manufacturers. You can also read e-books on your PC or laptop computer. (Please note that Ellora's

Cave does not endorse any specific brands. You can check our websites at www.ellorascave.com or www.cerridwenpress.com for information we make available to new consumers.)

3. *Mobility.* Because your new e-library consists of only a microchip within a small, easily transportable e-reader, your entire cache of books can be taken with you wherever you go.

4. *Personal Viewing Preferences.* Are the words you are currently reading too small? Too large? Too… ANNOYING? Paperback books cannot be modified according to personal preferences, but e-books can.

5. *Instant Gratification.* Is it the middle of the night and all the bookstores near you are closed? Are you tired of waiting days, sometimes weeks, for bookstores to ship the novels you bought? Ellora's Cave Publishing sells instantaneous downloads twenty-four hours a day, seven days a week, every day of the year. Our webstore is never closed. Our e-book delivery system is 100% automated, meaning your order is filled as soon as you pay for it.

Those are a few of the top reasons why electronic books are replacing paperbacks for many avid readers.

As always, Ellora's Cave and Cerridwen Press welcome your questions and comments. We invite you to email us at Comments@ellorascave.com or write to us directly at Ellora's Cave Publishing Inc., 1056 Home Avenue, Akron, OH 44310-3502.

erridwen, the Celtic Goddess of wisdom, was the muse who brought inspiration to storytellers and those in the creative arts. Cerridwen Press encompasses the best and most innovative stories in all genres of today's fiction. Visit our site and discover the newest titles by talented authors who still get inspired - much like the ancient storytellers did, once upon a time.

Cerridwen Press

www.cerridwenpress.com